The Big Hit

Dwight Mathieu

The Big Hit is a work of fiction. Names, characters, places, and incidents are the products of the author's imagination or are used fictitiously. Any resemblance to actual events, locales, or persons, living or dead, is entirely coincidental.

This book is for my father William, a man who believed that hard work is the best response to every challenge in life. Consequently, he worked harder than I knew to make sure I received the best education, of all varieties, that he could provide.

Any ability I have to tell a story, I owe to him.

ACKNOWLEDGMENTS

I want to recognize Professor Alasdair MacIntyre, who gave me the ability to analyze critically and write logically. Without my great fortune in having been exposed to his magnificent thought and challenging instruction, this book simply would not have been written.

To Sharon and our three children, Christopher, Kelsey and Dwight II: thank you for putting up with the years of my virtual absence while writing. I'm sure I would have been a better husband and father without it, and I hope that you are able to feel some recompense in finally seeing one of my stories brought to print.

I also want to thank my good friend and fellow author, Elizabeth Steynor, who applied her keen literary eye and deep editorial skill to shape this into a much better book than it otherwise would have been.

February 2014

Youth baseball is a very good thing because it keeps the parents off the streets.

-Yogi Berra

One

Wyatt stood just outside the batter's box, tucked the bat under his arm and tightened the straps on his gloves, making the pitcher wait; trying to ice him. He raised his left foot and tapped the barrel of the bat against his heel, knocking dirt from his spikes as if it were really there. He then repeated the tap on his other foot and stepped toward home plate deliberately, as if each measured pace was indispensable in preparing to hit. He used every last second he could, carefully digging his right foot into the hard clay in the batter's box while leaving his left foot out. Trying to pull the karma to his side, he held the bat vertical in front of him, making sure his hands were in just the right place on the grip. Then he extended the bat out to the opposite corner of the plate, holding it there for a perfect measurement before bringing his front foot around to plant it also.

He had everyone in the game waiting on him. The umpire grunted pointedly, urging him to cut the drama and get ready to hit.

The pitcher, pretending he didn't notice the theatrics, sensed that he'd finally be able to deliver and began to set himself in the stretch position on the mound. Just as everyone was fully ready for the pitch, the opposing manager stepped out of the dugout and signaled to the umpire for a time out. The mind game Wyatt started wouldn't be given a chance to work; there'd be a pitching change.

Wyatt O'Malley is a baseball player. He knows all the moves. He leans against the fence and chews seeds in bunches while talking with the other guys about the game; dissecting each play before moving on to evaluating the next. His natural baseball posture is obvious; he's one of those guys who look good playing the game. In fact, he looks good doing just about anything. He's not heavily muscular, but lean and trim and his arms display tone developed through careful weightlifting. A while ago he abandoned wearing his reddish brown hair long, trading it for a shorter cut which fits much better under his hat and doesn't require any fuss. Days in the hot summer sun have brought a golden hue to his light skin again this year, hiding some of the dirt the game casts upon him. He wears his uniform low at the waist and baggy at the butt, fitting loosely around the leg all the way down to his shoe tops and blousing at the ankles. His jersey vest is also loose and only partly tucked in, paying homage to the ghetto look and pushing the envelope of what the umpire will tolerate.

A fair amount of girls are in the crowd when Wyatt's team is playing. They sit in the soft grass outside the fence and pretend to care about baseball, but most of them are really there to see their respective baseball guys do something really cool. They scream when the team wins and they walk sympathetically with their guys after a loss. Some of them, guys and girls alike, lose their virginity here out beyond the center field fence late on a warm summer evening, proving that the ball park is truly a communal place both during and after the game. Wyatt has communed here several times. His prowess is legendary amongst his friends, which also adds to his mystique as a player.

But between the lines he's all business, all six-foot-two of him. When he pitches he can be un-hittable; grooving everything on the edges of the strike zone. And when Wyatt really has it going the only way a batter gets on base is if he somehow issues a walk or if the fielders make an error behind him. He once pitched a complete game no-hitter and *lost* the game 2-0. The other team scored their runs in the fifth inning on two walks, a sacrifice fly, and two infield errors. Such is the confounding nature of baseball. Afterward he told the two guys who made the errors that it was him and not them who screwed up; because the two runners couldn't have scored if he hadn't walked them in the first place. The pitcher is either the hero or the goat every time. Wyatt knows there's no in between and no sense pretending otherwise.

Tonight, he and the boys are trailing by one run in the final game of the Regional Championship. It's the bottom of the seventh inning with runners on second and third and two outs. A special opportunity is afoot. The winner will advance to the 16 year-old Babe Ruth World Series. One swing of his bat, Wyatt knows, a little gork he hits out of the infield; a sinking quail, a cue shot through the hole on the right side, any ball he hits that they don't catch will send the runner on third to home plate and at least tie the game. It will demonstrate once again that he's the right guy to be at the plate when the game is on the line, though he doesn't think of himself that way and would probably just shrug and say "that stuff doesn't mean anything" if you told him so.

The last minute pitching change is no big deal; Wyatt had been here before and seen the tactic on TV many times. He'd just find something to keep his mind off it

3

while the new hurler warmed up. So he walks back to the on-deck circle, rests the bat on his shoulder with one hand and looks past the dugout to a familiar cast of characters, the people who always show up: parents and others who've followed this team since he was eight and who are smiling at him now, urging him on. He takes stock of them while he waits.

Standing just inside the fence is Wyatt's old man, Rex O'Malley. He's been the manager of this team - the Nazareth Hawks - for as long as Wyatt can remember. Rex is leaning on the top rail talking strategy with Mark Berelli, the league President. Mark is some kind of lawyer, Wyatt recalls, and he has a lot of money. The other dads in the league always smile and nod their heads when they talk to him, as does Wyatt, but the guy seems like he lies through his teeth; which is true of course, since he's a lawyer. But Wyatt doesn't know anything about that stuff. Mark's son Alex is a pretty good ballplayer but his biggest asset, as far as the guys are concerned, is that he supplies most of the pot smoked in the high school. His mother is in therapy a lot, at least that's what Alex says, so she's not around very often. She actually spends much of her free time in an uplifting love affair with the high school Assistant-Principal, Tom Morton, who's also sitting in the bleachers. Wyatt doesn't know anything about that stuff either.

He looks over toward the home field bleachers where some parents and other managers from the league are sitting. Tom Morton is off to the side alone. It's his job as a Babe Ruth Board member to order and distribute baseballs to the teams during the season, and he takes it very seriously. He acts as if the balls belong to him personally; hoarding them and questioning it when a manager asks him for more. The other guys on the Board joke that he fondles them; the baseballs that is, late at night when he's home alone. Of course they'd never guess he's regularly fondling Mark Berelli's wife.

A few feet from Morton sits Becca Shea, the ex-wife of Jim Shea, a hot-tempered Irishman. Their son, the center fielder, is a good athlete but brow beaten and so insecure he can't perform well enough to make the school team. He plays well on Wyatt's Babe Ruth team though, because Rex gives him confidence and makes sure his old man stays away. Becca was also the target of emotional abuse for Jim, which is why she left him. She's now getting laid regularly by Mark Berelli. Becca is pretty hot looking for forty-five and an object of desire for most of the other Board members. Only the league President however, has the good fortune of batting leadoff on her team.

Since the new pitcher will be ready soon, Wyatt bends down to pick up a ring weight in the on-deck circle. As he slips it on his bat he hears one of the dads from a younger team, Peter Stenman, speak up.

"Get after it now Why-ett…" he says, "…earn your keep."

"No shit, asshole," Wyatt says under his breath.

Stenman is sitting with his group of league consumer advocates, as usual. If there was a Babe Ruth Public Interest Research Group, this bunch would be the charter members. They always have something negative to say and most of the other Board members are tired of hearing it. Stenman has been trying to over-throw Mark Berelli and assume control of the league for more than a year. He's called the IRS and Babe Ruth National headquarters and the Town Board and anyone else he can think of and told them that Mark pilfered money from the league. Then he filed a complaint with Office of the Attorney General, charging that Berelli "is dangerous to the welfare of the community." The AG's office investigated Berelli and league activities and found nothing out of place.

Despite being a troublemaker and anger management candidate himself, Stenman is also the league's chief fundraiser. He doesn't understand that most people can't stand him and they give him money just to get rid of him. When he doesn't get what he wants, he makes up a wild tale to disparage whoever is denying him. Berelli wants to throw him off the Board but can't because he raises so much money. Peter's son Justin is a decent ball-player but Mark is considering cutting him from the 14 year old travel baseball team out of spite. His wife Dale is a beautiful woman and using her charms on Mark in the hope of salvaging her kid's position on the team. Peter misinterprets what she's doing and suspects she and Berelli are having an affair.

Others in the stands have joined in the cheering now. Wyatt hears Becca Shea's sweet voice in the middle of it, saying, "Good luck Wyatt honey. Bring us home now…okay?" He likes the sound of that. All the guys like it when Becca calls them 'honey'.

The umpire yells "One more…." signaling to the relief pitcher that his regulation eight warm-up pitches are over. Wyatt takes a couple of full speed practice swings then knocks the ring weight off the bat and struts toward the batter's box again after the nearly ten minute delay. This is a big moment for sure. It's all about the team; it's about hitting the ball *someplace where they ain't* and getting the guy on third across the plate. He chokes up a couple of inches off the knob of the bat, digs his spikes in, taps the far corner of the plate and takes a rhythmic practice swing, then another and another; timing himself as the pitcher goes through his stretch.

He knows this pitcher, this lefty. They'd all faced him at one time or another. Their respective school teams play each other twice a season. His name is Peter Mirable, but the guys call him 'Peeks' because of the way he peeks over his glove at the batter before he goes into his windup. Wyatt is a career 9 for 17 against Peeks, though he doesn't know the numbers. He only knows he hits him well.

6

There's something about the way his looping curveball comes in; it seems to roll over right into his wheelhouse. Peeks always starts with a fastball first pitch and tends to miss the strike zone for a little while since it takes him a few pitches to settle down. So Wyatt isn't swinging at the first pitch here.

Jed Rounder, the fastest 16 year old in the county, is the runner on third. He's taunting Peeks by taking a huge lead, trying to draw a throw and generally being a distraction. But he's staying close enough to the bag to return safely if the throw comes over. JR Shea, Becca's kid, is the runner on second. He's bouncing back and forth tormenting the shortstop covering second base. JR is pretty fast too, but not the smartest runner. He sometimes gets himself picked off the bag because he underestimates the pitchers move. Wyatt is watching him from the batter's box, silently imploring him to stay close and not get picked off. There's no room for a dumb mistake now; not with two outs and the game in the balance.

"Baall," the umpire says in a loud grunt after Peeks first pitch to Wyatt, a fastball low and outside, pops into the catcher's glove.

If there weren't two outs, Wyatt wouldn't be quite as fussy. He'd be looking to put the ball in play, just hit a hard grounder somewhere or a long fly ball and Rounder would be able to score from third. But with two outs, he needs a clean hit. He needs to touch first base safely and that means hitting the ball out of the infield. He'll also take the walk if Peeks can't find the strike zone, so he won't swing on the second pitch either. Maybe he won't swing at all until Peeks shows he can throw strike one.

"Baaall two," the ump grunts again, this time after a screaming fastball a little high and inside, sizzled by Wyatt's hands and again popped the catcher's glove with a crack. Wyatt knows what it feels like to be unable to find the strike zone at a time like this. He knows Peeks will probably 'go home to mama' now and throw the looping curveball, the pitch he knows he can get across the plate. Wyatt looks over to Rex coaching at third base and gets the green light to swing.

Peeks comes set in his stretch and checks over his shoulder at Rounder bouncing around, doing everything he can to be a distraction, trying to draw the throw, trying to get the defense untracked so that even if Wyatt hits a ground ball they might make an error and allow the run to score. One little mistake and the game is tied. So Rounder and Wyatt are in this together, doing whatever it takes. They're so focused they don't even hear the crowd now, maybe three hundred fans total, screaming at every move.

The manager signals to the catcher to call for another fastball. Peeks gets the sign and shakes him off. The catcher puts the sign down again, as the manager wants, and Peeks shakes it off yet again. When he finally nods at the third sign, Wyatt figures the catcher changed the sign to one for the curveball - the deuce - and waits for the telltale spin. As the ball leaves Peeks' left hand Wyatt sees it, the pitch he's hoping for, the looping hook he's come to know and love.

The curveball hangs on the outside of the plate, not a bad miss most of the time, which forces Wyatt to lead the swing with his hands, go with the pitch and try to slap the ball to right field. Jed Rounder meanwhile, a few feet off third base, starts his thunderous advance toward home as soon as Wyatt starts to swing. Wyatt hears him coming just as the bat meets the ball. A sharp line drive rings from the bat and sails about ten feet off the ground toward the first baseman.

Wyatt bolts out of the box, his head down and digging. He needs only to touch first before somebody gets there with the ball. The first baseman reacts quickly and leaps into the air to make the catch but the ball deflects off the top of his glove and squirts obliquely into shallow right field, rolling away from all the fielders as Wyatt tries desperately to cross the bag ahead of the pitcher running over to cover.

Rounder crosses the plate and ties the game. JR is steaming around third; Rex is sending him home for the win. The right fielder finally gets to the ball, picks it up with his glove and in one motion transfers to his throwing hand and fires to home on a rope. Wyatt runs past first base then turns and stops, just in time to see JR slide on his belly around the back of the catcher and touch home plate with his left hand as the ball arrives. The umpire yells, "SAAAAFFFFE" with an animated sign palms down.

The game was over. In the dugout, his teammates, the coaches, everyone, jumped in the air or pumped their fists and joined Rounder in running out to swarm Wyatt and JR. All the Hawks fans raised their arms and yelled or screamed or hugged and in general celebrated in the euphoria that parents experience when their kids win a big one.

Wyatt and the other guys jumped up and down in unison on the field, their arms around each other and their faces beaming with the thrill of victory. The walk-off hit would be talked about for days to come, for weeks. It would be remembered the following season as The Big Hit, the one that sent the Hawks to the World Series for the first time in the fifty-two years that Babe Ruth Baseball had been played in Nazareth, New York.

Two

Wyatt rarely gets to sleep late on Saturday owing to the fact that the Nazareth Animal Hospital, where he works part time, is open from nine to twelve. Today, he also has baseball practice right afterward, so there will be no break in the action for the local hero. But Saturday morning means Saturday night is coming and that is always a big night for Wyatt and his buddies. It would be especially big tonight.

Rex O'Malley's young team is going to the World Series and they're riding high. They're in the big time; a bunch of celebrities going to The Show. The local weekly paper, *The Searchlight*, ran a special on them in Thursday's edition including a team photo on the front page and a brief bio of each player with his stats. Johnny 'MoJo' Morelli figures he's "gonna get laid on account of that article," due to his .474 batting average. He carries a copy of it folded up in his pocket for reference should any girl need a reminder of his prowess. Joe Morelli, his father, is the short, rotund owner of the local cleaners in need of anger management therapy. Joe yells at everyone from the stands: the umpires, the manager, the other players; anyone who he thinks is making the game go in a way he doesn't like. Johnny is the right fielder on the team. He's actually a little A.D.D. but likes to tell everyone he has Tourette syndrome, which gives him license to swear whenever he wants, question every call, lose control, piss off the umpires and get thrown out of the game regularly. The other guys on the team love his loony act and he gets big hits at the right time, which is why they call him Mojo.

The headline read "O'MALLEY HITS WALK-OFF." The article gave an inning by inning account of the game and highlighted the hit that sent the team to the highest level. In the days after the victory, Wyatt was asked to retell the story, how he knew it was going to be a curveball, how it felt when the bat hit the ball in the sweet spot, how it felt when he saw the ball deflect off the fielder's glove, what it feels like to have the game winning hit at such an important time.

"I just tried to see the ball well and make a good swing," he would say. And when they asked about being the hero on the team? "I got a little lucky. There were guys on base in front of me and got a pitch I could hit."

Rex O'Malley has managed his kid well both on and off the field. He had taught him to "say what they wanna hear but not say anything much at all." He also told him not to act in a way that would make his teammates think he was full of himself. When the old man talks, Wyatt listens. Well, most of the time, at least when it comes to baseball. He hadn't steered him wrong yet. But the kid was famous now, at least locally. And the way he figured it, he ought to be able to sleep in on Saturday morning. That's not the way O'Malley figured it.

"Hey Y-O" That's O'Malley's name for Wyatt, even though his initials are really W.O. Now everyone in baseball calls him that.

"Yeah Dad?"

"Gitchur butt out of bed, eat some breakfast, do your conditioning drills and get to work. You need to be at the field by 12:30. I'll be there early to set up the screens and the cage and I have to get some supplies first so I'm leaving now."

"I thought practice is at one?"

"It is. But you're the manager's kid. You get there early. It's your cross to bear."

"How am I going to get anywhere if you're leaving now?"

"Ride your bike."

"Aw come on Dad, I got to ride all the way to work and then to the high school?"

"You don't seem to mind riding all the way across town to get in your girlfriend's pants, so halfway across town to go to work is nothing."

This is what Wyatt likes most about his old man. As soon as he turned sixteen, O'Malley started treating him just like one of the boys. It's what all the players like about him; that and the fact that he knows more about baseball than anybody around. He's always showing them something they don't know.

"All right, I'll be there at twelve-thirty."

"I have your Gatorade and your bag, so you won't have to drag it with you on your bike."

"Thanks, Dad."

"Wear your pads, we're doing sliding drills."

"Oh great, can't wait."

O'Malley went out the door. As Wyatt threw one leg then the other out of bed, his cell phone rang. He struggled to find it and see who was on the caller ID. It was Alex Berelli, the pot dealer. He answered.

"Aurora Borealis, what up Dude?"

"The butcher came to town," Alex said in code.

"Oh yeah? Sweet. How are the steaks?"

"Primo… I had him cut you a half rack, that's what you wanted, check?"

"Check"

"K-O Paco. It's a honeybee a half, remember?"

"Man, the good steak is pricey."

"No so much. You'll get a lot more cuts off of this rack. You'll see."

"No problem. Where do I shop?"

"The usual place, it'll be there sometime today, could be early, could be late, maybe after my game. You probably ought to wait till after eight to go to the store. But it'll be there by dark for sure. Leave the cash in the register; I'll get it in the morning."

"It's all good," Wyatt replied, "peace."

"Peace," Alex returned, and hung up.

It was simple. Below the bleachers at the ball park, stuffed up under the framing for the top row, Alex would stash a half ounce of marijuana. Wyatt would retrieve it later and leave a hundred dollars, a 'honeybee', in its place. Alex would pick up the money in the morning.

He thought about going back to sleep for just a few minutes then looked at the clock. It was eight-fifteen and he had to be at work in less than an hour, so he sat on the side of his bed and made the final transition to being awake for the day.

By eight-forty he was peddling down the street feeling silly on the little fluorescent green bicycle that he'd been riding for the past year. He wasn't even sure where the bike came from. It was one that someone had left at his house a while back, after he had left another one at someone else's house, who had left yet another one at someone else's house, and so on. No-one knows the true

13

heritage of most of the bikes; they just pass them around as is convenient. Some were probably stolen at one time or another, or borrowed and never returned. But he was sick of riding a bike. He had his learner's permit for two months now and couldn't wait until he could take his road test in September.

He took a right off of his street, Willow Run, onto West Elm then cut across Oakwood at the four corners and through the parking lot for the Village Marketplace. Officer Victor Brunk was sitting near the intersection in his Nazareth Town Police car watching the traffic go by. Wyatt didn't notice the cop as he rode through, but Brunk saw him. "The O'Malley kid," the cop said to himself, "I wonder where he's headed." Even though Wyatt had his Hawks practice uniform on and was heading toward work, Brunk won't give him credit for doing anything except looking for trouble. They have a history.

Wyatt is a good student, he gets good grades. He's also a good baseball player, works for several neighbors doing yard work and odd jobs and puts in a few hours at the Animal Hospital each week sweeping, cleaning cages and doing miscellaneous clean-up. Most people like him. They're constantly telling Rex what a "nice young man" he is. They don't add, "especially since you've raised him alone."

But Wyatt has a habit of being in the wrong place at the right time. Not that he's different from any other teenager, occasionally getting into mischief and doing little things that are just a hair on the other side of the law, but he has a knack for getting caught or being around when someone else gets caught. Brunk was the investigating officer on several of his misguided adventures. There was the time he and his friends snuck out of the house on a sleepover, made puff bombs by filling coffee filters with flour, tying them off with rubber bands and throwing them at cars parked in driveways in the neighborhood. Brunk traced a trail of flour right to O'Malley's back yard.

Then there was the time when no fewer than four stolen bicycles were dropped off in the O'Malley yard, although Wyatt hadn't done any of the stealing. And there was the time he was riding on his friend Scooter's dirt bike as a passenger, when the kid decided to ride right through town on the shoulder of the railroad tracks. And there was the time Scooter decided to take his mom's car out for a joyride; Wyatt was there with him, in the passenger's seat. When Brunk found them out at the forest preserve, sitting and talking about their girlfriends, Scooter ran like hell into the woods. Wyatt wouldn't run, knowing if he did his father would be more pissed about that than anything else.

When Wyatt gets into trouble it's usually because he's in the vicinity. But he won't rat on his friends and so he suffers the same punishment as they do. It drives Brunk crazy that he won't cooperate, that he has more honor than to spill the beans about who was at the heart of such vicious criminal behavior. Wyatt once told Brunk he'd rather spend the night in jail than to squeal. His father was there when he said it. That part made O'Malley proud.

When Wyatt rode past Brunk sitting in his car, all of the history came to the forefront again. The officer watched the tall, muscular red haired kid peddle by on the bright green bicycle, Amazed at how he'd grown so quickly. He made a mental note to check the Babe Ruth ball field in a little while just to be certain the perpetrator was there. He didn't know that O'Malley's team was practicing at the High School today instead. Brunk's eyes followed the figure on the bicycle for as long as he remained visible, wondering if there was anything he could imagine that would warrant going after him. But Wyatt was just peddling his way to work. Brunk sighed and remembered the night of the stolen bike investigation at the O'Malley house, when he questioned the kid about where the bikes had come from. Wyatt refused to answer, denied knowing anything about it and at one point said, "If I stole the bikes, the last thing I'd do is leave em out in front of the house where you could see em." The fact was, Wyatt had no idea where they came from originally; he was sure his friends hadn't stolen them, although he did know, but wouldn't tell, who dropped them off.

At the end of it Brunk said, "I'm going to get you O'Malley; I know you're up to no good and it's my sworn duty to protect this town from delinquents like you. I'm going to get you when you least expect it." He pointed his finger at him and said, "When you look over your shoulder, I'll be there."

At 14 years old, this scared Wyatt pretty good and upset his father even more. The following day Rex went to the Town Hall and filed a formal complaint against Brunk, charging him with harassment. At an administrative law hearing Brunk was required to respond to the charges and defend his behavior. The judge found the conduct reprehensible and put him on probation for thirty days. But it was a farce; a wrist slap. As far as the court in the Town of Nazareth is concerned, Brunk is the biggest 'producer' on the police force. He always issues the largest number of tickets for speeding, cell phone use, and driving without a seatbelt. All of them stick. This generates nearly three times his annual salary in fines. He thinks of it as "earning his keep." They think of him as a cash cow.

Having for now survived surveillance by the omnipresent Brunk, Wyatt finished the final leg of his ride to the Animal Hospital and left his bike around the back of the office. The Doc didn't like it if he left it in front where patients could see it; said it made the place look trashy. He went inside through the back door and grabbed a lab coat to put on. Everyone has to have a lab coat, even Wyatt, though he never actually gets to work with the animals, except once in a while to help carry a big dog that has passed away. It's a sad time for him, seeing an animal die. He loves dogs, he loves all animals, which is why he works there. O'Malley would never allow a pet of their own, not because he didn't like them, but because he always said it wasn't right to keep a dog cooped up in a neighborhood; dogs need to run. Rex wouldn't have a lap-dog.

As usual, the Doc, old Tom Sheehan, left a list of chores for the day under a magnet on the samples refrigerator. Wyatt grabbed it and had a look as he walked to the janitor's closet. He knew that vacuuming the waiting room would be number one on the list. It always is. Item two was 'clean cages,' which meant the final hour or so of his time today would be spent doing the most unpleasant of all jobs. He grabbed the commercial vacuum from the closet, said "Good morning Doc" as he rolled it past Sheehan's office and went out to the waiting area. Mrs. Garret, the sour grey haired woman in charge of the front end of the hospital, was checking in a patient. The dog's owner, a pretty girl about Wyatt's age, blonde and sleek, stood in front of the counter with a worried look. Mrs. Garret didn't bother saying hello, but went right to the heart of the matter.

"If you would get in a little earlier, Wyatt, you wouldn't have to do that in front of the patients. And there's an extra little something for you over there in the far corner."

"I'm sorry," the beauty said, looking first at Wyatt, then at the puddle of diarrhea on the floor in the corner, "he can't control himself. He's usually very good, never goes inside, but he's sick now."

"It's not a problem," Wyatt said, "part of my job," gazing at her a little too long for Mrs. Garret's liking, and she cleared her throat at him pointedly. The beauty was pained, looking embarrassed.

"If you have some towels I'll take care of it. I'm so sorry." She said again. Wyatt shook his head, held up a hand in protest and smiled.

"It's okay."

"Yes, it's okay Sammy," the witch said, "you need to stay with Max… there's the nurse now, just follow her. That's right dear, go ahead."

Sammy led her big black Labrador retriever and followed the nurse toward the exam room. Max had to weigh nearly as much as his delicate owner. As soon as the dog realized where he was headed, he backed up against the pull of the leash and swung his head from side to side in opposition. She pulled him by the collar to get him to move and the extra effort he exerted while protesting caused another small shot of diarrhea to squirt from his rear; another extra little something for Wyatt.

"Oh no…oh god Max… I'm so sorry…." She looked at Wyatt again with her incredible blue eyes.

"No… no… it's okay… here, let me help." He walked over to Max, scratched him under the ears for a few seconds, then wrapped his strong arms around his front shoulders and rear and picked him up. Max couldn't protest. Sammy was impressed. Mrs. Garret smiled reluctantly.

After delivering Max onto the table in the exam room Wyatt returned to clean up the mess in the waiting area and then began energetically vacuuming the corners of the room with a crevice tool. He always thought it strange how animal hair could accumulate so quickly where the floor meets the wall. It was as if someone had pushed it there. He also noticed how badly the tile floor needed washing but decided not to bring it to the witch's attention. He couldn't stay late today to mop after closing and Mrs.

Garret had little regard for the foolishness of baseball. He hoped a good vacuuming would suffice.

With his back to the reception desk and the noise of the machine in his ear, he didn't notice that Sammy and Max had returned from the exam and were checking out. When he eventually turned and saw her there looking at him, they were both startled. She tried to pretend she wasn't looking. He didn't. Mrs. Garret broke up the buzz.

"You're all set dear, now the doctor wants a follow visit, what day is good for you?"

"I know. Well, let's see, I was supposed to return home to Westchester, I'm only here visiting my father."

"Yes," the witch smiled knowingly, "do you have a veterinarian in Westchester? We might be able to transfer…"

"No, I guess I can stay for a few more days. I don't want to switch him in the middle, can I get an appointment on Friday?" She glanced at Wyatt.

"Let me see. Yes, Friday, how about ten o'clock?"

"That's fine. And… uh….= can someone help me get Max in the car? He's a little woozy."

"Oh dear, we're short staffed on Saturday." She looked over at Wyatt reluctantly. "Wyatt, please help Miss Porter with Max, but don't dawdle."

"Yes maam."

Sammy pulled on Max's collar and walked toward the door. Upon reaching where Wyatt stood she smiled and extended her hand to shake, "I'm Samantha Porter."

"Hi," Wyatt wasn't accustomed to a girl so confident and forward. "Wyatt… uh… O'Malley," he shook her hand while Mrs. Garret rolled her eyes in the background. He moved toward the door also, opening it a little awkwardly while Sammy guided the stumbling Max. Upon smelling the fresh air the dog lurched ahead energetically, knowing he was getting free of the clinic. This pulled Sammy into Wyatt and they bumped as he tried to hold the door open from inside. There was an awkward pause while he tried to decide if he should grab her to keep her from being dragged down the steps by the beast. She managed to regain control and they walked toward her small blue BMW convertible.

"Nice car."

"Thanks. I just got my license a few weeks ago. I don't live here."

"Yeah, I heard. Where you from again?"

"Westchester, it's down by New York City. I'm here visiting my Dad, I come up every summer for a few weeks."

Wyatt got a slightly distant look on his face, trying to place the name Porter.

"My father's name is different. I mean, my name is different. My parents split right after I was born, so I took my new father's name, which is kind of unusual I guess. But I still visit my other Dad too, you know?"

"Sure, I get it. My parents are split too. My Mom's in California. I live with my Dad. I guess I should go see her sometime."

There was no struggle at all as Max jumped up onto the front seat and sat ready to go while Sammy closed the door.

"That was easier than I thought." She said with a weak smile.

"What's your Dad's name?" Wyatt asked.

"Brunk, he's a Policeman, do you know him?"

He nearly staggered, then felt a sinking feeling as he realized today would probably be the first and only time he would get this close to Samantha. He laughed nervously and she got a confused look. She wondered if she should be embarrassed about this revelation.

"No," he said quickly, seeing her face, "it's just that the guy hates me, thinks I'm a creep. Don't tell him you met me, he'll be coming after me," he chuckled, trying to be friendly about it, "but really, I mean it. He thinks I'm a criminal."

"Brunk thinks everyone is a criminal. You should see the wall in his office. It's covered with pictures of all kinds of people. I guess they're here in Nazareth. I wonder if you're up there too." She laughed genuinely.

"Guarantee, I am."

"I'll check tonight."

"Oh man."

"Why don't you give me your cell number, I'll call you, maybe we can hang out before I leave."

He smiled, he liked the idea. "Well, we'd have to leave town." He said as he pictured being seen with her out somewhere, then being chased around by Brunk after she leaves Nazareth and the word leaks back.

She looked at her car reflexively, knowing leaving town was not an issue. "I won't tell him I met you. You're right, he's a little nutty."

As she pulled out of the lot onto Oakwood with big Max the Lab perched up proudly in the passenger seat, Wyatt wondered silently how such a nasty old prick like Brunk could have ever fathered such a beautiful girl. Then he thought about genes, how recessive genes show up after skipping generations. He figured either Brunk or Samantha must have been a product of recessive genes.

After finishing his work for the day and being dismissed by Mrs. Garret, Wyatt rode his bike to the school ball field. He pulled up to the dugout to see O'Malley talking to a guy holding a microphone and another guy wielding a shoulder mounted video camera. The Press, the *real* Press, was interviewing him. Wyatt tucked in his practice jersey and straightened his cap, just in case.

"Well, we're fortunate in the Town of Nazareth to have many very good ball-players," O'Malley said in response to a question, "and we believe that's due to the overall quality of our Babe Ruth program, where every kid who wants to, can play good organized baseball."

The interviewer thanked him, said a few complimentary things about his ease in front of the camera, and added, "We'll see you at three o'clock then….and just let the players be natural. They don't need to dress for this; we want them just as they are."

"Right," O'Malley said, "Well, that's the way you'll get em, *au naturale*. And believe me, this bunch of hams will give you plenty of copy."

The news people chuckled and walked by Wyatt on the way to their van, nodding as they passed. He recognized the interviewer as the one who does *The Sports Board* on channel nine every evening at six-twenty-five and again later on during the late night news. He nodded and said "Hi," politely, then looked at his father in surprise.

"They're coming back later," O'Malley said, "to get some video of you guys during practice and do a couple of interviews; you'll probably be one of em."

"Jesus Dad, really? How'd you work that one?"

"I didn't do anything, they called and asked to meet me, I said sure. You guys are a big deal."

"Christ, we better win."

"Nah, don't think about that stuff. Just be…"

"I know, just be focused, stay in the moment and give… a… hundred… and ten… percent" Wyatt chided him.

"Hey, you're finally getting the idea. Imagine that, after all these years? Anyway, the rest of the guys will be fine. They're going to be looking at you. If you're relaxed and confident and FOCUSED, they will be too."

"You give me too much credit."

"You got The Hit."

"They give you any money for a hit like that?"

"Not in this league." O'Malley smiled.

Three

They don't usually keep the snack stand open at the ballpark after the District tournament is over. The baseball season that follows, the 'Travel Team' season, usually doesn't have enough parents interested enough to work the place. But since the 16 year old team had won the districts *and* the State tournament *and* then the Regionals, Peter Stenman kept putting up duty lists every week, trying to keep the snack stand open, requiring parents to continue to work in the grease pit well into vacation season. Many of them just didn't bother showing up; they were laying on a beach in Cape Cod or boating on Lake George instead. It came to be all about the money this year, cashing in on the success of the 16's team, so a few parents who still had the energy carried on and kept the place open. The snack stand is THE cash cow in the league. It makes tons of money, benefiting from a captive clientele and no cost of labor. But some parents think the league doesn't *need* any more money. The baseball experience in Nazareth is just fine; maybe even a little too captivating, as it is.

This morning, Stenman stood inside the screen door at the back of the small snack building pleading on the phone.

"I know you've worked every Saturday this month, Roger… but there are four sets of travel games today, all the fields are busy and I have no-one else who can do the shift. We'll have about 500 spectators here. If we can get each one to spend just five bucks, well, do the math…." Stenman implored the Board member, somehow believing the importance of what he said was automatically felt by everyone else in the universe.

"…don't say that Roger, you do give a shit, you know you do… and who's going to do the 50-50 raffle? You know you're the best earner in the league… no, I already called O'Malley, he has practice for the World Series. You're better than him anyway; he spends too much time flirting with the Moms… no, I don't mean the Moms don't flirt with you, you knock em dead too Roger."

In just three minutes Stenman managed to say something disparaging about one Board member and insult another. It's his way. He'd still get something good done. It would come as by-product, as many good things come to community baseball. In this case, he would manage to shame enough people to staff the snack stand on Saturday and thereby generate a couple of grand of sales, flowing directly to the coffers of the Babe Ruth program.

"…remember Roger, we're gonna hang that plaque on the new batting cages, your name's gonna be on there right next to mine. You want your kid to see it there don't you? It's all about the kids, Roger."

After convincing Roger Mann that his family's legacy was riding on how many burgers he flipped at the ballpark today, then making equally emotional appeals to the community conscience of two other Board members, Stenman had his snack stand staffed. Of course now he'd be able to hang around the games, watch the boys play and be free to remind everyone how the league would go to the dogs if not for his unsurpassed energy and skill.

"Yeah," he said to Jim Shea later, as he leaned over fence on the third base line of field number 5, pretending for a second to actually have some interest in the game being played. Shea was in the middle of coaching his 13 year old travel team. "I remember when we didn't even have this field," he continued. "That was before I got those Arabs over at Sabic Plastics to step up to the plate and do some good for this League. Told em their plant puffs an awful lot of smoke into the air around here, is what I told em."

Shea gave Stenman a look of impatience. "I've heard that shit a bunch of times Peter, why the hell are you telling me again now? I'm in the middle of a game."

"Just sharing how it feels, looking out across this field and seeing all the guys have so much fun."

"Yeah well, you oughta do a little more looking and a little less sharing. I heard Art Blaze had more to do with it than anybody." Jim Shea walked away, over to the third base coach's box in order to give signs to his first batter coming up for the inning. He rolled his eyes as he walked and shook his head slightly, trying to shake away the nonsense that Stenman had just put there.

Art Blaze is Regional Operations Manager for Sabic Plastics and a Board member with two sons in the league. His office is at the plant on the outskirts of Nazareth, a sprawling processing facility with 1,800 employees. It was Art, Jim Shea knew, that secured fifty thousand of the millions that Sabic spends every year on good will projects in the communities where their plants are located. It was that fifty grand which built field number 9. Art assured the Board that there's more money to be had, but they had to keep Stenman out of the process. He pissed off the Senior Executive VP pretty good with his 'puffs of smoke' comment. You generally don't get people to donate money freely when you tell them they smell.

"Yeah, well I made them feel guilty," Stenman said loudly at Shea's back as he walked away, "made it easy for Blaze is what I did."

Stenman decided he'd had enough of Jim Shea, the ingrate bastard, and walked over to the large stand of bleachers behind home plate. There, his two biggest supporters, Patricia and Joshua Grezudnik, were sitting watching their 13 year old son Lucas who plays on Shea's team.

"What's the hell is wrong with him?" Patricia asked as Stenman sat down, referring to Shea. "Lucas is a better shortstop than that other kid and this is the second game in a row he hasn't started. We didn't pay all that money to see our son sit, especially when he's the best player on the team."

"Shea is friends with Mark Berelli, Trish, you know that. Berelli's pissed at us for calling the Attorney General's office. Figure it out. He told Shea not to play your kid."

"If he's pissed at us Peter, it's because YOU called the Attorney General."

"Well, it had to be done. I knew they wouldn't find anything, Berelli is too smart. But he's converting funds; I know it. I can feel it."

"I don't know what it is you feel, Peter," Joshua spoke up, "but there was nothing there, no league funds mixed with his own; no improper tax reporting; no pitcher's mound built in his back yard; not even a few league baseballs in his garage. The guy is clean and we look like idiots. We can't even say anything about our kid's playing time now. People whisper about us."

"I'm telling you the guy is dirty." Stenman protested. "What about the trips to Disney with his Travel team last year? Those kids' parents didn't pay a dime for that trip. Think about what it cost! Where did the money come from?"

"The AG's office audited his records, Peter; he paid for the trip out of his pocket. He's a wealthy man."

"I don't believe it. He got the money from the league checking account. If not, what about all the money I've raised for this league? Where'd it all go? I worked hard for that money, I deserve some recognition. We should have those batting cages by now, something's wrong." Stenman ended shaking his head dramatically.

The Grezudniks said nothing further, but looked at each other as married people do, wondering in unison if Stenman had finally lost his marbles. Their blank gaze was interrupted by the umpire yelling "STEEERIKE THREE," as young Lucas Grezudnik, pinch-hitting for the other shortstop, struck out on three pitches looking. Patricia turned toward the field with gritted teeth, choosing not to look at Stenman, fearing she would really lay into him. In her anger, she connected Stenman's crusade with her son's lack of playing time and thus blamed him for Lucas' inability to hit the ball. She didn't change her gaze as he spoke further.

"I'm going to find out," he added, oblivious to her rage, "I'm going to find out what he did with all the money and make sure he's prosecuted to the fullest extent of the law. Did you hear about the new tractor? The league bought it from Grassworld, where they buy all their stuff. Guess who the lawyer is for Grassworld? That's right, Mark Berelli, and he's always playing golf at the owner's country club too."

Patricia stood abruptly and made her way down the bleachers toward the dugout where Lucas was standing inside the fence. Even she couldn't take any more and she was one of Stenman's supporters. She went to lick her son's wounds, help him regain confidence and get back into the battle for playing time. When she was out of earshot Joshua spoke up.

"Lookit Peter, I used to think your energy is good, you know, good for the kids. But I don't think so anymore. I don't think there's anything wrong with the league. There's nothing there. So I don't understand your motives, and I… that is, WE, don't want anything more to do with your campaign against Berelli. You're making us look bad." Joshua stood up and walked down the bleachers also, toward the snack bar.

"This is about what's right Josh, you know that. I'm all about what's good for the kids."

He was alone again, had found himself in that condition a lot lately. No one, he thought, understood him. His cell phone rang, interrupting his sulk. Someone was calling from home. Maybe Justin needed a ride to the park for his travel game. He flipped it open and listened to his wife Dale start right in.

"Whadya mean he's going to get kicked off the travel team?" he yelled incredulously, "That's nonsense, no-one can kick him off the team… I don't care what Mikey said in school, how would he know anything? Berelli's not going to kick him off the team. Hang on, I'll be right there, we'll get this straightened out."

He stormed down the bleachers, walking across the top of the seats in order to get down quickly and then stomped across the lot to his car. After the short drive home he came to a screeching halt in the driveway and barged through the back door. Justin was sitting in his baseball uniform at the kitchen table eating a bowl of cereal.

"What's this nonsense about you getting kicked off the travel team?"

"That's what Mikey's Dad says. He says Mr. Berelli is so mad at you, he wouldn't be surprised if I got thrown off the team."

"He can't throw you off the team."

"Why is he so mad at you?" Justin looked at him with a frown.

"Well, he and I disagree about how the league should be run."

"He's the President of the league dad, why don't you just let him run it? Why do you have to butt in? Now everybody thinks I'm gonna get thrown off."

"You're not going to get thrown off."

"That's what Mikey's Dad says."

"I DON'T GIVE A DAMN WHAT MIKEY'S DAD SAYS." Stenman was yelling. Justin was close to tears, but since he was fourteen he fought them off.

"I don't want to go to the game."

"You're playing baseball today young man, you made a commitment to the team and you're going to play. What would they think of me if I let you skip out?" Justin didn't answer. Stenman walked down the hall to the study where Dale sat talking on her cell phone.

Dale is a beautiful woman: long black hair, medium height, slender in the right places, soft and delicately curvy in others. She's a very young forty-two and not reluctant to use her looks and smarts to get what she wants. Her only mistake in life, her mother tells her, was using her looks and smarts to attract and marry that idiot…. 'Pete'

While 'Pete' was in the kitchen accomplishing nothing more than upsetting Justin further, Dale was talking with Mark Berelli, inquiring about what she had heard her son report, telling him she was certain it couldn't be true that a thoughtful and sincere man such as he would ever hurt Justin like that. She'd just finished asking him if he would like to meet for a drink, maybe downtown after work next week, so they could discuss it and he could feel her concerns in person. Stenman walked into the study and overheard her say the last part. She never spared him any anguish these days, ever, and didn't even blink when she realized he heard her flirting with Berelli. She continued chatting.

"That's so nice of you Mark… I want you to know that whatever issue you have with my husband, Justin thinks the world of you, as do I… wonderful, I'm glad you feel that way… so then I'll hear from you on Tuesday? Good, can't wait… you have my number right? Good… ciao then."

She clicked off the phone and stared at Stenman blankly, knowing he was seething but not caring. She lowered her voice so Justin wouldn't overhear.

"I'm not going to let your witch hunt spoil his baseball career." She said.

"His baseball career? He has a baseball career now? If it wasn't for me there'd be no baseball career."

"But for you, he wouldn't be hearing from his friends that he's getting kicked off the travel team."

"People say things Dale, they say all kinds of things about me."

"Yes they do," she said abruptly, "and what they're saying now is that you're an idiot, a power-hungry self-promoting jackass." She was nearly yelling so there was no keeping this from Justin. But he'd seen the movie many times before anyway.

Stenman's eyes became peepholes. His face was red and his lips were drawn tightly against his teeth. He raised his hand then stopped himself, waking up suddenly; perhaps remembering what happened the last time he hit her.

"Go ahead Peter, do it," she said cynically, "do it and I'll take my son and march right down to the police station. Then it'll be your baseball career that's spoiled."

He said nothing further but turned from her to see Justin standing in the doorway to the study. The kid was thinking he was going to have to protect his mom, steeling himself for what might be needed, and then sighed with relief to see his father walking away.

"Come on son," Peter said, "we need to get you to your game."

Justin let his head drop and looked at the floor. "I'm not going. I don't feel like playing baseball."

Stenman walked out the back door and got into his car without further discussion. As he drove to town he thought about what the marriage counselor had suggested last year, that maybe he should see a therapist, someone to help him control his anger. She gave him the name of someone as a reference, even made an appointment for him the following week, but he never went. "I need some therapy all right," he said to himself, and instead of turning left at the four corners to go back to the ball fields, he turned a hard right into the parking lot next to the bank, knowing that Grif's bar was open today, even this early. He needed to get away.

Officer Vic Brunk, sitting across the intersection in the lot next to the village marketplace, watched from his patrol car as Stenman walked into the small bar on the corner. "Some baseball guy," he said to himself in a whisper, "going into a bar on a Saturday. It's hardly past noon." He decided to wait around to see if Stenman would become a danger in any way, later on.

Four

Mark Berelli drove down Oakwood Avenue on his way to the ball park. He motored along casually, arm out the window, wearing his black travel team baseball hat with the silver profile of a hawk on the front, the logo of the Nazareth Hawks. He marveled at what a beautiful day it was and how upstate New York in July truly defines summer. There's something about the deep green of the rolling landscape and the smell of everything in full bloom, in contrast to the brutal winter, which makes each summer day special.

Things had settled down. The nonsense that the Attorney General's office had investigated was cleared up and over. Travel baseball season, the only season that he truly cared about, was underway. Everything was good in his world again finally. He also knew the humidity in the air presaged a thunderstorm in the afternoon and wondered if they would get all the games in today.

For Mark, Babe Ruth is just the minors. He supports it fervently and does everything he does in the name of Babe Ruth Baseball because it provides the raw materials for his travel league year after year. He hasn't actually managed a Babe Ruth team in over five years; he just can't be bothered with the kids who aren't special talent. But he's the first one at the table when the All-Star teams are chosen. The All-Stars make up the core of his travel teams at the different age levels. The beauty of this year was that the 16 year old Senior Babe Ruth All-Star Team, O'Malley's team, was going to play in the World Series. If O'Malley would push his kids hard enough, they could win some games there; maybe get to the semi-final round, which would really put his Nazareth Travel league on the map. It might gain him National recognition in youth baseball. The heavy hitters in Babe Ruth, Mickey Mantle and Connie Mack Leagues would come to recognize the name Mark Berelli.

Right now, he needed only to maintain an even keel, rebuild the peace and not allow anyone to persecute Stenman or the Grezudniks or others who had filed the complaint with the AG's office. There was no room for any more negative press or a discrimination lawsuit, though he detested the thought of those people continuing in the league. He couldn't stomach them, especially Stenman, questioning his every move. But it was the price of getting his program on the map. Maybe the rumor he planted that Stenman's kid would get thrown off the 14 year old travel team would be enough to get him to shut up. And now Dale wanted to meet him for a drink to discuss it. That was an unexpected bonus. His mind drifted from baseball for a second as he thought of what it might be like with her underneath him.

He was jolted back into reality by a flash in his rear view mirror. A Nazareth Town Police car with lights on was close behind him, clearly signaling for him to pull over.

"What the heck?" He drove onto the shoulder of the road. It was a busy Saturday on the main street in town.

"Christ, what the hell is this about?" He watched in his side mirror as the policeman opened the door and climbed out; stopping to make sure he was clear of traffic and to place his flat brimmed hat squarely on his head. It was Brunk. Berelli knew him fairly well; his nephew played Babe Ruth in the 15-year olds, but was never good enough to make a travel team.

"Do you know why I stopped you sir?" Brunk said at the window.

"Sir? Christ, Vic, it's me. No, I don't know why. I wasn't speeding, so why?"

"License, registration and insurance card please."

Mark handed the materials over and Brunk looked at it carefully, as if he needed to check this guy out thoroughly.

"Well Mr. Berelli, you were traveling 33 in a 30. I've been watching on radar as you drive by for years, always 33 or 34 in a 30. Just slow enough so you think I won't stop you. No one's above the law you know, no one."

"I don't think I'm above the law Vic. I was just driving as I always do."

"You need to adjust your driving habits. I'll be right back."

Berelli was incredulous. Brunk must have heard something about the AG investigation. This must be his way of being certain justice is served. "What a Nazi," he said under his breath and watched as one of O'Malley's players went by, his mother driving, rubber-necking to see who the subject of all the flashing lights was and then doing a double take after realizing it was him. This would be all over the ball park by six o'clock.

"Here's a summons for court on the twenty-fifth of this month." Brunk said when he came back. "Attached is my deposition, stating the make and model of the radar and that you weren't aware you were speeding. You're on your way to the ball park I assume?"

"Yes," Mark answered impatiently.

"Right, this other one here is for failure to use your signal when I pulled you over." Brunk gave him a stern look. "You can plead guilty if you check these boxes and send them in. Otherwise you need to appear at five pm on the twenty-fifth."

Mark nodded in acknowledgement as he took the papers, but maintained a blank look on his face.

"Now be sure to use your signal as you pull out again." Brunk said in closing, then walked back to his car and got in.

There's no telling whose side anyone is on in this town, Mark thought as he pulled out into traffic - with his signal on - and continued toward Home Run Road where the Nazareth Parks and Recreation Department had set aside land for the ball fields. When he reached the road he drove by without turning, knowing that everyone would be talking about Brunk pulling him over. He decided to wait to go to the park until later and dialed Becca Shea on his cell.

"Hey baby, it's me, are you alone?"

"Wow, I didn't expect to hear from you on a Saturday. Yes, I'm alone. The boys have games today and Jim took them to the park, why?"

"I need some lovin. Whadya think?"

"I think I always say yes," she said playfully "you know that."

"Uh-huh, and I'm a lucky man."

"Yes, you are."

"Uh-huh, and I would be especially lucky if you could meet me at the camp."

"Wow, you must really be taking Saturday off! I get you for the entire afternoon at the camp?"

"No, I get YOU for the entire afternoon at the camp."

She giggled. "Well, I have to take a shower; I've been working in the garden."

"Don't bother. Bring your suit and we'll swim. Then if you feel like you still need a shower, you can take it there. I'll wash your back.

"Mmmm," she said, "sounds wonderful, do I really need my suit?"

"Only for a minute," he chuckled.

He had her full attention now. "I'm so horny for you," she said, "I'm getting wet already."

"I can't wait."

"Me too. I can't believe this, on a Saturday? A baseball day? When do you have to be back?"

"I'm good all day, I just need to get to the ball park sometime before dark, take care of some things in the storage shed before the games tomorrow."

"What about Dana?"

"She went to the city shopping. Then to dinner with some people from her charity, so I have the A-pass."

"Wow, that's like seven hours. We never get seven hours together."

"I know, now hurry up. Let's not waste another second talking."

"Mark, I want you so bad honey."

"Baby, get in your car."

"Okay," she giggled, "I'm twenty minutes away, bye love."

The 'camp' is Mark's family camp, situated on a private mountain lake outside of Nazareth, a short drive from town. He and Dana spent a lot of time there when the kids were younger. But now that Alex was seventeen and playing baseball every day, or chasing girls, and Lonnie was in college and spending her summer working in Cape Cod, the camp was vacant most of the time. He and Dana had no interest in spending time there alone; in fact no interest in spending time *anywhere* alone. So the place became Mark's occasional love nest for himself and Becca when Dana wasn't around. At the moment he was happier than ever that he still owned it.

Arriving at the camp road, a long dirt driveway that begins at the main road encircling Parkers Lake and accessing his and two other camps on the east side, he turned left and began the fairly steep descent toward the parking area sitting above the camp. It's a short walk down a path through pine trees to the private setting overlooking the lake. The chalet sits nestled in the trees looking down the length of the lake, making sunsets spectacular from the second floor deck attached to the master bedroom.

Pulling into the parking area he was shocked to see Dana's car, a black Audi convertible, parked next to an older silver Saab near the opening to the path down to the camp.

"Shhhit. What the hell is she doing here?" He said aloud, and then took note of the other car. He was sure it belonged to Tom Morton, the Assistant Principal. He couldn't believe his eyes.

So as not to be heard, he shut off the car, called Becca and told her to stop where she was and wait for him to call back. Then he got out, closed the car door so that it only clicked shut and made his way down the path quietly, being careful not to scuff his feet as he walked, stopping occasionally to listen; to be certain no-one was coming up from the camp toward him. When the A-frame came onto view he stopped behind a pine tree off the side of the path, trying to see if they were about at the rear of the building. There was no sign of activity.

Because the chalet is actually built onto the hillside, one enters on the second floor at the rear, and then descends down stairs to the main area, kitchen and dining space, which in turn flow out onto a lake level deck with a small boathouse on stilts over the water. The second floor deck begins at the rear entrance, where Mark stood, and wraps around the building, joining with a deck that fronts the second floor master bedroom. He and Becca had lounged on that deck overlooking the lake several times, barely clothed, taking in the scenery and sipping coffee in the morning. They would make love to their hearts content there on weekdays, early, when the rest of the world was at work: when Dana thought he too was at work. They would stay until just after lunchtime, clean the bedroom carefully and then leave to return to the world. Becca would go home and wait for the kids to come home from school. Mark would go to his law office. By the time he arrived at home at six pm, the glow from his loving with Becca would have long since departed. He was sure that Dana had no clue.

He removed his sneakers and walked quietly around the second floor deck, stepping carefully while listening for sounds of activity. He stopped to listen just before turning the front corner of the building. The sliding door at the front of the bedroom was just a few feet away. He heard a dull noise, not legible from this distance, but definitely there and continuing. Turning the corner carefully and making his way to within inches of the open screen on the slider, he stopped and listened again.

"God yes Tom, uuuuhh….

oh yes….

yes…uuuuhh….

yes….uuuuhh…

god…you feel…good…

you're so hard…mmmuuuuhh….

god…yes…harder…

uuuuhhh…mmmmm….uuuuhhh…

fuck me harder Tom….

that's…it…harder…uuuuuuhhhhh…
mmmuuuuuuuuhhhhhaaaaahhhh.

Just after the crescendo of orgasm she giggled. Then a loud groan followed, that of a man losing himself in the same way. Berelli didn't need to hear more to understand the harmony of this. 'Christ' he thought to himself, 'I just heard Tom Morton have an orgasm.' It repulsed him more than anything else.

He stepped back to the corner, turned quietly and tip-toed to the back deck. Then he stepped onto the path and quickly moved away in bare feet until he was out of sight of the house. He put his sneakers back on and half jogged back to his car, got in quickly, started the engine and drove away; all the time Amazed that Dana and Morton had heard nothing.

"Becca, you're not going to believe this," he said into his cell phone, almost laughing.

"What honey? What happened?"

"Dana and Tom Morton were at the Camp."

"What?"

"Yup, and I snuck around front by the bedroom, heard them going at it, you wouldn't believe it. She was getting it good, and lovin it."

"Whaaattt? You have got to be kidding."

"Nope."

"WOW," she exclaimed

"She never came like that for me." He laughed.

"Well, you aren't an Assistant-Principal. She only gives it all up for guys with real power. But she doesn't give it up like me, does she?"

"Nuh-uh baby, nobody gives it up like you."

"And I don't give it up for anybody BUT you."

"This is Amazing," he said, "I feel so liberated. After all these years of worrying about being THAT kind of man, I didn't need to worry at all. She's banging Tom Morton for Christ's sake!"

"Yes, and in OUR place. I hope they're considerate enough to change the sheets."

"Well, we can't have them in our place; I'm going to have to tell her to find somewhere else to bang that crusty old fart. Hey, do you think he ever brings along a case of baseballs and they fondle them together?"

She laughed loudly, and then said, "Damn, we were going to have it to ourselves this afternoon, she always wrecks it. Go back there and tell her to get her bony ass to a motel; you had plans for the camp today."

"Nah, I'm going to love you up so good, won't matter where we are. I'm feeling released Becca, you're really gonna get it."

"I can't wait. I want you to just cover me up Mark, drown me in sex. Where are we going to go? Damn, I want to go to the lake."

"Let's just go to the Days Inn over on Delatour. It's close by. I'll stop at Dunkin Donuts and get a couple of coolatas and some creamy donuts. We'll put on an old movie and lie around and eat donuts and lick and suck, okay?"

"Oh God!"

"Look for my car," he told her.

"Okay, whipped cream and two Splendas."

"Got it, see you there."

"Mark?"

"Yeah baby?"

"I want you"

"I want you too, Becca."

search

Five

Brunk returned to the parking lot at Village Marketplace after giving Mark Berelli his two tickets and remained there until four o'clock. During that time he gave out two more speeding tickets, one ticket for no seat belt and three tickets for talking on cell phones. He knew the fines for the seat belts and cell phones were $125 and $250 respectively. He guessed the speeding tickets would be reduced to failure to obey a traffic signal or something like that and would cost the offenders $250 each. He figured that the failure to use his turn signal would cost Berelli another $50. A quick tally put him at $1,425 in revenue. Not bad for a Saturday afternoon.

At a little after four he called dispatch and volunteered to work the evening shift if they needed him. The duty sergeant usually says yes to this because Brunk always pays for his time in citations. On a Saturday night he'd probably process at least two DWI arrests, which bring big dollars in fines. Dispatch cleared him to stay on patrol until eleven o'clock and approved an early dinner break since he hadn't taken lunch that day. He made his way over to the Village Diner which is tucked in behind the bowling alleys on Oakwood, and sat at the counter. Although no one much cares to talk to him, there's a special waitress there with nice legs and chest and she gives him free soda. She makes sure he gets a few peeks at her cleavage, as insurance against a speeding or cell phone ticket. He could probably just get up and not pay his check at all, but Vic Brunk pays his way. He wants everyone to know that his protection does not come at a price, unless of course you're one of those scofflaws who dare to travel a couple miles per hour over the speed limit, then you know his protection comes at a big price.

He ate dinner and read *The Searchlight* cover to cover, paying special attention to the *Blotters and Dockets* section which chronicles the DWI arrests and any other crimes charged in Nazareth during the previous week. Then he read the front page article about Wyatt and the team with skepticism, at one point shaking his head about the fact that the paper made the kid out to be a hero He finished his meal, paid his bill, strutted back to his cruiser and drove by the front of Grif's to see if Peter Stenman's car was still parked in the bank lot. It was gone.

"Shit, I missed him."

Knowing where Stenman lives, he decided to cruise by the house to see if the car was parked in the driveway. If so, the worst case scenario would be that the lucky son of a bitch got away with DWI and he'd have to find another pigeon to cite tonight. He remembered the last time Stenman got all liquored up; a couple of the guys from another shift responded to a domestic violence call at the house. He'd slapped that pretty woman Dale around in his drunken rage and they carted him off to the holding cell to sleep it off. It wouldn't hurt to check out the house, just to make sure Stenman wasn't doing a repeat performance tonight. Plus, maybe he'd get a chance to see her. She sure was a pretty one, he thought.

The house sits on a quiet street in a section of town

called Old Nazareth, shrouded in mature hardwood trees, scribed by picket fences and adorned by shiny European cars sitting in clean black driveways. A police car cruising through this neighborhood is out of place, except for the hint that something may be up once again at the Stenman's. Brunk cruised by number 133 Chestnut Street and looked carefully into the driveway and around the front of the house. Stenman's red Volvo SUV wasn't in the driveway and the house looked peaceful enough. Brunk now felt a genuine concern that he was out there driving the streets somewhere, drunk out of his mind and an authentic danger to other people. He hoped that perhaps the guy found another bar and would stay put until he could be found and removed in the name of public safety. He considered putting out an alert on the car so that another cruiser could spot him, but then the others might question why he let Stenman out of his sight to begin with.

He drove around Nazareth slowing at every bar he could think of. He drove past the house two more times and found no sign of him. He drove to bars on the farthest outskirts of town, checking to see if he had ranged out there, to no avail. Finally, as darkness was approaching, he drove out to the ball park, where he hadn't been all day, to see if the Volvo was around. Maybe Stenman had driven there, parked, and passed out. During this time Wyatt finished practice at about four o'clock, posed with the team for some video for the six o'clock news, did a short interview with the guy from 'The Sports Board', then rode his bike home to chill for a while until he needed to leave to go get the 'steaks' and meet Scooter and the boys for a night on the town. He called his girlfriend, Kelly, told her was going to hang with the guys tonight, which didn't win him much favor, took a shower, had a sandwich and watched some of the Red Sox game with O'Malley. At about seven-forty-five O'Malley sensed he was getting antsy and knew he'd be heading out soon. "Y-O, where you going tonight?" He asked.

"Probably hang over at Scooter's for a while, or maybe JR's house. Becca is supposed to make those great pecan chocolate chips, if she ever gets home. JR's waiting for her to find out if the cookies are going to happen." He surely didn't know that Becca might be a little too worn out to be making cookies from scratch tonight.

"If she makes them, bring me a couple willya?"

"Sure, but I won't be getting home until right at eleven, we're going to play Texas Holdem at JR's."

"That's okay, I'll be up."

"Dad, you don't have to wait up for me. I'll be home on time."

"Not a problem. I'm not going anywhere."

"It's Saturday night, why are you just sitting home?"

"No place to go really; I'll watch the game, maybe catch a movie on pay per view."

Wyatt didn't say anything else for a moment, thinking about his Dad, feeling sad that there wasn't a woman around; then asked a question that had been nagging at him lately. "You ever think about finding a woman, you know, that you can be with a lot?"

"There are a couple of women who I see occasionally.

But not anyone I'd want to bring into our lives."

Wyatt understood, but still couldn't imagine him being without a woman companion forever. "What do you think about Becca?"

"Becca? She's a nice woman, pretty, seems happy with life. Why?"

"Johnny Morelli thinks she's got it for you."

O'Malley cracked up, laughing out loud, "Becca, got it for me? You gotta be kidding. She's not interested in me, believe me." He continued to laugh, but didn't want Y-O to get the wrong idea. "Listen, Becca is a good person, very thoughtful and smart, and talented. Did you know they show her paintings in a gallery downtown? And she's really pretty too."

"Yeah, she is."

"But we're not interested in each other that way. We have great sons who are close friends. That's good enough. We're lucky as it is, wouldn't want to screw it up."

He knew O'Malley was being politically correct. Saying the right things for public consumption, pretty much what he always does. People love him for it, except that as Wyatt grew older he figured it out and knew there was always more in the background somewhere.

Wyatt told O'Malley he'd see him later and left the house, got on his adopted bicycle and rode toward the park. It was time to pick up the steaks. Scooter had text messaged him several times in the last two hours, to check if he'd gone to get it yet. Wyatt was the only one in the group with a job, so he was the only one with enough money to buy pot. He would front some of the guys a few buck's worth, enough for a couple of joints and let them owe him. He usually collected his money reasonably soon, but most of the guys always owed him some money. He kept a sheet, nothing really organized, but little notes in his wallet about who owed him what and who had paid him what. It got to the point where JR would ask, "Can you lend me a couple of bones and put it on the sheet?" Or Scooter would ask, "What's my number on the sheet?" Some of them found other ways to clear up or reduce the sheet. Taylor Best swiped some condoms from his older brother, gave them to Wyatt and got ten bucks credit on the sheet.

Every week or so he'd get another steak from Alex. He'd usually sell off enough to his friends to pay for most of it and then have a stash for himself. After he'd sold them a share, he'd get to smoke some of it with them, so he was sharing pot he'd just sold, which wasn't a bad arrangement. And though he wasn't really dealing to make money, he had so much out there on different sheets that it seemed like he was making something on all the transactions.

He took the back way to Home Run Road this time, going through the Town Park which borders the ball park. He didn't want to be seen riding down main street toward the fields. He rode past the pool, between the soccer fields and down the path through the woods and appeared from the bushes at the rear of field number 5. He looked around quickly, saw that the fields and the lot were deserted and rode quickly to the bleachers, leaning the bicycle between the seats and the fence so no one who happened to drive through the lot would see it. He slipped into the end of the bleachers and climbed over rail after rail until he arrived at the spot where he and Alex traded drop-offs. Reaching up into the framing of the top row he found the baggie full of goods right where it was supposed to be. In the gloaming he took just a second to open the bag, smell the musty sweet contents and run his fingers through it to make sure he'd gotten a good count. He'd never rejected a bag of pot that Alex had left him, but he went through the routine anyway. Deciding this was once again a fair deal; he pulled five twenties from his pocket and stuck them up in the spot where the pot was. Then he rolled the baggie up and put it in his pocket.

He heard the sound of car tires on crushed stone in the parking lot. Looking through the slats of the bleachers he watched as Mark Berelli drove up and parked. This wouldn't do. If he walked out now, Berelli would be full of questions. There was no explanation for being under there and it was too late to pretend that he was hanging around for anything related to baseball. He thought about the bike leaning against the fence. Bicycles were often left overnight at the park, in fact it wasn't unusual to see one lying around for days. He sat down in the dirt below the stands and remained perfectly quiet, deciding to simply ride it out until Berelli finished whatever he was doing.

Berelli went directly to the shed, about thirty feet from where Wyatt hid, unlocked the large swinging door, went inside and rattled around in there for what seemed like an eternity. He would stop for a minute and be silent, then start moving things around again. Wyatt sat with his head resting against an upright and thought about other things. Within minutes another car drove in. This time the driver passed through the lot, drove up the footpath and stopped directly in front of the shed, ignoring the sign, not bothering to park and walk the path. When Stenman got out of the car Berelli appeared at the door.

"Why are you here so late, Peter?" he asked.

Stenman left his car running and stood outside between the open door and the driver seat. Wyatt strained to see, but could tell he was disheveled, his hair was all messed up and he leaned awkwardly against the car.

"Well, well," he said, "what are you doing, counting your stock in there, keeping an eye on your kingdom? Ha ha ha…you're such a fuckin sleaze Berelli."

"Stenman, you're drunk, as usual. If you came here to make trouble…"

"I came here to kick your ass is what I came here for."

"That stuff is for kids Peter. Be a man. You lost. You thought you were going to get me out of the league so you could take over, and you lost. Trying to kick my ass won't change that. Wait until next year when my kid moves on to twilight league, then you can take over for me and screw things up anyway you want. And get your car out of here. See that sign over there? It says NO VEHICLES. It figures you would drive up here anyway; you're special, right? That's part of your problem Peter; you don't want to play by the rules. You think they don't apply to you." Mark turned and walked back into the shed.

Stenman stumbled out from behind the car door and grabbed a spade leaning against the side of the shed.

"I'm going to teach you some rules," he said, drooling, slurring his words loudly; and then swung the shovel like a baseball bat against the side of the small building, making a loud bang as it struck. Wyatt was dumbstruck. These guys were going to fight. Berelli came out of the shed again, also in disbelief. When he appeared Stenman took another wild swing with the shovel, this time with him as the target, but missing the mark by several feet. The momentum of the swing without striking anything made him stumble. He tried to catch his balance but tripped over his own feet and fell down. He laid there a drunken mess, struggling to get back on his feet. Berelli laughed at him.

"Christ, I don't have to fight you Stenman; you can get beat up all alone. You're so pathetic." He laughed at him again. "Go home and sleep it off. Tell Dale I'll see her Tuesday night. And don't wait up for us, okay?"

Berelli had gone deep. Even in his stupor, Stenman heard the mocking tone and the reference to his wife energized his anger.

"You fuck; I'm gonna fucking kill you. Everybody in the world thinks I'm an asshole because of you." He got to his feet and stood there more solidly now, incensed, his intoxication replaced by the adrenalin of rage. He went at Berelli again, swinging the shovel more directly this time, grunting like a rabid animal. His tongue stuck out of his mouth and his eyes were ablaze.

As Berelli jumped around to avoid the flailing shovel, Brunk arrived in his squad car and drove up behind the Volvo. The cop got out of his car and ran to the side of the shed and yelled loudly, "STENMAN, PUT THE SHOVEL DOWN!"

"Get out of here Brunk or I'll fuckin kick the shit out

of you too." The madman swung the shovel at the door as Mark tried to close himself back in the shed. Stenman got his foot in the jamb and poked the handle of the tool in the crack, finding his target and jabbing Mark with the blunt end of the stick as he tried in vain to pull the door shut. Brunk came from behind and wrapped his arms around Stenman but his frenzy was much too strong. He whipped his elbows against Brunk, pelting his stomach, flailing wildly at him in a circle. One of his flying elbows struck the old grey officer forcefully below the jaw and stunned him. He fell back several feet, then drew his gun and yelled.

"Stenman, hold it right there. STOP!!! Put the shovel down and get on the ground, on your stomach, NOW!" He held the gun directly at him with his right hand and pointed to the ground with his left.

Wyatt remained perfectly still under the bleachers. He couldn't believe what he was seeing, but had his wits about him enough to realize if he went out there nothing good would come of it.

Stenman stopped and swerved in place, staring at Brunk standing there with the gun, as if sizing him up; deciding if he should take him seriously. He must have come to the conclusion there was no way he would actually shoot, because he advanced on the cop with the shovel raised in the air, pointing the sharp end of the spade at him; taunting and jabbing as Brunk moved to get out of the way. Mark ran out of the shed to tackle Stenman from behind, thinking together they could get him under control. But it was too late. Swinging the shovel quickly with both hands, Stenman managed to catch Brunk on the left arm with the back side of the spade. Reacting to the blow in anger, or in fear, or in some combination of the two, Brunk pulled the trigger before Mark could arrive.

Wyatt had never heard the sound of a gun except on TV. Mark hadn't heard it since his hunting days. Brunk had shot the occasional rabid raccoon and he maintained his skill set with mandatory range practice four times per year; but he had only pointed his gun at a human once before, a long time ago. The boom filled the air, echoed off the trees at the rear of the park and stunned them all. Stenman recoiled from the impact and fell to the ground in a slump. They stared at him until Mark came to his senses first and ran over, rolled him on his back and felt his neck. There was only a weak pulse.

"Stenman," he yelled, "Christ, Stenman!!!"

He looked at Stenman's chest. In the short time since Brunk fired a large spot of red had developed at the top, directly below his neck. Mark tore open Stenman's shirt and saw a hole there, pumping blood out. He put his hand over the hole, but the blood continued to run out the sides.

"Jesus Vic, what the fuck are you doing? Call an Ambulance, get on your radio. What the hell were you thinking? He's just a drunk. He's dying. You SHOT him. I can't believe this, shit."

Vic Brunk, *Patrolman* Victor C. Brunk, twenty six year veteran of the Nazareth police force, said nothing. He watched as a pool of blood began to form by the side of the man he'd just shot, hoping it was a dream; realizing it wasn't. Within seconds his mind left the reality that he had ended a human life to the notion that by doing so he'd destroyed a career's worth of vital law enforcement. All the good he performed for this town would soon come to an end. He shot and killed a drunk who was threatening him with a garden shovel. It would never sell. He raised his eyes to Mark Berelli, frantically pumping Stenman's chest, knowing he was now a witness and wouldn't say anything redeeming about this later. The knee-jerk liberals in this town would be all over him and the force; screaming foul, demanding that he be suspended at the very least. There would be a full IAD investigation after which he'd be riding a desk until they forced him to retire. His career ended two minutes ago. This town would not survive without him.

Wyatt sat frozen, shaking, gasping for breath, trying to decide if he should go out there. Brunk made his decision for him. As Mark was bent over Stenman vainly trying to revive him, Brunk raised his gun again and fired. The Bullet entered just below the shoulder blades, sending Berelli tumbling over Stenman's body, finally landing flat on his back and staring straight up. His left foot twitched and he gasped for air as his heart also beat blood onto the grass beneath.

After the second explosion decayed away, Brunk lowered the gun and looked at the two of them lying there in the near darkness.

"Sometimes the ball of Justice takes a funny bounce," he said without remorse.

Six

Rex O'Malley thought about it being Saturday night, that Wyatt must think it strange he has no love interest. Maybe part of it was that since the kid has no mom at home, he might have felt he was missing something. At times, Rex felt guilty about letting her leave all those years ago, but they both would've been miserable if he'd talked her into staying. She hated baseball. Why the hell did she marry a baseball player if she hated the game so much? It was another one of those things about her that made no sense, at least to him. But deep inside he knew it wasn't only about baseball, it was about his job; she hated his job. The last time he spoke with her she seemed happy with her new man and new life in San Diego. She was forever asking Wyatt to come out there to visit, stay if he liked, promising that California is a great place to play baseball. Wyatt never wanted to go. He told O'Malley that when she left him, she left both of them. Regardless, he knew the kid suffered over her absence.

The Red Sox game was pretty boring tonight, it was the top of the sixth and they were beating the Orioles 11 to 2. It wasn't anything worth watching. He decided to go out after all, down to Grif's for a couple of beers and see who was around. There was sure to be some fun as the entire town was buzzing about their trip to the World Series. He was as much of a hero as the boys and it reminded him of the old days. When you do something big, everybody wants a piece of you.

The place was lively. At the door he took a right and went to the bar instead of a left to the restaurant area, full as it was with families and kids. He could have stayed outside on the patio, a parking area they turned onto a street side café, but it was populated mostly by couples. The bar is where the guys hang out, the other baseball dads, coaches, a few female baseball groupies and girlfriends. None of the regular women there interest O'Malley, at least not to date, but the bar is warm and congenial and a good place to have a few.

The first guy he recognized was Harry Strauss, a small man, the Vice-president of the Little League in Nazareth. His kids have all grown out of the league but Harry stays involved anyway, mostly because he has no life and partly because he's a bit of a letch who likes to flirt with the team moms. He calls it the 'mom factor,' a concept he made popular. When a manager is drafting his little league team and it gets down to the final ten draftees or so, the kids who couldn't catch a baseball if their life depended upon it, by Strauss's rule, you apply the 'mom factor.' You draft the kid with the best looking Mom. It really is the deciding criterion sometimes, though no one admits it except Strauss. At the Little League Park, the moms often catch Strauss staring at them through coke bottle glasses, extra thick on the bottom. He's so blind that when he talks to you he has to stretch his head way back so he can look up at your face through the bifocal part.

"Hey O'Malley," Strauss said, looking up when Rex walked in, stretching his head back. His large nostrils flared with the effort. O'Malley noted that Strauss was especially in need of a nose hair trim tonight.

"Hey Straussey, how's it going?"

Harry shrugged and looked over at the bar where Bobby Barone's mom Wendy was sitting. He calls her the Red Baroness. Bobby graduated from Little League to Babe Ruth this year. Wendy, a red-haired beauty, was a tremendous loss to Harry's league. O'Malley noticed her too, from the corner of his eye.

"Things could be worse I guess," Straus said with a crooked perverted smile, glancing over at Wendy. "Are the boys ready to go?"

"They looked pretty good in practice today," O'Malley said, "the Channel 9 news people were there doing some video. The main challenge is to keep them on a level plane. It's tough when they're sixteen."

Ethan Ward, a news writer for *The Searchlight*, walked up to them. His wife left him last year; rumor has it, because he's gay. But he's not really, O'Malley knows the truth. He ran into Ethan in a bar in the city back in the spring, sitting with a very pretty and apparently very loose woman in a corner booth. It's his and Ethan's little secret and the cause for a smile between them occasionally. His son is fifteen and a decent ball player. The other players roll their eyes when they hear he is on their team, because of the rumor. They figure he's gay too. Ethan is a Board member and in charge of distributing all the team uniforms, which he stores in his garage over the winter. This weirds some people out a little; thinking about him thinking about the boys in uniform. O'Malley is fine with it.

"You gonna give me an exclusive?" Ethan asks with a smile.

"Before or after the World Series?"

"After."

"It depends on how we do."

"Aw come on Rex, you know you guys are gonna win at least a few games. You haven't even been tested yet. Those guys you beat last week went all the way to the semi-final round last year."

"That was last week. Hey, I need a beer. You guys ready?"

Harry and Ethan both had full glasses and indicated so. O'Malley turned to the bar where Jim Shea, a regular at Grif's, was leaning.

"Hey skipper, what you want?" Shea asked.

"Bud Light Jim, thanks."

Shea is one of the people in the league that O'Malley considers reasonable, although he does have an anger issue and needs to be reined in from time to time. It seems funny that Becca often accompanies Jim to the bar even though they're divorced. But it's safe for her to hang at Grif's with him, nobody bothers her when he is around and she isn't looking to meet anyone else. She wasn't there now, which seemed strange. Rex knew Becca better than Wyatt imagined. He knew she was involved with Mark Berelli, but he was the only one who did. He would meet her for lunch occasionally. They'd talk about the boys, about life, about happiness. They talked about whatever they wanted to talk about, which was the best thing about their friendship. It was honest and open and valuable. They liked each other. They never crossed the line from there, though they had both secretly thought about it. Becca is a complex woman and O'Malley understands her. She told him her relationship with Mark was a dead end street; they just hadn't arrived at the end of the street yet. He guessed she was with him tonight and took a long pull on his beer.

"You know," Shea said to him, "Peter Stenman is a pain in the ass. All he wants to do is promote himself and bring Berelli down. We ought to get enough votes together to throw him off The Board."

"We can't do that right now."

"Why? There are enough members who think he's destructive…"

"Yeah" O'Malley interrupted, "but he'd turn around and sue us for retaliating against him, about the Attorney General thing and all. We'd have to spend thousands with lawyers. It'd be crazy."

"Skipper, this is screwed up. Stenman and his bunch of activists have no business being involved with the league. All they care about is tearing it down. The baseball, the thing we're doing here, doesn't mean a thing to them."

"They care about their own kids playing time, right?" O'Malley said with a sarcastic look.

"Oh yeah, that too. The Grezudnik woman lit into me today. She said her son struck out twice in a row because I didn't start him at shortstop and he was upset. I told her he struck out twice in a row because he won't stay in the box when the pitcher throws a curve ball. They know he's afraid of it, so that's what they throw."

"She's got him all twisted up Jim, afraid to fail," O'Malley said. "You could take a lesson from that."

"Whadya mean?"

"What do I mean? Jim, you oughta see JR play when you're not around. He's a different kid; confident, relaxed, poised. You get him tighter than a piano wire."

"Why, because I yell?"

"Hello? Yes because you yell. He can't focus because he's thinking he's gonna fuck up and you're gonna yell, then the other guys are gonna laugh at you yellin at him. What a dumb thing to have to think about when you're trying to play baseball."

"I know, but I yell at all the players, not just my own kids."

O'Malley twisted his mouth up, the way he always does when the answer is so obvious he can't stop himself. "And what's your record so far this season?"

"Well we haven't played well these first few games, but the guys are really having fun."

"What's your record?" Of course, O'Malley already knew.

"We're 0 and 5." He said, knowing where this was headed.

"People who don't know much about baseball like to think it's some kind of course in the humanities, that somehow it's fun for the guys just to be a part of the team;

that learning the game and sportsmanship and teamwork are the most important things. And all that is important. In fact, working hard at this game will make you a better human being. But I never heard a player say they had fun losing."

"I know, I know. Winning isn't everything, it's the only thing." Shea thought this summed it all up.

"Nope, and you know what? Vince Lombardi never said that. What he said was 'Winning isn't everything, wanting to win is.' Your guys need to experience winning so they can get past losing. Your job is to make them want to win. If you do that, they will. They'll learn from failure and then forget it. They'll be dying to get back on the field and try to win again. That's when the fun begins."

"I push them really hard to make the plays, to execute, so they have a chance to succeed."

"And then you yell at them if they make an error or strike out."

"Well, yeah, well I don't yell every time."

"Don't ever holler about mistakes Jim. Holler about effort, after the game. Don't make them afraid of trying. Teach them to be afraid of NOT trying."

Shea became distracted by a pretty blonde sitting at the end of the bar. He'd seen her here a few times but never had a conversation with her. The woman was looking in their direction at the moment and Jim picked up the vibes like a radio antenna. She would come here with a girlfriend nearly every Saturday to get her fill of guys stepping over themselves to talk to her. O'Malley saw the change in Shea's interest then looked in her direction and smiled.

"Yeah, I got it skip," Shea said, trying to wind the conversation up, "I'll do some work on that, be right back." Being divorced and a bold Irishman, he walked down the bar to make a move on the blonde.

"Has anybody seen Peter Stenman?" Chris the bartender announced loudly. He had the bar phone in his hand with the mouthpiece against his chest so the response couldn't be heard on the other end.

Someone yelled out, "Why? Is that his boss at the IRS?" Several people at the bar laughed.

O'Malley watched as Chris put the receiver to his ear and spoke while shaking his head no. He remembered that bartenders protect their customers more than anybody, even when the customer is a jackass like Stenman. He looked down at his beer and was nearly ready for another so he upended it and motioned to Chris for a refill. Art Blaze, the Sabic Plastics VP, sat with his wife and another couple about midway down the bar from where O'Malley stood. Art waved his hand at him, motioning him to come over and O'Malley obliged. Art is another one of the reasonable ones.

"Rex, please say hello to my sister Karen and her husband Jack, they've been dying to meet you." O'Malley offered his hand and smiled while they exchanged how-do-you-do.

"We understand you played for the Red Sox," Karen began, "how lucky this community is to have you."

"Well thank you," O'Malley said honestly, "I was in the Sox minor league system for a few years, after college. That was before they paid guys big money to do nothing. I was one of those they paid nothing to do nothing." Everyone laughed.

"Rex is the manager every kid around here wants to play for. Of course, it helps their cause if they drop off plane tickets to exotic places at his house," Art joked.

"Yes, and the Caribbean is big on my list right now. We don't play much baseball in January. How old is your kid again Art?"

Jack and Karen chuckled at the friendly banter.

"But in all seriousness Rex," she said, "the players are very lucky to have such a talented coach. The paper said the boys are good players, but it's generally known you bring out the best in them."

"Well, again, in all seriousness Karen, I'm just happy to be here, baseball is a game of inches, you win some and you lose some, and I couldn't do this without them."

"Are you in public relations Rex?" Jack asked while laughing, "Because we could sure use you on our team."

"Jack is a candidate for Town Supervisor in Mitchell," Art told him. Mitchell is another town on the other side of the city, similar in size and character to Nazareth, though not as old.

"Ah, I see. Well, if you'll build a big ball park with a team clubhouse, I can be bought."

At that moment, Tommy Hunter put his hand on O'Malley's shoulder from behind, smiling demurely as he sought attention. After O'Malley turned to greet him, Karen said "Isn't he an interesting character?"

They all agreed. Art shook his head and smiled at the coach's success, "His son Wyatt is a good ball player too; he had a big part in this advance to the Series."

"I read about that," Jack said, "a walk-off hit. That's something he'll remember for the rest of his life."

Tommy was a little ashen faced as usual, owing to the fact that he drinks a little more than is good for him, but he's a big burly bear of a man with a kind heart and deeply connected in Nazareth town politics. He used to be married to the town supervisor, Melissa Hunter, before she left him and married the town attorney. It was a big story around the community, her leaving the modest life as the wife of a plumber, getting into politics and remarrying into influence. Now she drives to the town offices in a mid-size Mercedes coupe, while Tommy continues to drive to his jobs and the ball park in his service van. He remains one of the real workers for the league, at the fields constantly; mowing, raking and fixing the pitchers mounds. He always wears a smile and has nothing bad to say about anyone. Tommy is a quiet, unpretentious man who loves his drinks after work at Grif's. He's one of a dozen or so with a house account at the bar.

"Can I talk to you Rex?" Tommy turned his head to the side when he realized the others heard him and spoke in the opposite direction before he said the rest. "Kathleen's not doing well." Kathleen is their daughter, Melissa's and Tommy's, sixteen and institutionalized at an eating disorder clinic in Boston.

"Yes, of course Tommy, I was thinking about you guys the other day, what's going on?" Rex asked warmly, genuinely concerned. Tommy confides in O'Malley occasionally, sort of a counselor for him. He understands things from a guy's perspective, gives him a place to vent and gets him back into the 'glass half full' mode. It has never been more truly said that a coach is so much more than just a coach.

"She's down to eighty four pounds. She's six feet tall Rex. They had to give her intravenous electrolytes yesterday, they were afraid her heart was going to stop."

"Tommy, why are you still here?"

"Melissa is over there. They told me that whenever I come to see her, she has an episode. She always asks for me, emails me, calls me, asking to come get her out or at least bring her something, you know? But when I go to see her, she has an episode as soon as I leave."

"What kind of episode?"

"They have to put someone with her seven-twenty-four, because when she's alone she just exercises, she'll do hundreds of jumping jacks, or she'll run in place; whatever she can do to take off weight. After I left her the last time she put all of her food down in her pants at dinner, hiding it, so they would think she ate it."

"Good God Tommy, I'm so sorry. When we last talked you said she was doing better, she came home for a while; I don't understand?"

"Well, she was doing better, that's why they let her come home. But it seems that it's me, when I'm around she relapses. She had to go back. I don't understand either. She says she loves me."

"Tom, everyone knows she loves you. I've seen her at the ball games, when she makes a basket she always looks to you for approval."

"Maybe that's the prob…" Tommy's cell phone rang. "It's Melissa, I gotta go, thanks Rex." He was backing toward the door, putting the phone to his ear.

"No problem Tommy, go…go ahead, call me later."

Jim Shea came back over, in need of a beer. O'Malley promptly obliged, and asked. "So what happened with the blonde?"

"You mean the good widow Anastasia?"

"She's a widow?"

"Yeah."

"Man, she sure looks young."

"Forty one. Her husband was older, a banker, had an aneurism and dropped dead last year." Shea looked at him with a sarcastic grin. "I didn't have a chance; she kept looking over here and asking about you."

"I gotta go." O'Malley said, "Y-O will be home at eleven and I need to be there."

"Why do you need to be there?" Shea asked

"Because I told *him* to be there."

Seven

Wyatt sat in the mud while water dripped around him. It had been hours since he first made his way under the bleachers. In the meantime the thunderstorm had come up as forecast, drenching everything. A puddle built up where he was sitting. He was soaking wet, tired, scared and shaking.

The storm was timely for Brunk though, it served his purposes perfectly. During the deluge, he went into the shed and found a roll of plastic. Taking his time, he closed the door and cut four pieces about twelve feet by twelve feet. He also cut a piece about five feet wide to sit on. After the storm broke he put everything in the shed back the way he found it then went to his police cruiser and put on overalls, his field issue boots and latex evidence gloves. He opened the hatchback to Stenman's SUV, put the rear seat down and lined the cargo compartment with the sheets of plastic. Then put the smaller piece on the driver's seat where he would sit. Wyatt watched him working.

The forecast called for continued thunder-storms throughout the night and Brunk could feel the breeze pick up again as the next line approached. He lifted two fifty pound bags of lime, the material used for striping the baselines, from the stack in the shed and loaded them into the car. Then picking up his pace he dragged the two bodies over to the SUV and struggled to lift them into the back. Both men weighed nearly two hundred pounds so it took some doing even for Brunk, a man in much better condition than most police officers at nearly fifty five years old. He was careful not to let any of the blood get on his overalls or the gloves so that there'd be no chance of dragging some with him. The bleeding had stopped oozing from the wounds after the hour or so since he shot them and *rigor mortis* would begin soon. After closing up the car he went back to the grass where the bodies had lain and looked carefully with his flashlight for any signs of puddles of blood. The rain had washed nearly all of it away and he was sure that the next storm would take care of any that still remained.

Brunk is familiar with nearly every piece of town property in Nazareth. Directly adjacent to the baseball fields sits a pet park, an area of grass about an acre in size that the town had fenced in, used by residents for walking their dogs without a leash. This is not a place where the dog owners themselves tread very often as the grass is strewn with pile upon pile of dog manure, big and small; an area of 'land mines' in a sense. So most owners usually stand just inside the gate and let their dog run. The town crews come by occasionally, every two weeks or so, and use an agricultural rake to mix up the surface. The grass has gone bare in some spots from all the urinating and defecating. The field of dreams, Brunk decided, would be a perfect resting place for Stenman and Berelli.

He started the SUV, backed out of the path to the shed and instead of turning left in the lot to go back out to the main road; he turned right and went straight to a dirt service road that connected the ball park with the back of the doggie park. He would leave the SUV there, out of sight, and return later after he went to the station, turned in his patrol car and completed his reports at shift's end.

Wyatt saw this as his chance. He knew that Brunk could not get to the main road from the service road so he had the opportunity to slip away, but he had to move quickly. The quickest path to safety and the way least likely to be seen by Brunk would be to go out to the main road and ride home that way. Once he saw the SUV out of sight he stood up. After sitting motionless on the wet ground for so long, his legs had gone partially numb. At first, he struggled to step over the framing of the bleachers in a coordinated way. Panic was settling in as he felt the urgency to get out from under there before Brunk returned. Although he knew the place by heart, he slipped twice and fell again in the mud, finding himself careless in his fatigue and desperation. Finally out in the fresh air and clear of the bleachers, he hopped on the bicycle and rode feverishly toward the road.

Meanwhile, Brunk left the SUV behind the maintenance barn at the doggie park and began his walk back to his patrol car in the dark. He nearly reached the parking lot in pitch black when he heard the sound of a bicycle chain rattling as it bounced over potholes. Standing perfectly still, he heard small tires rolling over the gravel and searched the darkness in the direction of the sound while it trailed off. As a car passed on the road in the distance, its headlights shone on the silhouette of a bike and rider at the end of the ball park entrance. Brunk knew the color, he'd recognize it anywhere: a small fluorescent green bicycle lit up brightly under the lights of the passing car.

Wyatt rode as fast as he could; faster than he'd ever peddled in his life. He took every side path he knew; cutting across the church lot and backyards and riding the railroad tracks where it would keep him out of sight and represent a more straight line to home. He didn't want anyone to see him and connect him with being at the ball fields. Whatever became of Brunk killing those guys, he'd kept himself out of it so far and wanted nothing to do with it going forward.

It was eleven-ten and he was late. A few minutes would be no big deal to O'Malley, but as he leaned the bike against the tree in the side yard, he realized he looked a mess. His cargo shorts were filthy, he was soaking wet all over and his sneakers, the brand new Nike Air Force that O'Malley had just bought him the week prior, were soaked and covered in black mud from under the bleachers. He had to think fast. He opened the garage door and stashed the baggie of pot in his ski boots sitting on the shoe rack. Then he stopped by the door to the house, removed his sneakers and shorts and carried the shorts in the door with him.

"Sorry I'm late," he said as he walked in from the garage in soaking bare feet and just his boxers."

"What happened to you?"

"I was waiting until the storm stopped to ride home, but I got caught in it anyway." At least he wasn't stoned, he felt like O'Malley could see right through what he was saying, it would have been ten times worse if he was buzzed. O'Malley looked him up and down; then saw the mud all over the back of his shorts.

"Were you guys playing football in the mud again?"

"It was really muddy…"

"O'Malley interrupted him, "Well get your clothes right into the wash, Mrs. Perkins will be in to clean and do laundry on Monday."

"Okay," he said, relieved, and walked toward the door to the laundry room, "I'm gonna get in the shower and go to bed, I'm beat."

"Did Scooter find you?"

Wyatt didn't say anything in return, pretending he didn't hear while he thought of what to say.

"Y-O, did you hear me?"

"What did you say?" he asked from within the laundry room.

"Did Scooter find you? He called here about a half hour after you left. I told him I thought you were going to his house."

"No, we never did hook up, because of the storm and all."

"Isn't your cell phone working?"

"No, the battery is dead."

"Did you bring me some of Becca's cookies?"

"It was pouring rain Dad."

"You bum."

"Sorry."

He figured if he got through this he'd done pretty well,

because he hadn't lied yet, he just didn't tell the whole story. O'Malley made it easy for him by the way he asked the questions. If he only knew what he'd seen tonight.

The adrenalin was still coursing through his veins. There hadn't been time for all of it to sink in. The hot shower slowed him down as he sat on the floor, letting the water pour over him. It felt so good he forgot his situation for a few minutes. The comfort and security of being home provided a short reprieve; assisted him in denying the event. But as his pulse slowed while he showered, a dull ache began to rise up in his belly. He dried off, brushed his teeth and went to his room, saying an abridged 'good night' as he walked by O'Malley sitting watching Sports Center in the living room. If he could just go to sleep now he would find an answer in the morning. The 'what ifs?' were knocking on the door to his consciousness, but the trauma of seeing the whole crime unfold had exhausted him mentally. It's a testament to nature's genius that young people are able to sleep during the most trying of times. The mind simply 'checks out' for them, while the same disturbing event would render an adult sleepless for days. Wyatt was sound asleep within seconds of slipping under the covers.

Brunk, on the other hand, went to the police station and filed his reports, then returned to the doggie park and opened the maintenance garage. He needed digging implements; a shovel and rake. He knew that the doggie park, like most land in the area, is comprised of loamy sand. So the digging would be easy. He used his penlight to find the tools and went out into the grassy area, walking carefully to avoid leaving tracks in bare dirt areas or stepping in dog manure. Once he located a large section of turf void of grass, he planted the shovel to mark it and went to the SUV and retrieved a piece of the plastic, then spread it out on the ground to catch the spoils where he would dig. He estimated he'd need a hole three feet wide by seven feet long by three feet deep to serve his purposes, so he shoveled steadily, setting a pace he could maintain without over exertion. Though wet from the rain, the sand came out of the ground easily without forming mud. After about an hour the hole was complete.

He returned to the garage, withdrew a wheelbarrow and took it to the car to fetch the bodies. He grabbed them one at time by the ankles and pulled them covered in plastic out of the car, letting them drop out the back and into the wheelbarrow, and then carted them coarsely to the grave site. Struggling mightily, he finally succeeded in getting both bodies into the hole side by side and face to face. He chuckled that these guys would never have imagined they'd spend eternity so embraced.

He went back to the car and retrieved the lime, then returned to the hole and emptied both bags over the bodies. He hoped this would help prevent the scent of decaying flesh from leeching up through the soil and being picked up by the visiting dogs. Then he went back to the garage and found a hand tamper, returned to the hole and began to fill it in. After spreading about six inches of dirt onto the bodies he tamped the dirt, knowing he would have to pack it tightly, hoping somehow he'd be able to return most of the soil into the hole from whence it came. He repeated this process every few inches until the hole was filled to the top, pounding the last of it vigorously with the tamper, adding more dirt, and then pounding again. He was pleased to see he had only about three wheelbarrow loads of soil to dispose of, the Amount which represented the space taken up by the bodies in the hole. He raked the top smooth, then loaded the remaining dirt onto the wheelbarrow and dumped it deep in the back of the park, spreading it around in a stand of trees out of sight.

Thunder rumbled in the distance and the wind picked up again, foreshadowing another storm about to arrive. It was approximately four thirty a.m. on Sunday the 14th of July. He smiled, knowing the rain would soon be teeming down again, removing evidence. He also so knew that being Sunday, no town workers would be at the garage for at least another thirty hours or so.

After cleaning up carefully and putting the tools away, Brunk drove home letting his thoughts turn to the chain clanking in the dark and the little green bicycle in the headlights. The question bore in of whether it was Wyatt or someone else. He couldn't be sure and wondered if whoever it was had witnessed what he'd done to Stenman and Berelli. The scene returned to his mind. He pictured the shed and the cars parked there, the fight and the shooting, as if he were looking through someone else's eyes. Where could that someone else have hidden? The woods behind center field came to mind and the port-a-john by each field, and the rear of the shed. A chill came over him in a wave as the scene replayed in his mind. He remembered seeing just the rear tire of a bicycle, mostly hidden from view by the bleachers. The bleachers... of course, the bleachers.

He turned the car around abruptly and drove back to the park. With his small black flashlight he walked to the bleachers. It was nearly five am and the sky was beginning to lighten. He didn't have much time before he could be recognized by someone, a jogger, or another cop cruising by. It started to rain again, a final morning downpour from the departing storm, as he stood by the bleachers and peered underneath with the flashlight. Rain pelted his back and head, making it difficult to concentrate on what he was looking at. The ends of the bleachers were open; the only way someone could get underneath. He peered below in the rain, moving the flashlight to see past the odd soda can and the weeds growing at the edges. About midway down the back of the structure he spotted a trampled area, muddy and churned up, indicating someone had lingered there for a while. He entered at the end and climbed underneath the frame, over the cross supports, avoiding hitting his head, until he arrived at the spot. There were footprints formed from the water raining down through the seats; fresh footprints in the mud.

The tracks were inconclusive. He thought it could remain muddy under there for days after a rain, and the footprints could have been made the night before last, another rainy night. The Cop in Brunk made him consider other factors. Someone riding a bicycle at the ballpark at that time of night would be unusual. The ballpark is not a short cut to anywhere, it's a destination. The kid was not riding through, going home, or to a friend's house. He was either arriving or leaving. He wasn't arriving. He had been there.

Eight

One of the great things about community baseball, at least if you're a ball-player, coach, parent, or board member, is that there's something going on at the ball park every night from the first of April to the middle of August. It's the perfect excuse for fathers and sons to get out of the house, night after night, to play baseball, talk baseball, hang around and watch baseball, work on baseball fields, to do everything and anything baseball.

But Sunday practice is unusual. If Wyatt's team wasn't in the big tournament, they'd be playing a travel game somewhere, maybe a double header. Once travel season starts there's no time for practice. They'll often play five games a week, so O'Malley lets them get away the rest of the time; lets them be kids. But travel season was postponed this year for this team, as there was still business to do in Babe Ruth. They needed to prepare to play teams from all over the country beginning on Monday. The fortunate part for them was that the tournament, the sixteen year old Babe Ruth World Series, was being hosted just twenty miles north in Ridgewood Park. This was one of the reasons that the Regional tournament was played in Nazareth and hence partly the reason the Hawks were so successful in it. They had home field advantage throughout the Regionals - lots of 'home cookin', as they say.

It was 11:00 a.m. and the team was assembled at the

field for practice. O'Malley had them sitting in the shade in deep right field next to the fence while he talked. He would've held the rap session in one of the dugouts, but spectators - supporters and parents - had shown up for practice. They'd followed the news coverage yesterday and were here to see if any more media appeared. O'Malley chuckled about it. 'A day late and a dollar short,' he said to himself. But now that spectators were around he had to take the guys away so they could speak openly without worrying about outsiders listening in.

"What we have to say to ourselves," he said while pointing a finger to his ear, "is that the upcoming series is no different than any other we've played this year."

"Well, tell it to them skipper," big Patrick Burns the first baseman said as he nodded toward the thirty or so people who had gathered to watch practice, "Cripe, you could run a fifty-fifty here today, for PRACTICE." Everybody laughed, it felt good.

Patrick plays first base. His father Ricky is a little guy who disagrees with everyone about everything. Ricky is a mortgage broker with a lot of spare time and hence he runs for miles every day; runs in every marathon on the east coast. The guys joke that he's trying to prove he's got the biggest heart, but they really mean he's trying to prove something else is bigger. He and Joe Morelli come close to a fist fight nearly every season, mostly because neither of them will let the other have the last word. Ricky thinks his tall and overweight kid should hit a home run every at bat, but he never does. Big Patrick benefited from most of his mother's genes- he's happy-go-lucky and confident just like her. But he'd have been better off without the ones that made him fat.

"Let it be different to them Burnsy," O'Malley said,

"but when we walk onto the field Monday night, remember; for us this is the same game we play every day. The teams are going to be better, they might be as good as we are, but this is the same game. We need to block out the crowd, the noise, the difference."

"There's gonna be a lot of babes there, skip, a friggin lot of babes, that's a big difference," John Morelli said as he held up a clipping from The Searchlight the one with his picture and his stats on it. "And I'm ready for em." They all cracked up.

This is good, O'Malley thought, they're behaving normally. Except for Y-O that is, he sat at the end of the row looking distracted. He flopped his glove against the ground rhythmically as he sat there, not hearing much, looking uncomfortable, as if he needed to get out onto the field quickly but couldn't because of some unknown force field holding him down.

"Hey Wyatt, we boring you dude?" Jed Rounder asked.

Wyatt looked up from his trance, ashen faced, trying desperately to eke out a smile. He said nothing, just shook his head and squirmed as everyone else began talking again. This let him off the hook but O'Malley noticed; he knows his boy. Wyatt is never loud in the group but he normally has a loose demeanor, easily connecting to any joke or conversation when the game isn't being played. He shifts gears when it's time to play and down shifts again when there's a break in the action. So seeing him uncomfortable here at practice, when nothing in the world could be wrong, caught O'Malley's attention and became a concern. He elected not to draw further notice to him at the moment, but would dig into it later.

"All right, we'll do about thirty minutes of infield-outfield, then work on bunt and pick-off coverage, then batting practice. We good?" O'Malley asked.

They roundly approved and began to stand up. Wyatt was first off the ground and walked toward third base without speaking. As he strolled over to his position, feeling a little better no longer cornered against the fence, he saw Brunk out in the parking lot leaning against his car staring in his direction. Brunk always watches carefully whenever Wyatt is around and Wyatt always pretends not to notice. The game was no different today. Though of course, it was. He walked around third base as a player normally does, took a throw from the second baseman and forwarded it to the catcher at home. They warmed up while waiting for O'Malley to get his fungo bat and step near the batter's box for infield practice.

"Get ONE." O'Malley yelled finally, meaning the infield should field the ball and make a routine throw to first base. He always started with third, so Wyatt knew a grounder was coming his way. The ball cracked off O'Malley's bat and bounded in Wyatt's direction, requiring a move slightly to his right to field it. He wondered, as the ball skipped toward him, why Brunk was out there staring in toward the field. Then instead of making a clean scoop on the grounder, it slipped underneath his glove and skittered out into left field, disturbing the rhythm of the exercise before it even started. "Hey Y-O," O'Malley yelled, "I can guarantee that ball will NOT jump off the ground and into your glove. My experience has been that you need to reach down far enough to get the real thrill of catching it. Do it again."

O'Malley hit him another one. This time, Wyatt fielded the ball correctly but made a high throw to first, unreachable by the first baseman.

"Never mind," he said, "I'll come back to you."

As O'Malley continued hitting ground balls around the rest of the infield he knew something was wrong.

Over the next half hour Wyatt misplayed three other grounders out of the fifteen or so Rex hit to him. The sloppiness was contagious and he realized that as he went, so went the rest of the players. O'Malley couldn't believe it, in all the years of coaching this group of players, he hadn't seen them this bad since they were twelve. He finally stopped the infield practice and asked Art Bastau, his coach and whose son Danny plays second base, to throw batting practice. O'Malley walked toward the dugout; thinking maybe today was just a bad practice day. The thirty or so parents and Board members who were watching looked at him as he walked. Jim Shea came over to the fence.

"JR looks awful today."

"That's because you're here."

Shea laughed. "No, really skip, they stink."

"Yeah, they do today. Maybe it's all the attention turning into pressure."

"Yeah, maybe that's what it is." Shea was distracted by Brunk and a detective standing and talking next to Mark Berelli's car. "Hey, did you hear about Berelli and Stenman?"

"Hear what?"

"They're missing."

"Missing?" O'Malley gave him a twisted look and pointed to the car, parked in the lot where Mark left it the night prior, "Whadya mean missing?"

"Yeah, I know. But they can't find them."

"Since when?"

"I guess Dana called the Police sometime late last night, Dale reported on Stenman this morning."

"You gotta be kidding me. So the car has been here all night?"

"I guess so." Shea shrugged.

"Where'd you hear about this?" O'Malley now watched the two cops snooping around Berelli's car.

"Becca called me a few minutes ago. I guess the news is going through town pretty quick. She was pretty shocked."

Rex paused for a few seconds. "I imagine."

Another Nazareth police car pulled into the lot, and then another. Now three patrol cars were parked at Mark's green Jeep SUV. A fourth stopped where Brunk was standing. He had a brief conversation with the officer driving and pointed to the dirt road leading to the rear of the doggie park. O'Malley and Shea watched the car zip away and disappear into the trees. The players stopped what they were doing and looked at the gathering. John Morelli and Jed Rounder, who were preparing to be the first two in batting practice, walked over to the backstop fence to get a closer look.

"What's going on Skip?" Jed asked, "why they foolin with Mr. B's car?"

"I don't know," Rex said. He and Shea looked at each other and he didn't want to address the issue now and so returned to baseball. "Okay guys, where's our first batter? Coach you ready to go?"

"I'm ready Rex, let's get a hitter up there." Art Bastau said.

"Johnny, you number one?" Morelli nodded his head, "alright well get in there then, let's go. Give me two bunts to start, then ten swings."

The order for batting practice was established early in the season, so everyone knew where they stood and when to come in to be on deck. Coach Bastau threw each of the players about fifteen perfect strikes so that they could take smooth contact swings. He was like a machine. After the process started O'Malley slipped out through the gate beside the dugout and walked down to where the police were convening around Berelli's car. Wyatt watched anxiously as he walked away though didn't let on to any of the others. O'Malley strolled up to Brunk who was standing apart from the other cops, appearing like the master of ceremonies. It seemed they were all waiting for something.

"Hi Vic," O'Malley said, "got any information yet?"

"This is a police matter Mr. O'Malley. If there's anything to be announced, the Chief or the Town Supervisor will do it later."

"I understand Vic; I wasn't looking for anything official. Stenman and Berelli are a part of our league and important to a lot of people. It'd be nice to have facts instead of rumor. I'm hearing they were reported missing?"

"That's right."

"When?"

"Between 3:45 a.m. and 10:15 a.m.."

"So you mean one of them was reported at 3:45 a.m. and one of them was reported at 10:15 a.m.?"

"I didn't say that, don't put words in my mouth," Brunk said, and stared at him with cold black eyes.

"I'm not putting words in your mouth. I'm trying to get a straight answer."

"I didn't take the call, so I'm not sure. As soon as the press gets wind of it, you'll have all the answers you want."

O'Malley walked off in the direction of the doggie park, following the road the police cruiser traveled. He shook his head as he took the first few steps, unconcerned if Brunk saw him or not. As he walked around a bend and up a shallow incline the police cruiser and then Stenman's red SUV came into view. The two cops, a uniformed patrolman and a plain clothes detective, were looking in through the smoky glass but not touching anything or opening the doors. Seeing O'Malley walk up they stopped snooping and assumed a more official guard-like stance. The detective spoke. "I'll have to ask you not to touch the car Mr. O'Malley. Since the missing person report was filed, the vehicle is going to be dusted for evidence."

"No problem detective, I understand. It's funny that Stenman's car is up here, isn't it?"

"Yes sir, when was the last time you saw Mr. Stenman or Mr. Berelli?"

O'Malley pulled his hat off by the brim and scratched his head, thinking. He watched with detachment as three dogs ran around playfully inside the doggie park fence. "I guess the last time I saw Mark was Wednesday at the board meeting, though I spoke with him on the phone Friday. I haven't seen Stenman since last Sunday at the ball game; you know the finals of the regional tourna…"

"Right, the big game," the cop smiled. "And what did you and Mr. Berelli talk about on the phone?" He pulled out a little note pad and was writing now as he talked.

"Baseball stuff, the World Series, game plans, some items that were on the meeting agenda, nothing personal."

"Did he seem normal to you? Was there anything that was bothering him?"

"No, he was his normal self. In fact I would say he's been in an especially good mood lately because that AG investigation is over, you know what I'm talking about?"

"Yes sir, I'm aware of it. Now Mr. Berelli and Mr. Stenman don't get along very well do they?"

O'Malley chuckled. "Well you can't say whether they'd get along because they refuse to speak to each other. Stenman's the one that filed the complaint with the AG." He looked out at the doggie park as the officer was writing. One of the three dogs in the doggie park, a large Shepard, squatted over the top of the dirt area that Brunk had filled in about 12 hours prior and grunted out a bowel movement, leaving a huge going away present on top of Stenman and Berelli laying face to face just three feet below.

"Do you think they'd ever go somewhere together?"

O'Malley chuckled. "Not willingly." He glanced at the Shepard, who'd finished his business and moved away kicking dirt behind him, as if to cover up the mess. Another dog in the group came along, smelled the pile closely then hiked his leg and urinated on it, having the last say in the matter.

Nine

By the time O'Malley returned from the doggie park, the guys had finished batting and were hanging around, some sitting on the bleachers waiting for him to return. A few of the parents had gone out onto the field to smooth out the mound and plate area that the players had dug up and chatted about what was going on with the cops. Wyatt sat alone on the grass behind the visitor dugout, watching Brunk. A tow truck came and removed Berelli's car, then another tow truck came in and went down the road toward the doggie park. He figured that O'Malley had seen the bodies by now, having been gone for so long.

'I think they call it *Corpus delicti*' he thought to himself; the investigation at the doggie park had produced the bodies. Now that they found the *corpus*, he figured, it wouldn't be long before they traced everything back to Brunk who would then be on the hook for the murder and Wyatt could go back to living a normal life. The last he knew, the bodies were in the back of Stenman's SUV. He couldn't imagine they were still in there at this point though, that wouldn't be very respectful, just carting them away on a tow truck. The more he thought of it, the more it seemed strange that there wasn't an ambulance there by now. And Brunk sure looked calm. O'Malley came out of the woods and approached where Wyatt was sitting.

"Hey, what was the matter with you today? You

played like you just got back from a month off." O'Malley said when he walked up.

"I don't know Dad, I'm all right; maybe a little tired is all. We're sick of practice; we want to get on with the World Series. Hey, what's going on with all the cops?"

O'Malley sighed, knowing he had to level with Wyatt. "Well, Mr. Berelli and Mr. Stenman were reported missing last night."

"Missing? You mean nobody knows where they are?"

"That's right."

"By missing, do you mean dead?"

"They don't know if they're dead, they're just missing at the moment."

"Did they see anything in the cars that might tip them off about where they are?"

"They're probably going to go through them with a fine toothed comb. But it looks to me like they have no clue. The detective up there asked me a bunch of questions. I don't think I was much help."

Wyatt suddenly felt ill. A cold sinking feeling came over him almost as if he was caught in a lie. He was sure O'Malley would notice he was shaking. He tried to come up with something that sounded casual, but all he could think of was the fact that there's no *corpus delicti* yet and it's no wonder that Brunk was acting so normal. The bastard has nothing to worry about. Then he also considered Alex, what it would be like to have your dad just not show up at home one night. "I wonder how he's doing," he said finally.

"Who?"

"Oh, I mean Alex, you know, his dad missing and all."

"It's probably rough around the Berelli house right now. Hey boy, are you sure you're feeling ok? You look pretty pale."

"Yeah, I'm okay, just tired."

"Alright, well I'm going to check in with coach Bastau and then we'll shove off, okay?"

Wyatt nodded and O'Malley walked onto the field, where he was immediately noticed by a group of parents who wanted a report on what he had seen. Little Ricky Burns, father of big Patrick Burns the first baseman, turned to greet him first.

"We were thinking Rex," Ricky said, "maybe the two of them are gay and they ran off together. They kept it secret all these years and now they're sitting on an airplane, holding hands, dreaming about a bungalow on the coast in southern California." Ricky laughed his nasty little laugh.

The others were mildly amused the first time they heard it, but the second time around it sounded crude and they didn't join in. Ricky and Berelli only barely tolerated each other, owing to the fact that Ricky was President of the league until Berelli came along and took it away from him a few years ago. The little man never quite got over the ignominy of it. And like everyone else, he couldn't stand Stenman. So he was making jokes about the disappearance of two men who represented to him, no great loss. O'Malley figured he'd be happier if they were never found. He looked at Ricky and wondered how such a good kid like Patrick could have such a complete jackass for a father.

"You'd feel pretty stupid if Dana or Alex got wind of you talking like that."

"I'm only joking, come on," he slapped Rex on the shoulder, "geesh, you know I love those guys." Ricky turned suddenly solemn and concerned. "So what's going on over there, what do they know?"

"Not much, it's early and they're not saying much."

Joe Morelli, Johnny's dad chimed in. "Maybe one of them killed the other and then got scared and took off. I bet if you search those woods over there real careful you'll find a dead body." They murmured over Joe's grisly notion. Some chuckled and shook their heads.

O'Malley paused to consider the possibility and said, "Took off how? Both cars are here."

"Maybe he flipped out and took off on foot. People do strange things when they kill somebody."

"How the fuck do you know Joe, you ever kill anybody?" Ricky asked and laughed.

"Not since Desert Storm," Joe protested indignantly, "but you have no idea…."

"Yeah, yeah, you were probably smoking wacky weed." Ricky interrupted, sparing everyone the pain of listening to yet another of Joe's Desert Storm experiences.

"You ought to write a book Joe. One of those two guys didn't kill the other one; neither of them is strong enough to do it." Ricky said, hinting there was only one guy around who is fit enough to do something like that, and they were looking at him.

"I will write a book if one of them did it. I damn well for sure will. What a great story huh?" He looked to the others for support in the idea. "You may be in there too Burns," he added, "you'll be the little guy who runs 3 miles each way to the drugstore to pick up his Viagra." Joe belly laughed at his wit. The group also chuckled.

O'Malley was concerned this would degenerate. Burns and Morelli had been close to fisticuffs several times over the years. Usually alcohol was involved and the altercation usually followed a reference to Ricky's size. He couldn't believe these two were behaving this way now. He changed the subject.

"I imagine the place will be crawling with cops in a little while, so if you don't want to get interviewed you ought to bug out now."

Joe Morelli perked up again. The possibility of them wanting his expert opinion was too delicious to resist. "I guess I'll hang around for a while," he said, "make sure they know to search the woods real good."

"Yeah, they'd never figure that out without you," Ricky responded. Everyone chuckled as they walked off the field loosely, all of them choosing to hang around by the fence to make it clear they were available for an interview if needed. O'Malley walked over by the dugout to talk baseball with Art Bastau.

Wyatt sat with Patrick Burns outside the fence waiting for O'Malley. They were talking about Alex. He looked up casually at Brunk from time to time, to make sure he didn't miss anything.

"You think we should call him?" Burnsy asked.

"Well imagine if your old man turned up missing, would you want to be talking to anybody?"

Burnsy looked over at Ricky, his father, standing by the fence in tight black spandex running shorts, the type worn by a marathon runner or a cross country cyclist. No-one else would play baseball in such things. "Hey, if Ricky disappeared, I'd be driving around in that," he laughed and pointed at his father's car, a black 500 series Mercedes coupe.

"You're such an asshole," Wyatt said.

"What? What's the matter with you Y-O? You're all uptight dude."

Wyatt realized he had to loosen up; that he was the only one that knew Berelli wasn't just 'missing.' He couldn't expect anyone else to have respect for the dead when they didn't know the truth. "I just hope they find him and he's ok, Mr. Stenman too I guess. It's so weird, both of them being gone like that."

"They hate each other you know."

"I know, Alex told me that his father said he was gonna sue Mr. Stenman if he didn't stop spreading rumors about him, said he was gonna 'own his kid.'"

"You can't take somebody's kid, can ya?"

"I don't think so Burnsy, I've never heard of it have you? I think it's just an expression, meaning he's really gonna get him in court."

"Can you imagine that, taking somebody's kid?

Nobody would want me, I eat too much."

Wyatt chuckled for the first time in a while. While Burnsy talked, Wyatt watched Brunk take a call on his cell phone and then walk toward his car. He glanced at Wyatt before opening the door and set his hand on his gun briefly while looking at him, sending an instant message, then got into the car. Wyatt quaked reflexively as if the message slammed against him when he received it. Then it sent his mind whirring about what he meant by it. Maybe he was just adjusting his holster before he sat in the car. Maybe it was Brunk's latest way of telling him he better behave. Maybe....no, it couldn't be. How could he know?

Burnsy chattered on about Alex this and Alex that. Wyatt heard hardly any of it. He watched Brunk pull out of the parking lot and onto the road, then tear off with a screech.

"Uh oh," Burnsy said as he saw Brunk roar off with his lights flashing, "there must be somebody without a seatbelt on somewhere."

Wyatt's cell phone rang. It was a strange number, another area code, he thought he recognized it from somewhere but couldn't figure it out. He decided to answer.

"Hello?"

It was Samantha Porter.

"Oh, hey Samantha, I'm at baseball practice, can I call you back? Yeah, in a little while... okay, bye."

Burnsy looked at him. "Who's Samantha?" He asked.

"Just some girl, she doesn't live around here."

Burnsy went deep in thought for a second. "You mean Samantha Porter, Brunk's daughter?"

"Jesus Christ Burnsy, how'd you know?"

"Brunk lives on Clermont Street, right behind my house. Our yards butt up. Ricky's at the back fence all the time talking to him. I see her when she visits every summer. I don't know of any other Samantha that doesn't live around here. They call her Sammy and she drives a Beemer you know."

"I know."

"Well how the hell did you meet her? She's a serious babe man. How come you always get the babes? You don't even have a car."

"What are you talkin about Burnsy, you've got Cindy, and she's pretty hot."

"No way man, she just likes me because I get to use the old man's Mercedes sometimes. She likes to ride in it."

"Wait, you were making out with her at JR's house the other night."

"Yeah well, what's fair is fair."

"So if she wants to ride in the Mercedes she has to make out?"

"Yeah, pretty much."

Wyatt chuckled. "I met Samantha yesterday at the animal hospital. I told her not to tell Brunk, he'd hunt me down like a dog."

Burnsy laughed, "Yup, he sure would. What did she

want?"

"Just to hang out, I guess."

"She wants to hang out and you blew her off?"

"I didn't blow her off. It's complicated."

"Yeah, it's complicated all right, about as complicated as this," Burnsy made like he was putting a phone to his ear, "'Hi Sammy, so you wanna pick me up in your Beemer and take me for a ride? Oh, I don't know, I need to think about this, one-thousand-one, one-thousand-two. Okay, I'm in,' that's about how complicated it is."

"I got a thing with Kelly. I can't just hang with another girl. It's a thing."

"Oh yeah, I forgot about Kelly. Yeah she's pretty hot too, you got a real problem here dude."

"Well I'd be pissed if she was hanging with somebody else," Wyatt added with a 'fair is fair' expression.

"Why don't you trade her one?"

"I can't *trade* her one. She won't do that."

"But you would if she would, right?"

"Well, yeah, maybe, it would depend on who it is."

"You mean for you or for her?"

"Both, I guess. I don't know Burnsy, this is nuts. It doesn't matter because she'd never do it."

"How do you know? Maybe there's some guy she'd want to hang with but doesn't because of the thing with you. Here's what you could do, you could go hang with Sammy and then tell Kelly about it. Tell her she can go hang with another guy for a day if she wants to, then you'll be even. If she doesn't want to, that's fine, but at least you gave her the choice."

"You're fucked up."

"It's pure logic dude, pure logic. You can't argue with logic."

O'Malley walked up, finally ready to leave. "Burnsy, you need a ride home?"

"No thanks Skip, I'm good. I'll wait for my dad."

"You may be waiting a while."

"Yeah, I should have driven myself."

Wyatt stood up, "Seeya later Burnsy. Dad, I'll meet you at the car, I gotta make a call."

"Y-O, you've been sitting here waiting for me, why didn't you make your call then?"

"I was talking to Burnsy," he protested.

"All right, hurry up. I wanna get home, I'm hungry."

O'Malley slung his practice bag over his shoulder and walked off to the car. Wyatt walked behind him and to the side, then dialed Samantha and made some small talk at first. In about two minutes he forgot all about Kelly and realized he really liked the sound of Sammy's voice.

"I have a girlfriend you know," he said smiling, "she'd be pissed if she knew about this... I know you're leaving next week... all right, we'll hang out. I need to shower, so give me a little while, maybe an hour or so? Yeah, three o'clock is good. Your old man CANNOT know about this, he'll kill me I swear. And when you get there just come on in and meet my dad, he's cool, you'll like him... all right, later."

Ten

"The thing is Ms. Shea, it's just like you see on TV, we can do this the easy way or we can do it the hard way. I get the same paycheck either case." Detective Byrd ran his large right hand over his shiny bald head out of habit, as if he were smoothing back hair that wasn't there. Becca had seen him around town before. At the station they call him Mr. Clean. He's a stark character, strangely good looking and large, burly, she put him accurately at about forty-two.

They sat in her living room after she invited him in and offered him a chair, not realizing at first that the conversation would turn adversarial. But she abruptly stood up again when asked about her and Mark, wanting her to tell him everything about yesterday - Saturday - from the minute she woke up to the minute she put her head back on the pillow again last night. She stared out the window to the front of the house, eyeing the unmarked grey Ford sedan in her driveway knowing someone in the neighborhood would see it there.

"You see, there's some stuff I know," he continued, "and I know because my wife's niece Larissa? She's going to college in the fall. But this summer she's working at the Quality Inn over on Delatour, she cleans there."

He paused for a second to let this sink in.

"And since she knows your sons, yours and Mr. Berelli's that is, well she recognized the two of you there at the motel yesterday. I guess you didn't recognize her. Why would you? It's an honest mistake. Anyway, she called and told me when she heard about the missing person reports. I figure you must've been one of the last to see him before he disappeared, but I don't imagine you were planning to run right over to the station and talk about it."

Becca exhaled loudly and covered her eyes with one hand. "Am I a suspect or something?"

"There can't be a suspect unless there's been a crime. Has there been a crime?"

"No, God… I mean, I don't know. Everything was fine when he left me, about eight. He said he was going to the ball park for a little while. He does that all the time, later, after the games are over."

"What did you do then?"

"I came home. JR, that's my son, he was here with his friends playing football out by the garage. When it started raining they came in. I made cookies."

"How many boys?"

"Well there was six or maybe seven playing football, only four came in. The others went home."

"Can you name them?"

"Of course…"

"We'll come back to that. Is there anything going on in Mark's life that might help to explain where he is?

"God, what isn't going on in Mark's life?" She made a pretend laugh. "Do you know about the thing with Stenman?"

"Yes."

"His wife is having an affair, uh… too." She held her head low with crossed arms, one hand supporting her forehead.

"With who?"

She grimaced. "Tom Morton, the Assistant Principal."

Byrd didn't say anything, just looked at her and blinked his eyes twice quickly, trying to digest this without seeming flabbergasted.

"Mark walked in on them yesterday, before he met me. They didn't know he saw them."

"Are you sure?"

"Yes, I mean, that's what he said. He caught them at his camp on Parker Lake. They didn't know he saw them there. We were supposed to meet there but when he got to the camp before me, they were already there. They were in bed. It's weird, but he was happy about it; made him feel like what we …uh… are doing isn't so bad."

"Do you think she knows, Dana Berelli that is, about the two of you?"

"If this gets out it will ruin our lives," she said darkly.

"I don't want to do that. Look, let me put it this way, if I can find out what I need to know and no crime has been committed; there's no reason that certain things have to be made public. If there's been a crime….well….you're going to have to roll the dice." Byrd paused with a shrug, as if to say that events could take it out of his hands. "I can tell you this, if you don't cooperate with me the chief's gonna wonder why you won't talk; that maybe you're hiding something. If he starts asking those kinds of questions there's no chance that your relationship with Berelli can remain a secret."

Becca paused and looked at him intensely trying to determine if she had any choice but to continue. "I don't know what she knows," she said finally, "the way Mark talks, I'm not sure Dana would care as long as it doesn't become a public spectacle."

It had been some time since Byrd was happy in his own marriage. He wondered briefly if it would ever come to this for him. He looked at Becca and confirmed that Berelli was a lucky man. "And what about Mrs. Morton, do you know her?"

"Loretta? Only to say hello; I have no idea of what she knows about Tom and Dana. What would she have against Mark?

"We have to cover all the bases."

She nodded. "She seems much older. I never see her at the games. All her sons have graduated and moved on to college."

"How long have you been seeing Mark Berelli?"

This deflated her. She was ashamed to admit it. "About three years," she said after gathering the will. "We spend nearly every free minute together. Except when he has baseball things to do, which has been a lot lately with the AG investigation and all."

Byrd remained stoic. "Does he ever talk about his relationship with Stenman?"

"He tells me everything. He detests Peter Stenman. The man has made life hell; not only for Mark but for everyone else involved with the league. We used to have a fun program, simple, just tons of kids having a great time playing baseball and their parents having fun putting it together. It's so formal now, there's so much concern about liability and following the 'Not for Profit' laws. It used to be when the league needed something, a bunch of us would go out and raise the money or even throw in the money. Now they can't do anything without consulting an accountant or attorney. It's not about baseball anymore. Mark blames Stenman for that."

"Is there anything else that might have been bothering him yesterday?"

"Not really. He got a couple of traffic tickets. It was Brunk, do you know him?"

"Yes."

"He gave Mark a ticket for going like 33 in a 30 and another for not using his signal when he pulled him over. It was bogus, just Brunk going overboard as usual; you chuckle when you hear about him from someone else, you're pissed when it's you."

Byrd thought it strange that he hadn't been told about this yet. Well, he hadn't seen Brunk yet either. He changed direction. "Is there anybody else who knows about you and Mr. Berelli, someone it might bother?

"Bother?" she asked indignantly, not understanding what Byrd was driving at.

"Yeah, someone who might take offense or be

jealous."

She caught on. "There's only one person for sure that knows about us, because we're good friends and we talk about things that are big in our lives."

"Who's that?"

"Shit, do we have to bring yet another person into this?"

"I gotta know."

"There's no way he would try to hurt Mark or be jealous."

"Who is it?"

She exhaled hard and shook her head at herself, then said, "Rex O'Malley."

Byrd wasn't quick enough to stop his eyebrows from rising, but he moved on and said, "There are some people who believe that Mark Berelli is just as aggressive about his position in the league as Peter Stenman is about his. Do you think those two could have gotten in a fight, I mean a violent fight?"

She quaked at the visual of Mark lying somewhere beaten and dead by Stenman's hand. "Maybe," she said with a sigh.

"Is Mark Berelli a violent person? Does he have a bad temper?"

"No, not Mark, he's never upset for more than a few seconds and even then you'd think he was just in a bad mood. But Stenman has an awful temper. The cops had to go to his house a few months ago because he hit Dale. Did you talk to her yet?"

"We will."

"She's such a sweet person. She never supported Peter in his inquisition into the league you know, she distanced herself from it."

"Yes maam." Byrd's cell phone rang, "Yeah, it's Byrd." His face betrayed no emotion while he listened, "yeah… all right… I'll call you back in five." Which meant, to Becca's relief, he would soon be gone and she could try to figure out what the hell had happened to her world.

He finished writing the last sentence, closed his small notebook and put it in his back pocket then handed Becca his card and cast a friendly face. "Keep yourself available okay? And if you think of anything we should know, call me."

"What does that mean?'

"Don't leave town without telling me."

"You mean I'm grounded?"

"Technically, no."

"I'll be going to the game on Monday, the World Series, my son is on the team."

"We'll be talking before then, I'm sure."

"Great, I can't wait." She managed a cynical smile and pulled the screen door closed behind Byrd as he walked out.

"Oh, I almost forgot, the names?" he pulled out his pad again and prepared to write,

"The names?" she was confused.

"Yes, the boys who were here when you arrived home last night?"

"Oh yeah. Well, there was Jed Rounder, Scooter, Burnsy, JR of course, they came inside when it started to rain. The other two, I think it was Johnny Morelli and Will Toomey, went home. Wyatt wasn't there for some reason."

"Scooter?" he asked, "and Burnsy?"

"Yes, Scott Daggett, they call him 'Scooter', and Patrick Burns."

"You say that Wyatt wasn't there. Is that Wyatt O'Malley?"

"Yes"

"Ah, the famous one," he smiled.

"Yes, he's the only one with a steady girlfriend right now, so he's hit or miss with the boys."

When Byrd returned to his car he immediately dialed back one of the other investigators conducting interviews in the case. Nazareth has a staff of four detectives and all of them were called into the station within an hour of the MP reports. The chief was uneasy over the coincidence of the two men being reported missing nearly simultaneously, so they were on duty this Sunday afternoon rather than waiting the twenty-four hours customary for a MP case.

Detective Romundo was the one who called Byrd while he was with Becca. Romundo had been over to the Stenman home and conducted a full interview with Dale and Justin. They told him about the argument and the rumor that Justin was going to be thrown off the travel team. Dale also informed him of her plan to meet Berelli for lunch on Tuesday to discuss Justin's 'career' and how that really set Stenman off. He was raging with anger, stormed out of the house and didn't return. She figured he went to the ball park or to Grif's, as there hadn't been a Saturday in summer in years when he wasn't at one or the other. She called the police later, at night, after she grew fearful he was drunk and run off in a ditch somewhere. Romundo then went over to the Berelli residence and spoke with Alex and Dana. Alex hadn't seen his father since Thursday night, though they did talk on the phone Saturday morning. Their schedules are simply different this time of year. Alex figured he would see him at the ball park Saturday afternoon, at his game, but he never showed. At first Dana told Romundo she was in the city shopping yesterday and then went out to dinner with friends. Then she realized this was a non-starter and as soon as Alex left the room she told the truth, knowing Romundo was going to check with the friends who wouldn't corroborate the story. She was with Tom Morton, she confessed, until about 10 pm last night. Romundo had yet to interview Morton to confirm this, but he was next on the list.

Byrd filled his partner in on the conversation with Becca. They agreed that Romundo would locate and interview Morton and then talk to the staff at Grif's, to see if there were witnesses as to whether Stenman was at the bar yesterday and for how long. Byrd would continue checking out Becca's story by interviewing the boys and Rex O'Malley. They agreed to compare notes again later and decide what direction they would take next. But it was beginning to look like there was no smoking gun early on. Byrd knew the Chief had some of the uniformed cops out knocking on doors in the neighborhoods to find out who might have seen either of the men last. There may be some news from that front later as well.

Byrd looked at his watch, it was nearly five o'clock. He decided to drive to O'Malley's house and try to interview the coach. It seemed like this might be a good time to catch him. When he pulled into the driveway, O'Malley's Black Ford SUV was sitting there as he hoped. They'd known each other since high school.

"Well Byrd, I was wondering if it would be today or tomorrow," Rex said as he opened the door and saw the flat-foot standing there, "did word get back already that I was trying to get information from Brunk out at the park?"

"I don't normally talk to him O'Malley, but maybe I should ask him to keep an eye on you huh?"

"I already have enough problems with that lunatic," O'Malley said, "he can't stand my kid, always harassing him."

"I'm not here to harass you Rex, just ask some questions."

"About Becca I imagine."

"She and Berelli are involved?"

"Is that what she told you?"

"Do you think she would hurt him?"

"Becca?" he laughed, "hurt someone? She's a gentle and peaceful woman."

"You know her pretty well, eh?"

"Well enough"

"Why are you playing games with me O'Malley?"

"Because I figure you're here to find out stuff about people that they wouldn't want you to know. If you want to know about Stenman or Berelli, I'll tell you everything I can. If you want me to talk about Becca, it's not happening. She didn't have anything to do with the disappearance of those two guys, believe me. And my kid was over at her house last night until late, probably eleven o'clock, eating cookies and playing football in the rain."

"Your kid? You mean Wyatt?"

"I only have one kid."

Byrd pulled out his notebook to check what he had written down, just to be certain. "Becca says Wyatt wasn't there last night, at her house."

"She must have made a mistake. I was here when he came in, he came from her house."

"I have a list of the boys she said were over there playing football, he wasn't one of them."

"Byrd, is my kid a suspect or something?"

"No"

"Then why are we talking about him?"

"Rex, let me start over okay?" O'Malley didn't say anything, he had no respect for the Nazareth Police Department, whatsoever. But he was somehow engaged by what seemed to be sincerity coming from Byrd. "I know you've been through some bad stuff with Brunk. I won't elaborate, but let me say that his methods and mine are different. You might even say our objectives are different."

This brought a cynical frown to O'Malley's face. "Okay, so you're not a shithead Nazi, I feel so much better."

"I'm a detective. It's my job to get the complete story. When a story isn't complete it usually points to something wrong. Not that Wyatt did anything wrong. But inconsistency is often a symptom of something bigger. When all the loose ends tie up, I move on."

"I hear you." O'Malley was burning inside, wondering why Wyatt hadn't told him where he really was or if Becca was simply mistaken, "Well we can't talk to him, he isn't here."

"Where is he?"

"I'm not sure exactly, a girlfriend came and picked him up, they went for a ride."

"Maybe he was out with the girl last night and didn't want you to know?" Byrd suggested, trying to show he could consider all sides of the story.

"Maybe," Rex said with a sigh, "but he has no reason to lie. He knows I wouldn't care if he was out with her, as long as he's home by curfew time."

"He has a curfew?"

"Yeah, eleven o'clock."

"And he was home by eleven?"

"Yeah, well about a quarter after, which is fine. It's

close enough."

"And he said he'd been at Becca's?"

O'Malley reconsidered the conversation he had with Wyatt. Thinking hard about exactly what he did say. He realized he never actually specified. He said he was going there earlier when they talked, he didn't confirm he was there later. He said only that they were playing football in the mud. At best, O'Malley realized, he drew the impression. Then there was a hollow feeling as he remembered how strangely the kid behaved at practice this morning.

"I'm not sure that he did say he was at Becca's. That was the plan earlier in the day. I just assumed that that's where he was."

Byrd looked at O'Malley and raised his eyebrows, then spoke, "I need to talk to him. Any idea when he'll be back?"

"It's summer. There's no school tomorrow, but his curfew is eleven."

"Is there any way to reach him? Does he have a cell phone?"

"Yeah, I can try." Rex pulled out his own cell and dialed Wyatt. The call went directly to voice mail. "Nope, he's either out of range or he's talking. I'll have to keep trying. I'll get him back here and call you when he's here."

"Rex, I came here to follow up on Becca's story. I'm going to talk to the rest of the boys too. But I need to know about Becca's relationship with Berelli. She says you're the only other one who knows about it." He told

O'Malley about the sighting at the Quality Inn, to establish he wasn't blowing smoke.

"They've been involved for a few years, maybe three or so." O'Malley said with resignation, "She never volunteers specifics, I never ask. I know she loves him. We're good friends, she talks to me about love. I think she would go through whatever she needed to in order to be with him. I'm not sure he would do the same for her and I think she knows that. But she could never harm him. If he told her tomorrow that it was over, she'd just continue living her life quietly with her son. She'd be miserable for a while, but that's what she'd do."

"Was there ever anything between the two of you?"

"Just good friends, that's all. You have any women friends Byrd?"

"Yeah, I get it." Byrd said, knowing there's no way his wife would ever tolerate him having a woman friend, "Do you want to try Wyatt again before I leave?"

"Sure." O'Malley dialed the cell and again it went directly to voice mail. "Still no answer," he said.

Byrd left without asking anything further. He drove over to Jed Rounder's house next, looking to find another kid who could substantiate where Becca Shea was last night. He almost felt as if it wasn't necessary after he'd gotten a feel for things. His instincts told him the Becca Shea trail was a dead end. She was not involved in the disappearance of the two men. Wyatt O'Malley however, had piqued his interest. He figured the Rounder kid could speak to that query also.

Eleven

"He's not my real father you know," she said as she drove the smooth road winding through the foothills outside Nazareth.

Wyatt stared at her, watching the wind gently alter the fall of her hair in the convertible. The drive threaded alternately between stretches of forest shrouded curves and vistas exposed over the mountain edge, laying out the valley below them. At one point he saw the water tower in Nazareth from the distance, giving him a familiar perspective of where they were.

"Nobody knows that, except for me and the three of them, Brunk, my mother and my step dad." She looked at Wyatt in between focusing on the road, "and now you."

Sammy is older than Wyatt, by a few months. She'd just recently celebrated her seventeenth birthday, for which she received the shiny new blue BMW convertible. Wyatt guessed that her mom and step-dad were not lacking. But she seemed much older by the things she said, her confidence, her ability to make him feel comfortable immediately and her willingness to express what she wanted without hesitation. He felt lucky all of a sudden, wondering how it came to be that he was here riding with her. He decided to just accept whatever it was she saw in him.

"My mother was in love with another guy and got

pregnant with me. She left Brunk for him when I was two. That didn't work out either, I mean, her and my real father, he was killed when I was three. Then she met my step dad, he raised me. I have a half-brother and sister too."

"Why do you come here to visit?"

"I don't know. I've always come here in the summer. When I was little my mom would bring me and I'd stay with Brunk while she went out west to visit her sister. I guess he likes me around."

"How did he die?"

"My real father? It was a hunting accident. He was out in the woods alone and somebody mistook him for a deer. That's what they think anyway. They never caught the guy."

"Geez," Wyatt said, "so he was…."

"Yeah, murdered. Weird, isn't it? Brunk says the other hunter probably didn't even know he shot him. It took a few days for the searchers to find his body. He was way back in the mountains."

"Was Brunk a cop then?"

"Yeah, he's been on the Nazareth force for thirty years or so. My real dad was a cop too."

"So your father and Brunk worked together?" Wyatt swallowed hard.

"Yes."

"That must have been tough for them, I mean, because of everything."

She nodded and started to slow down. Wyatt thought about Brunk. The visual came back from two nights prior when the old cop pulled the trigger on Berelli. It didn't bother him at all. He just let him lay there and die.

"Hey, do you know how to drive?" She pulled the car over onto a wide part of the shoulder and stopped.

"Yeah, I have my permit," he answered, a little shocked.

"Good." She opened the leather covered hatch on the armrest between them, reached in and pulled out a carved wooden box about the size of a pack of cigarettes. It had a band of inlaid mother of pearl running up the side. She rotated a small door at the top exposing the hollowed out body of the box, filled with finely ground reddish marijuana. The other hollowed out section held a short slender pipe, a one hitter.

"You drive and I'll get this going for us." She smiled close to his face as they both leaned in and looked into what she was holding. Then he smelled her. Maybe it was her perfume or her shampoo, or just her body musk in the warm summer afternoon. He didn't know. But he was so intoxicated by the aroma that he could only sit and let it embroil him, smiling, gazing at her aura, forgetting where he was or what he was supposed to be doing.

"Well?" she asked as he sat paralyzed.

"Huh? Oh, yeah," he opened the door and got out. She slid over the console and sat in the passenger seat.

As Wyatt drove Sammy filled the little bowl for them, taking a hit herself and then refilling it and passing it to him. After three turns on the little pipe he held up his hand to signal he'd had enough and smiled. She looked at him, took one more herself, and then put the box back into the console. They enjoyed the buzz together mostly in silence as he drove. As a small dirt road came up on the left he slowed and turned in, knowing the road led to a path down to the south end of Parker Lake, a spot he and his buddies had visited for years. They'd ride their bikes there in the summer, making a day trip out of it, or get somebody's mom to drive them. A huge old swamp maple grew out of the shoreline with a rope swing where they would vault off of the bank and drop into the water. He pictured what she would look like letting go of the rope and falling. She'd probably scream the first time, they always did.

There was no time now, but it kept coming to him, the thought of Brunk and how difficult it was to visualize doing the right thing. He imagined the look on Sammy's face if she learned that he went to the police and told his story, even if the old man wasn't her real father. She'd be devastated. If the world believed him, his word against a policeman, she might eventually come to wonder as he had a moment ago, that maybe Brunk had killed her real father in a jealous rage. There would be speculation that her young dad was stalked in the woods then shot in a revenge and left to rot alone. They don't even let deer rot in death; that much he knew. She might wonder if he died quickly or if he suffered in pain. He couldn't imagine what this might add to her unusual life. He looked over at her as the marijuana fully kicked in and he turned the corner onto the dirt road. She smiled in the glow of a fresh mild buzz. The vibes she emanated were those of companionship with him. She was having fun. It was all over her face.

He thought more as he drove, buzzed himself, feeling the marijuana concentrate his focus and magnify his fears. What if they didn't believe him? After all, it would be his word against Brunk; a famous cop, a doer of justice. He'd have to tell them why he was there under the bleachers. In the middle of the World Series he'd have to spill the whole thing. Alex Berelli, after losing his dad, would be guilty of dealing marijuana. There would be a huge letdown for the team; no-way they'd win, not with a stoner for their ace pitcher, not with a murder witness on the team. Wyatt himself, the guy who got the hit, would be convicted along with Brunk. Maybe they would let him off, he thought, since he solved the crime. But then again how would he solve the crime? They wouldn't believe him, not his word against Brunk, not without the bodies. Where the hell did Brunk stash the bodies? What felt like an hour of thought to him really consumed only about a minute on the clock. The pot was really good. He was stoned.

"Where are you taking me Mr. Big Shot baseball guy?"

She giggled at her own sarcasm. She liked the sound of it. She liked the thought of riding in the mountains with Wyatt, somewhat of a celebrity, somewhat of a lawless character, at least according to Brunk. She was appreciating him as she might appreciate Huck Finn. Her warmth pulled him away from the agony of his state. He smiled between gazing at her and keeping his eyes on the dirt road. She was loose and leaning between the corner of her seat and the door, playfully challenging him to take her further on this adventure. He imagined they'd known each other for a long time. Or, long enough anyway.

"The swimming hole at Parker Lake. You want to swing on a rope?" he asked casually.

"It's not muddy or weedy is it?"

"No, it's deep, you don't touch bottom. Then you just climb out again on the rocks." He smiled and didn't tell her the part about trying to stay shallow when you hit the water so your feet don't go into the top of the weeds.

"We don't have bathing suits."

He grinned slightly and shrugged, as if that small detail were one they would easily survive. "We come here lots of times. It's quiet. We just swim in our underwear." He wasn't yet aware that her underwear consisted of just a thong. She knew she had a long tee shirt in the trunk.

"Okay," she said. He hoped there was no-one else at the spot today.

They swam and swung on the rope and dropped into the water. Wyatt showed her how to release at just the right instant to get the most air time. She marveled at how he made everything into a game. Striving to go higher at the apex of the rope arc became instant fun. On the other hand he had never seen a woman, not a girl but a *woman*, wearing only a thong and tee shirt swinging from the rope at the swimming hole. He never imagined he'd see such a thing. None of the guys would imagine such a thing and they'd never believe it if he told them. She was beautiful and sexy and smart and carefree and she wasn't a girl. She would soon arouse him as no girl ever could.

"You got a boyfriend?" he blurted out, catching his breath when they sat down on top of a big round rock.

The rock was warm from the sun beating on it all day, though the sun itself had slipped below the trees behind them as the afternoon wore on. She pulled her legs up under the wet tee and stretched it out so that she was comfortably covered, relatively speaking anyway. The warmth of the rock felt good on her bare buttocks and heat filled the cavity made by her stretched out shirt. He sat leisurely in his boxers. She saw the little barking dogs in the print and chuckled.

"I had one before I came here. He didn't want me to come up this summer. I come here every summer for a couple of weeks. We may get back together when I go back. I don't know," she smiled and shook her head slightly, "you know how it goes. He wanted me to come to his parents place on Cape Cod next week. He's pretty boring really; never stops talking about himself. There are a lot of guys like that in Westchester. It's because of the money, you know? My parents have money too, but I'm not full of myself, you think?"

He shook his head, "Definitely not."

"What about your girlfriend, are you tight?"

"She's cool."

"She must not be too cool. Or you wouldn't be here would you?"

"She'd never come here, she's too fussy for that."

Sammy chuckled, "Why not? That's silly, this place is great. I'm having so much fun."

"So am I." He realized that Kelly spends hours doing her make-up, fixing her hair and making sure each outfit is just so. Sammy is prettier than her by doing nothing. In fact he looked at her and thought he had never seen such a pretty girl, well maybe in the movies but not for real. "And it'll never be the same for me now." He laughed at himself, at everything. He felt okay again for an instant, detached from the world sitting on this rock.

"Why not? What do you mean?" She laughed too but was confused at his laughter.

"Well, I mean, you're here with me, and like all you have on is a thong."

He was smiling, but realized that he'd made her self-conscious, as if she wasn't doing the right thing. She adjusted herself a touch, her body language suggested uncertainty, the free spirit of their flow interrupted.

"No, I mean it's great, I feel great here with you. I've never met anyone like you."

She never considered that what she *wasn't* wearing was improper, it was so private there and he was so easy to be with. Didn't people go skinny dipping all the time? What she had on was way more than that. She was just feeling free. "Oh…well I thought you said it was okay." She answered.

His naiveté caused him to dig himself a hole that he never intended. This was new territory, expressing his feelings to a girl. She brought it out in him. It had never happened before. He's usually indifferent about a girl's feelings. But with her he wanted to fix it; to let her know what he really meant.

"Sammy I'm sorry, I didn't mean to make you feel

funny. I think you are really pretty. I just feel lucky, that's all. I mean I'm lucky that I met you and you want to hang with me. And I mean it's so cool that we just met and you feel like we can swim together with almost no clothes on. You're way different than the other girls who take their clothes off. No, I don't mean *that*, I don't know, I feel like I'm making it worse. Is anything I'm saying making sense?"

She was charmed and laughed. He was making perfect sense and she was mature enough to rise above his clumsiness. "The other girls who take their clothes off?" she asked, jumping right on it and giving him a needle, "Do lots of girls take their clothes off for you Mr. Wyatt O'Malley the BIG baseball star?" Her gentleness made him feel good, like she 'gets' him, and curiously it seemed she was inviting him to say, 'yes'.

"Don't you like baseball guys?" He asked with a devilish grin.

"I love baseball, and I really like the baseball guy who is sitting on this rock."

He smiled again, "Okay, but I'm not a big star really. People don't get it you know."

"Don't get what?"

"That when you forget about everyone one around you, when you just get focused on the game, that's when you do good stuff."

"I know, you get in the zone," she said.

"Yeah, the zone. How do you know about the zone? Do you play a game?"

"I don't play sports, I'm a dancer."

"What kind of dancer?"

"Classical Ballet, I've been doing it since I was three. It's pretty intense; I have an agent now in New York. He and my mom want me to turn pro but I don't know if I want it that bad."

"Wow, you mean you can stand on your toes?"

"Yes," she laughed, "it's called *sur la pointe* meaning, literally, on the point of the toes."

"That is so cool, I could never do that."

She laughed again. "Jump in the water."

"Huh?"

"Go on, jump in the water, off the rock. Go on, I'll show you. You need special shoes to do this perfectly but you'll get the idea."

He jumped in the water and swimming away from the rock confused, he yelled, "Why am I doing this?"

"Stay right there," she said, "and be quiet for a second," with which she stood erect, the grace and strength of her legs brought forth a serenity as she posed in her thong and wet tee shirt. She raised her arms elegantly at soft opposite angles, threw her head back smoothly, and standing on the rock, elevated to her tip-toes. "*Sur la pointe,*" she said.

He was astounded at her beauty, dumbfounded by her poise and caught up fully in the aura of her profile. "*Sur la pointe,*" he repeated.

She held the pose for several seconds, spread her arms roundly for balance, pulled one leg up and to the left into a ninety degree angle and stood there perfectly on the balls of one foot. Then she came to the flat of her feet and jumped into the water toward him, both of them laughing as she hit surface in coarse messiness compared to the grace of her previous position. She swam to him and floated close, ran her arms around his neck and allowed him to kiss her gently and support her as the floated. She felt his hardness well up against her inner thigh as she curled her legs around him.

"*sur le point*," she said, with a 'le' this time, the masculine form of the concept.

Twelve

"I can't imagine what good it would do," O'Malley said when it came time for him to speak, "for all we know, Berelli could have run off to Vegas with his secretary and Stenman could be holed up in a hotel in a drunken stupor."

"It would show respect for the families and demonstrate that the community cares about its own," said Gino Rinalli magnanimously, serving as chairman of the meeting in Mark Berelli's place. Rinalli called the special meeting of the Board of Directors for Nazareth Babe Ruth league in order to strategize about their response to the circumstances and discuss what would be appropriate now, on the eve of the 16 year old team's impending visit to the World Series.

"I agree with O'Malley," said Joe Morelli, "I was in Grif's yesterday for lunch. You know, they got the two burgers for five-dollars special on Saturday right? I still don't get how they do that. I ordered four of em. But I could only finish three so I took one home with me. I had three burgers and a beer for twelve-bucks and I still had one more for later. You can't eat at home for that."

"You want to tell us why you agree Joe?" the chairman

said with no hint of impatience. Everyone else had gone brain dead on the burger discussion. But Rinalli, a man known for his never-ending tolerance, gently nudged Joe back into the present. O'Malley wondered what the meetings would be like if Berelli never came back. Rinalli, the current VP, would succeed him as President and the meetings would turn into encounter sessions.

"Well yeah," Joe answered, "Stenman was in there and all churned up about something. He must have had three or four beers while I had one; didn't even eat. You could tell he was pissed or really down. I figure he's just off on a binge somewhere and he'll be back Monday or Tuesday. Anyway, there's no way we should withdraw from the World Series on account of him."

"Did you tell this to the police?"

"Yeah, sure I did. They got a whole list of people who were in there when Stenman was there. I left after my burgers. Of course, he didn't speak to me, he never does."

"That's because you told him you were gonna call the cops on him," Jim Shea chimed in, everyone chuckled.

"Well he took the damn mower from me right when I was in the middle of mowin the field for my kid's game. I stopped to get a drink of water and when I came back he had started it and run off. When I tried to take it back he chased me with it. "

"Who'd you tell about Stenman being at Grif's?" O'Malley asked.

"Brunk, he came to the house this afternoon to interview me cuz he knew I was there yesterday."

"How'd he know?"

"He saw me, that is, I saw him. He was parked outside in the Bank lot. I figured he was waiting for guys to leave Grif's. You know how he does that shit. I'm Amazed Stenman got away without a DWI."

Chris Toomey, generally thought of as Berelli's lap dog, cleared his throat and gave the signal that now was the appropriate time for his insider's point of view. "Well as you all know, Mark and I are very good friends and rest assured that I speak for him when I say this tournament must go on. He would never want to be the cause of the kids missing something special. Maybe we should let it be known we're moving forward in his honor. If it's agreeable with everyone, I'll call *The Searchlight* and craft a statement to that effect. We are very close you know…."

"If you're so close then why don't you know where the hell he is?" O'Malley said before he had the chance to think better of it, then back-pedaled. "I'm sorry Chris. I'm just a little frustrated by all of this. Of course you're close to him. That's good by me. You tell everyone after we decide."

"Tell us your frustrations Rex," Gino said in a priestly confessional voice.

Rex wondered for a second if he could be busting on him, but looking at his face he could see the man was serious. "Aw Christ, it doesn't mean a hill of beans next to what those families must be going through." Rex paused for effect and everyone focused on him. "But a big part of me is thinking about the players. They've worked hard to be in a position like this, going to the World Series. I'll tell you what, does anyone here know someone who's played in a World Series of any kind?" No one said anything. O'Malley nodded his head and said, "That's what I mean, this is something special. Here these guys have such a great opportunity, a dream come true, then this happens. It stinks for them too."

Art Blaze, whose sons are younger, raised his hand and Rinalli recognized him. "It seems to me it's a simple choice. We either drop out of the Series or we play. The Babe Ruth people aren't going to postpone the tournament because of this. I feel pretty sure that if Mark and uh....Stenman were here, they'd say we should play no matter what. I make a motion that we move forward with the tournament, then call *The Searchlight* and tell them to run an ad saying we're dedicating our season to those two guys. Chris can take care of the verbiage. Hopefully before it runs, they'll turn up and it'll all be moot anyway."

Tom Morton, who had been characteristically silent to this point, raised his hand, "second," he said.

"All in favor," Rinalli said formally. Everyone there, which was all the members of the board except for the two missing, raised their hands. "Motion passed."

The meeting adjourned and the members made their way out solemnly. Some lingered and chatted in small groups. O'Malley, grateful that the Board had done what he thought was the right thing but secretly worried about Wyatt, left without talking to anyone. Outside he dialed Wyatt's cell phone and got his voicemail yet again. He wondered if the thing was working at all since it had gotten wet on the night of the disappearance. Then he remembered that Wyatt had used his phone today after practice, so that couldn't be it. He began to worry. Becca came to mind and he called her house next.

"How you holding up?" he asked when she answered.

"I'm okay," she said in a low key voice, "confused and scared. Do you think that Stenman did something terrible and then took off?"

"I don't know. How was Mark when you were with him?"

"He was fine, we spent the day together."

"I gathered. I'm so sorry Becca, you don't deserve this."

"Yes I do."

"Why?"

"It's God's way Rex. I've been sinning all this time. If Mark is with God then I'm not worried about him, he's in good hands. I'm left to suffer for my sins."

"Well if that's the case I hope you don't suffer too long."

"I miss him, which is to say I miss knowing that he's there. More than anything though, I feel awful for Alex."

"I know, me too. Hey, tell me something will you?"

"Sure, what?"

"Was Wyatt at your house on Saturday night?"

"That cop Byrd asked me that too. Is he in trouble?"

"No, I don't think so, but before he went out he led me to believe he was going there. Then he came home late, soaking wet, supposedly from playing football in the rain."

"He wasn't at my house, at least not when I got home.

"What time was that?"

"Around eight. Why don't you just ask him?"

"Yeah, I will. I just want to find out everything I can first."

"The boys were playing football in the back yard, JR and Jed and a few others. Wyatt wasn't there. When it started raining they came in and I made cookies and they played some poker in the basement. Everybody left about ten thirty."

"Okay," O'Malley said despondently, hoping there was some revelation that would clear up what was becoming a nagging concern over where Wyatt was and why he hadn't been forthright. It wasn't like him.

"Did he lie about where he was?" she asked.

"He didn't exactly lie; more like didn't tell me the facts. I'll figure it out, thanks for the help. And hang tough, okay?"

"No other way to hang. I know I'm going to need your company pretty soon, can I count on you for lunch next week?"

"Next week is going to be crazy with the Series starting on Monday night, but if I get any free time at all, it's yours."

"Thanks Rex."

"Why don't we try to have a drink and a bite to eat

tomorrow after the game?"

"Okay," she said, "Bye."

Rex hung up and drove the short distance from the VFW Post where the Board meets to home. It was about seven-thirty and he figured Wyatt would be rolling in around sundown, in about an hour. He thought of a strategy for what he was going to say to him. Wyatt would have to call detective Byrd and set up a time when he could answer questions. He didn't know that Sammy and Wyatt were also on their way home at the moment, having left Parkers Lake when O'Malley was talking to Becca. Wyatt even tried to call him but Rex was talking with Becca at the time.

In fact, they were just crossing over the town line into Nazareth, motoring down Route 43 from the mountains. Becca was driving which was a good thing. Just as they crossed over the town line, where the road leads down a long slope out of the hills and where everyone must slow down to thirty-five miles per hour, Brunk sat in his patrol car tucked behind a stand of trees. It was a perfect place to trap speeders who had not yet slowed to the limit because of the hill. Sammy cruised by unaware of his presence. Like most other people coming down the hill, she crossed the town line above the speed limit. Brunk's radar read forty-four. He looked up and recognized her car and saw the back of Wyatt's head; the reddish hair.

"It couldn't be," he said, then started the engine and pulled out behind them, staying some distance back, just close enough to could keep the BMW in sight.

"By the way," she said to Wyatt as she toed the brake

bringing her speed under forty, "you're up there, on Brunk's wall."

"You looked?"

"Yes, I had to see if you were on his hundred most wanted." She chuckled.

"I guess I Am." Wyatt didn't find this humorous but did manage a polite smile.

"And I couldn't spend a lot of time in his office but he had a few pictures of you lying on his desk this morning. It looked like you at different ages. Are you like some kind of delinquent that I should like, stay away from?"

"I didn't do anything wrong," he said, "not really anyway, he's always trying to pin something on me." His stomach began to ache and he got a sinking feeling again, like the feeling you get when you know the bully is going to beat you up after school. Or like the feeling you get when you have a nightmare that your homework is late every day and the teacher yells at you and gives you detention, day after day. Sammy could see it on his face.

"Listen, the guy is psycho," she said. Wyatt looked at her and thought she had no idea just how right she was. "That's why my mother cheated on him all those years ago. That's why I was born. If she had been faithful, I wouldn't be around."

"It oughta be against the law taking pictures of people like that," he said, "think it is?"

She looked at him and shrugged, "Weird? Yes. Illegal? Maybe." But you can't tell anybody about this. If it ever got back he'd know it was me that told you. Nobody ever goes in his office."

"I'm not telling anything, the guy's already after me, especially now," he slipped.

"Especially now?" she asked, "what does that mean?"

Wyatt threw up his hands in frustration at himself and looked away from her, out the right side of the car. "Nothing. It doesn't mean anything." He tried to cover himself quickly, "I mean now that I know you…"

"Oh shit," she interrupted.

"What?" Wyatt turned to see her staring at the mirror, squinting. Then he looked out the back and saw the cruiser in the distance. "You gotta be kidding me, is that him?"

"Could be, probably not though, there's a lot of Nazareth cop cars around. I can't tell. I'll take a turn somewhere, see if he follows us."

As she approached town, passing by the Sabic Plastics plant, she took a left on a back road that cuts across former farmland but also leads to Nazareth from a round-about direction. Wyatt watched out the back to see if the car followed. As she motored slowly along he saw the car turn in the road.

"Fuck, he's following, whoever it is."

"It could be just a coincidence," she said.

"No, it's him. I know it is. I can feel it. He can't see me with you, Sammy. He's gonna kill me, he'll kill you too."

"Lookit," she said, "he's not going to kill either of us.

We didn't do anything wrong. I'm just going to drive you home like normal. We don't even know for sure that it's him."

"It's him." Wyatt was shaking.

"You're acting all mental Wyatt. What did you do? Why are you weirded out like this?"

"You don't understand."

"Well then make me understand." She was nearly yelling at him, adding to his anxiety.

"I can't," he said, "he's your father....well whatever he is."

He was weakening, needing to tell someone. She came out of nowhere and gained access to his insides somehow, getting him to drop his guard without knowing it. Now he felt the need to talk, wanted to talk to her. How could he do this? How could he tell her? He was Amazed at how they were able to talk so earnestly after such a short period of time.

"You must have done something really bad to be freaked out like this."

"I didn't do anything, I swear it."

"Well then chill. I'm going to tell him you're a really good guy. He may even let his guard down and get to like you too. He listens to me."

She took the back way around the high school and traversed through a couple of neighborhoods en route to Wyatt's house. Brunk followed in the patrol car as if he knew where they were headed. Though they lost sight of the cruiser from time to time as they twisted through the quiet side streets, he always reappeared, each time confirming again it was him. At the last sighting Wyatt's fears reached a crescendo. He could take it no more and spoke.

"Listen, Sammy, you have to get me to my house fast. My street is a cul-de-sac remember? Don't drive in there. Just drop me at the end of the street and keep on going. He won't follow you."

"Wyatt? What the hell? I'm not going to do that. I don't care if he follows me. He doesn't own me and he can't tell me what to do. I can see anyone I want and I don't care what he says."

As they approached his street Brunk had drawn closer. She looked in the mirror again.

"It's him for sure, I can see his face."

"Just let me out here, NOW."

"Tell me why you are so afraid of him."

"I can't. Just let me out."

"No way, if you won't tell me he can follow us in. I don't care." She turned onto Wyatt's street and pulled into the driveway.

"I'll call you and explain later. Don't tell him anything about us talking about this."

"Okay, I won't"

When Wyatt got out of the car and stood, Brunk pulled over on the street at the end of the driveway and rolled down his window.

"Why are you following us?" she asked.

"You were speeding when you came off the mountain." He looked at Wyatt with an evil smile, intimating that he was closing in.

"I slowed down in time Pop; you didn't have to follow me here. It's so embarrassing. Now drive away and leave us alone."

O'Malley heard the commotion from inside the house and came out, stood in the open door and said, "What's going on?"

"I just wanted to make sure everyone got home safe." Brunk said. Wyatt made his way to the house, not willing to be an object of the cop's invasive glare any longer.

"Why wouldn't they?" O'Malley asked sarcastically.

"She's my daughter Mr. O'Malley and I worry about…"

"I'm not your daughter Brunk and if you want me to come here to visit again you'll leave right now." Sammy said bitterly.

Brunk said nothing further but ran up his window and started off, taking a loop around the cul de sac in order to turn around. As he drove back by the house he glared in at Wyatt. O'Malley caught the look. Sammy backed out of the driveway and mouthed to Wyatt, "Call me." O'Malley saw that action as well.

"You have some talking to do pal," O'Malley said once they were back inside.

Thirteen

Byrd isn't used to working late on Sunday. When a case hits the office they'll work it pretty much around the clock if it makes sense, stopping only to catch some sleep or eat. But capital crimes are few and far between in this quiet suburb. There's no need to push the envelope on the occasional burglary, vandalism, or pot bust. He wondered what it was he would do if he went back to the station that night. He could stretch it and continue interviews until around ten pm, but most people would tell him to get lost after that, and success in a missing person's investigation depends upon cooperation from the community. He wouldn't be able to use incriminating evidence to strong-arm anyone, there wasn't any evidence. At the moment, two guys were missing and that's all. So there wouldn't be much to do after hours that Sunday night, even though the Chief was expecting them to stay hard on the case non-stop.

He went back to the ball park about an hour before dark, just to think, maybe look around for something as the sun set. It was one of the places the two men were last known to be presumably, since both cars were parked in the vicinity. He stood in front of the shed, not knowing he was nearly on top of the spot where Brunk pulled the trigger. He looked around at everything trying to imagine Berelli getting out of his car where it was parked. Why would he have parked it there? According to the other coaches who were at the field on Saturday, Berelli wasn't there during the day. Clearly he was working in the shed after everyone else had gone. Byrd went over to the door and opened the lock. Inside were garden tools, equipment bags, baseballs, signs and all manner of baseball utensils. Nothing stood out.

At the office earlier, he was briefed with various progress reports and interview results. According to witnesses at Grif's, Stenman was at the bar until nearly seven o'clock. He had been in there drinking since just after noon time and the bartender finally cut him off. He refused various offers for a ride home and wouldn't call a cab. He was belligerent and very vocal about his dislike for Berelli, although he made no threats that anyone could remember. He stumbled out the door and no one saw any more of him. Officer Brunk filled out a report that he had sat outside Grif's for some time, apparently concerned about Stenman's safety, but missed him when he left the bar during dinner break.

Brunk's report also contained two traffic tickets issued to Berelli earlier in the day, which was the last public sighting of him. Becca Shea was in fact the last person to have had contact with him. Byrd chuckled to himself that no matter where Berelli had gone off to, Becca Shea probably gave him just about the best send-off a man could ask for. But the most that everyone else knew at the moment was that Brunk was the last to see Berelli. It wouldn't be long, though, before his own report would have to include the affair with Becca. That would be bad for her and bad for the family as well.

By late afternoon the lab technicians the town contracted from the city had provided a preliminary report on the analysis of the cars. There was nothing found in the carpet, on the seats or in the way of fingerprints that pointed to anything other than normal use by the owners. Many fingerprint groups appeared, far too many at this point to make a determination that any one of the groups was the result of foul play. There was significant work left to be done there.

All things considered, he was limited to pure speculation, which is something he became good at over the years. Make a theory, he thought, and then test it. Decide what didn't happen and by process of elimination center on what might have.

Both wives, he figured, might have a reason to want their husbands gone. Dana Berelli is allegedly banging Tom Morton, which is not by itself necessarily a motive for murder, but there may be more to it. Dale Stenman gets slapped around occasionally by a husband who, by all accounts, is a complete abusive asshole. Were they acting together? The fact that the cars were found in exactly the same place might suggest the wives are associated. Nothing else ties them together. Was this a professional elimination? Maybe it was. Hence both men simply disappeared without a trace. Could it be a coincidence that both women planned to get rid of their husbands on the same day or hired professionals without the other's knowledge? Not likely. Becca was with Berelli at the motel. His car was there, then, also. Did she murder him then drive his car back to the ball park? If so, how did she get back to her car, then back to her house in time before the rain to make the boys cookies? And how would she do all that without being seen at the park or anywhere else, unless of course she had help. But what was her motive? And where is the body? Picturing Becca Shea as a murderer didn't work for him.

Maybe the two men ran into each other here, argued, got into a fight; Berelli killed Stenman, dumped the body somewhere, drove his car up to the doggie park then took off on foot. Pictures and names of both men had been circulated at the airport, train station and bus station. Neither had bought a ticket or left town by any of those means. If one had killed the other and then fled, he'd be found somewhere: on the streets, holed up, or trying to get out of town. This was a plausible scenario, but there was a deafening silence about this case; he sensed finality in the air, in the vibes. He had no other gut feeling, no intuition about what caused the silence.

Everyone was numbed by the twin disappearance. No one has a clear motive except the victims themselves. The wives, who might have a motive, seem too detached from the event to be involved. They just don't fit.

"Something decisive happened here," Byrd said to himself, then thinking about the two cars, "or maybe somebody wants me to believe that."

He walked out of the shed, locked the door, and started to circle the building, looking carefully at the grass and increasing the circle as he went, searching for something, anything. As he increased the circumference outward he eventually came upon the wooden bleachers under which Wyatt was trapped on the fateful night. He stood at the open end, looking out across field number five and thought about all the youngsters who had played here over the years, imagining what the fence and bleachers would say if they could talk; wondering if they had witnessed anything Saturday night that would help in his quest.

Looking down at the open end, the muddy path under the highest section became visible to him. He wasn't surprised at the footprints in the mud, in the dark shadows of the structure. He could imagine back when he was a young kid, following his buddies under there to hide from adults or have a secret meeting. He visualized a group of kids, there at the park to watch older brothers in a game, finding fun under the bleachers in the mud. Looking closer though, he didn't see the footprints of small boys, but rather those of a large foot, a man-sized foot. He thought about the weather, the rain that had caused the mud. It was Saturday's rain. The foot prints were fresh.

Byrd stuck his head into the darkness and waited for his eyes to adjust. The light shining from the other open end both helped and hindered. It allowed him to understand the shape of the cavity underneath the bleachers but the glare prevented him from seeing any detail in the churned up mud of the pathway along the back wall. He stood there with his head stuck into the space for some time, trying to sort out what he was seeing and to determine if there was any significance for him in this hiding place. The man-sized foot prints confused him. Why would a man walk under here in the mud? The incongruity of it was enough to make him sling his leg over the cross frame and go in.

After pulling out his pen light and holding it in his mouth, Byrd made his way into the interior, climbing over each cross frame as he moved and, looking down to the mud, observing the footprints as he progressed. After crossing three frames he noted that there were two sets of prints, those of boots with cleats he had seen first and a second set, those of sneakers, made apparent by the Nike 'swoosh' sign in the middle of the sole. When he reached the spot where Wyatt had waited in the dark watching Brunk perform his mad act, the prints became jumbled and went no further toward the other end. He stood there in a semi-crouch shining his flash-light around the trampled spot, then the walls, and then looking through the cracks in the wood framing, noting he could see the shed and the rest of the area pretty well through the slats. He backed away and shined his flashlight up at the framing above his head. There where Wyatt had left it, lay the five folded twenty dollar bills meant for Alex Berelli. Byrd reached into his hip pocket and retrieved a pair of latex gloves. After stretching one onto his left hand he reached up into the framing and gently pinched the folded money, lifting it from where it rested and lowering it to where he could count it in front of his face. Then he carefully refolded it and tucked it into the other latex glove, which would temporarily serve as an evidence bag. After a thorough inspection of the rest of the framing he left the hiding place, carefully stepping around as many of the footprints as he could and feeling relief at being able to stand up fully again once he was outside.

In the fresh evening air he looked at his feet. They were covered in black mud, not the kind that's found in mud puddles, but dark organic mud; the kind that resides in years of darkness, made rank by a lack of air circulation and fermenting organic material. He scraped the sides of his shoes on the grass in order to clean them, then went to his car and got two evidence bags, one for the folded money and one for a sample of the mud.

"What did I just find?" he asked out loud. He decided to have a patrolman posted here, out of sight somewhere, so that if the intended recipient showed up, this might be followed one step further. After retrieving a mud sample and stashing both bags in his car, Byrd decided to walk over to the doggie park to see what that area might turn up as well. His cell phone rang.

"Yeah, this is Byrd," he said. He listened while the caller explained who it was.

"Yes, Wyatt, thank you for calling back. I need to ask you some questions, are you at home?... no... who said you did something wrong? I need to talk to you as part of my investigation into the disappearance of Mr. Berelli and Mr. Stenman... yes right now. Is your father at home also?... he needs to be there with us... okay fine, I'll be over in a few minutes... okay?... okay good, I'll see you then, bye."

Byrd continued his walk up the road to the doggie park but quickened his pace. He would limit this to just a quick look at the spot where Stenman's car was found, then get back to O'Malley's to talk with Wyatt.

The sun was nearly all the way behind the trees to the west of the park. It was a beautiful summer evening, cool and dry for July, perhaps seventy-five degrees and almost no humidity. He stood at the spot where the red Volvo SUV was parked, where Brunk had driven it and dragged the bodies to the hole he dug. The heavy rains of Saturday night had washed away all evidence of what had occurred.

The fact that the car was left up here at the town maintenance building was very confusing. There was no reason for Stenman to be up here. He wouldn't have parked it here himself. The car had to have been brought here by someone else. Maybe it was their way of attempting to confuse the issue, lead away from a trail left somewhere else. He stood there and looked across the lot at the garage, at the fence separating the doggie run from him, and then at the gate into it. He walked over the gate and noted that it was unlocked, even though this was not a gate used by residents to walk their dogs. It was a large double swinging fence gate with a latch holding the two gate halves together. He looked over the gate at the bare ground with patches of scraggly grass still trying to grow despite of piles of dog manure and what was surely constant drenching by acidic dog urine.

A few residents were down at the other end of the park, down the hill at the normal gate. He saw two dogs running and playing together. The dogs spotted Byrd standing there and were distracted by his presence, stopping their playing and standing to look at him. One of the dogs, a large golden retriever, put his nose to the ground and followed a scent which had drawn his attention. The dog ran around searching for more, weaving around patches of grass, determined to find the source of the interesting smell. It stopped on top of the spot where Berelli and Stenman were buried and started to dig as if searching for a bone it had put there previously. His owner appeared a short distance away, walking up over the edge of the hill whistling to the dog.

"Come on Buster, let's go, no digging here. You're not getting back into the car all dirty." He noticed Byrd standing outside the fence and nodded, "Sorry, he likes to dig."

"No problem by me," Byrd replied, "it's what dogs do." Buster pulled up from his digging and ran to the owner who was clapping his hands. Byrd turned from the doggie park and walked back down the road to his car, then got in and set off for O'Malley's house. As he pulled out of the spot near the shed where he was parked and started out the lot toward the main road, Brunk pulled in. Byrd lowered his window and waited for the Patrolman to drive up next to him.

"You find anything?" Brunk said through the open window.

"Maybe," Byrd answered, "under the bleachers. There are a couple sets of footprints, fresh ones, and I found this," he held up the evidence bag with the money in it, "stashed up underneath the seats."

"Cash?"

"Yeah, looks like a drop off, probably a couple of kids making a drug swap."

"Really?" It was all starting to come together for Brunk.

"Can't imagine any other reason somebody would hide a hundred bucks there, can you?"

Brunk just shook his head. "What's this town coming too?"

"Nazareth is just like every other town Vic. Certain kids are gonna do whatever the bad thing to do is at the time. This probably belongs to some ballplayer you'd never suspect."

"Yeah, I guess you're right." Brunk said agreeably, maybe too agreeably. "But nothing on the missing persons though?"

"Nope," Byrd said, and then something that had been nagging at him came to mind. "You were watching Stenman at Grif's yesterday afternoon right?"

"Yeah, it was in my report."

"How did he get out of there without you seeing him?"

"He must have taken off when I broke for dinner; I was doing other things you know."

"Why didn't you call in for back up? He was there for what was it? Like Seven hours? He must have been pretty loaded in that Amount of time."

"I didn't have probable cause," Brunk replied with a trace of indignation.

'Since when do you need probable cause?' Byrd thought but didn't say. Then he pressed further. "What were you doing, traffic stuff?"

"Yup, two seat belts, a cell phone and two speeds, then I broke for dinner," he replied, feeling confident that what he was doing sounded important. "Sometimes you just can't cover all the bases."

"Sounds like you were busy, too bad though, huh?"

"Who knew?" Brunk shrugged his shoulders.

"Yeah, who knew," Byrd sat there nodding his head,

looking out the windshield. Brunk was nodding also, both of them in fake agreement. A pregnant pause followed.

"So, what's next on the agenda?" Brunk asked collegially, sounding like he was interested from a teamwork standpoint.

"I'm going to the O'Malley house, there's a loose end that needs tying. Hey, you worked a double yesterday right? Did you see Wyatt out and about?" From talk around the office, Byrd knew Brunk was constantly harassing Wyatt. He figured that if he was on duty and the kid was on the street somewhere, he'd know about it.

"Nope, and we keep a close eye on him. He's a bad one."

"Really, has he ever been charged with anything?" Byrd asked.

"Can't make anything stick," Brunk said a little too aggressively as his anxiety showed through, "he's slippery and his old man puts up a stink every time I question him."

"That's what I hear." Byrd went to nodding again, trying to bring the conversation to a close by agreeing.

"Let me know how you make out," Brunk said, "but don't trust anything he tells you. The kid lies like a rug."

"I'll keep my guard up."

"You want me to come with you?" Brunk asked, "he's scared of me and it might help you get whatever it is you're looking for."

He had the feeling that Brunk was fishing. "No, I'm

good for now," he replied, "I'll call if I need you."

"Alright, I'm on until eleven tonight again." Both men drove away.

Brunk pulled into a parking spot facing the shed and stared out across the field, the sun was now almost fully set and the park was immersed in gloaming. He was near panic state and sweating from the stress. The money under the bleachers told him what was going on there last night before he arrived and he was now certain that the kid riding the green bicycle was in fact Wyatt. Things got close unexpectedly. Byrd was shifty, he knew that. And now he was over at the O'Malley house talking to the kid. He began to sweat as he considered whether Wyatt would confess to what he had seen and if he had been successful in scaring him enough that he wouldn't dare talk out of fear for his life. There were no bodies to point to. It would be the kid's word against his. It wouldn't fly in court. It would make things nasty though, if Wyatt caved in to Byrd. There was no doubt about what had to be done and soon.

Byrd pulled into O'Malley's driveway and saw the light go on in the garage, where the overhead door was open. O'Malley had seen him drive in and turned on the light as a welcome. He got out of his car and walked into the garage. Rex opened the door to the house before Byrd reached it. "Hello Detective," he said in a friendly but formal tone. Byrd simply nodded. As he approached the door he looked at his feet to make sure they weren't dirty before entering. Some of the black mud was remaining on the side of his shoes so he reached down to untie them, gesturing that he would remove them before walking in the house. As he did so, he noticed Wyatt's brand new Nike sneakers where they had been left the night prior, when he removed them before coming in out of the rain. He saw the same black mud smeared on the sides and paused, but said nothing.

"That's all right Detective, you can leave them on," O'Malley said, "hell we probably have half a ball field of dirt in here."

"Nah, I'll take them off. My wife makes me do it all the time."

"Your call," O'Malley said and while Byrd was untying his shoes he yelled for Wyatt, who was in his room, to come front and center. When he arrived in the living room O'Malley introduced him to Byrd and Wyatt stuck out his hand to shake. He gave Byrd a firm and sincere handshake as Rex had taught. The detective was impressed by his confidence but said nothing. O'Malley motioned for them to sit, putting himself between Wyatt on the couch next to him and Byrd in the chair to his right.

"What did you want to ask my son?" O'Malley asked.

Byrd had his little notebook out and flipped through a few pages as if searching for notes he had written on the subject of this interview. "When you left here last night Wyatt, where did you go?" he asked eventually.

Wyatt looked away at the floor, then toward the door to the garage, then turned back, shrugged his shoulders, sighed with frustration and said, "I went a bunch of places."

"Was one of those places the Shea house?" Byrd

asked.

"You already know I wasn't there."

"Why did you tell your father you were?"

"I didn't."

"You told me you were going there earlier, before you left," O'Malley interjected, "you even said you'd bring me home some cookies."

"Yeah, but I never made it."

"Where did you go?" Byrd asked again.

"Is one of my friends in trouble?" Wyatt asked, looking directly at Byrd without a hint of fear.

"Who said anybody's in trouble?"

Wyatt paused and looked at O'Malley, then down at the floor again, then started to shake his head slightly. "I'm not tellin," he said finally, "you're tryin to frame me or one of my friends, I'm not tellin."

"I'm not trying to frame anybody, but if you don't tell me then I WILL think you did something wrong."

"I don't care what you think; I didn't do anything, so it doesn't matter."

The three of them sat in silence for a moment. Wyatt stared at the floor, refusing to yield. O'Malley looked at Byrd and shrugged, sending the message that if Wyatt wasn't going to answer, he wasn't going to force the issue. If he did do something wrong, O'Malley figured, he wasn't going to make his son talk without counsel. This wasn't Brunk. Byrd was a detective; if this guy was interested in

Wyatt's whereabouts then it probably wasn't about flour bombs or stolen bicycles.

Byrd decided to take a harder line, see if he could get the kid to fold. He really didn't have anything to charge him with that would hold up, so one last effort to scare him was all he had.

"Where'd the mud come from on your sneakers?" Byrd asked dramatically in a monotone.

O'Malley's head moved to Wyatt then back to Byrd then back to Wyatt. "What's this about?" he asked.

"What mud?" Wyatt pretended, though he felt a shudder through his stomach and his head began to shake. Then he got it under control.

"The same black mud that's on my shoes," Byrd came back, "the mud I got on them from walking under the bleachers out at the ball field. You see, I figure you were under those bleachers last night. You got a Nike sign on the bottom of your sneaks?"

"Lots of guys have those." Wyatt said defensively. O'Malley knew the swoosh symbol was there too, he looked at it when he bought the shoes last week, as he was handing them to Wyatt fresh out of the box.

"What's the money for?" Byrd asked, hoping to snare him.

"What money?" O'Malley interrupted.

"I don't know what you're talking about," Wyatt answered, then wondered immediately if Byrd had gotten the information from Alex Berelli. In a flash he couldn't figure why Alex would squeal about the pot deal, especially now, being so screwed up with his dad missing and all.

"I think you do," Byrd responded, "and I have a sample of the mud from under there and if it matches what's on your shoes then we've got a problem now, don't we?"

"You're not going to be matching any mud without a warrant," O'Malley said, "and lookit detective, I consented to let you talk to Wyatt because I was thinking you were just trying to get straight about Becca's story and all that. But if you think Wyatt's done something wrong then you better file some charges or something and I'll call my lawyer and we'll see what's what."

"I'm not going to file any charges Rex, not at the moment at least, but eventually we're gonna see what's what. Can I talk to you outside please?" O'Malley looked at Wyatt and then nodded and rose to his feet.

"Wyatt," Byrd said as he stood, "you think about this son, if you didn't do anything wrong then there's no reason not to tell me what I want to know. If you didn't do anything wrong, no one's going to hurt you."

Wyatt stared at him, knowing full well that Byrd had no idea what he was talking about.

Outside, O'Malley stopped at the garage door. He wasn't going to walk Byrd to his car, not sure if the guy was an adversary or what he was. Byrd turned to him and said sincerely, "you want to know what I think?"

O'Malley shrugged, "sure."

"I think Wyatt was under the bleachers last night and either picked up some drugs and left money, or left money for someone else to take when he dropped off the drugs."

"My kid's not on drugs."

"I don't imagine he is," Byrd shook his head, "at least not hard drugs. I've heard good things about Wyatt, from people I trust. He's probably smoking pot like millions of other kids, like we did when we were kids." Byrd looked at him with a 'let's be real' look. "That's probably what the money was for."

O'Malley didn't say a word, trying to decipher where Byrd was heading with this, or if he was just trying to disarm him.

"But even if that's the case," the cop continued, "where was he all night and why isn't he saying?"

"He doesn't want to get busted," Rex said, "or get his friend busted."

"Talk to him Rex. Tell him I don't care about the pot and I'm not going to bust him. But let me tell you something about me. I don't like it when things don't make sense. I don't quit shaking the tree until they do. And right now he won't talk, so this ain't makin any sense."

Byrd got into his car and left. O'Malley watched him pull out of the driveway and then walked back into the house. He had to admit, the cop was right.

Fourteen

"I had fun today too," he said into the phone. He was in the basement, speaking softly so O'Malley wouldn't hear him and then find an excuse to come talk to him. "I can't talk about it now...yeah, I can probably get out...Alright, I'll see you out front in about fifteen minutes...okay, peace." Sammy was coming to pick him up. He closed the phone, got up off the couch and walked up the stairs slowly, trying not to draw attention to himself. O'Malley was seated at the counter in the kitchen, watching the Sox game and eating an orange.

"You been thinking about baseball?" he asked as Wyatt appeared at the top of the stairs.

"A little, I'm looking forward to getting away from all the stuff that's going on."

"Me too, I just wish they'd find those two guys, then things would settle down. We have a world series to play."

They hadn't discussed the interview with Byrd. When O'Malley came back inside after Byrd left, Wyatt had already escaped to the basement. O'Malley let him be, knowing Wyatt never responded to the need to do the right thing by being forced to do it. If he came around, he did so after thinking about it and deciding he'd behaved wrongly. If he didn't come around right away, O'Malley would wait a few days and then approach it in a different light.

"I'm going out with Sammy for a while."

"So what's the deal with this girl Sammy anyway?"

"Why, don't you like her?"

"I don't know her, how can I not like her?"

"She's Brunk's step-daughter, sort of."

"I gathered that."

"She moved away a long time ago, when her mom got divorced from Brunk."

"I see."

"She visits him every summer. She's going back to uh, what is it? Westchester, that's it, on Friday."

O'Malley stared at him and smiled. "She's pretty. I guess you must be a real hit at Brunk's house now."

"He yelled at her when she got home."

"What for, being out with you?"

"Yeah, he's a weirdo, I mean a real weirdo Dad; you have no idea. Even Sammy says he's nuts."

"All kids think their parents are nuts at one time or another. Did you ever think I'm nuts?"

Wyatt looked at him for a moment, thoughtfully. "Nah, I don't think so."

"Well, you're due. So when you finally do decide that, remember how good I've been so far and cut me some slack."

Wyatt smiled but shook his head. "He really is nuts, it's bad," he said and turned toward the door. "Thanks for not pushing before."

"Yeah, no problem, but you're gonna have to clean things up with Byrd. I don't think he wants to give you a rough time, but you gotta talk."

"Yeah, whatever, I'll be back at eleven."

He went out the door and sat with his back against the maple tree that shrouds the driveway in front. While waiting for Sammy he tried to further steel himself to the loneliness resulting from being alone with his burden. No one could know about what he had witnessed. He would probably get over everyone in the friggin world finding out that he was there to pick up drugs, well, not exactly drugs, marijuana. He thought hell; almost everyone smokes pot these days. Some guys might even think that what happened, what he saw and the reason he saw it, was pretty cool. But some people - the most important ones at the moment - would never believe him. Or it would take maybe weeks for them to figure out he was telling the truth. And in that Amount of time Brunk would have plenty of chances to find him alone someplace and kill him too. The picture of him pulling the trigger on those two guys kept playing before his mind. If he killed them so easily, he could do it again.

If they found the bodies, he might have a chance. They would see the bullet holes. They knew the cars were left at the park. He could describe what happened exactly, what they were wearing, how they fell when the bullets hit them. It would all make sense. They might even arrest Brunk right away based on his story, which would give him protection. But without evidence, it would be his word against Brunk. They couldn't arrest him on that. He shook again when he thought of Brunk killing Sammy's real father, out in the woods someplace, making it appear to be a hunting accident. She had to live her entire life without a real dad. It must be tough for her. He wondered how it would affect her if she knew. Would it screw her up so bad she'd never be right again? He tried to put himself in her shoes. Nah, he decided, it wouldn't screw him up if somebody killed O'Malley, but it would really, really piss him off. He'd want to kill that person in exchange, at least. Would that be justice? He didn't know and didn't really care. He was more than scared now, he was angry, for Sammy.

Immersed in thought as he was he didn't see her headlights as she turned the corner and drove toward him. She was almost in the driveway when he came to his senses. She pulled in, stopped, and looked out the window at him. She had the top up this time, even though it was another gorgeous summer night. He stood and walked toward the car making a move to get in the passenger's side.

"You want to drive?"

"Yeah, but it's probably not a good idea on account of Brunk."

"I know a place down by the river," she said, "I go there alone sometimes, it's pretty and peaceful and there's no way he'll find us."

"Anywhere you want," he answered as he pulled his seatbelt on, "let's just get out of here."

She drove out of Wyatt's neighborhood the back way so they didn't have to pass through the center of Nazareth, then she went across the main town by-pass, down the hill toward the Hudson River and turned onto the River Road.

They said nothing as the car motored along, though when Wyatt looked at her she smiled back a couple of times. At one point he raised his hand to her hair and tucked the silky blonde strands behind her ear then let his hand rest on her shoulder as she drove. She turned her cheek and kissed it resting there and he gently rubbed the side of her face with the back of his fingers. They were falling for each other. The anxiety of what had transpired and the urgency she felt to know everything were combining to push them toward desperate love. Still they said nothing until she pulled the car to a halt at the end of a narrow dirt road which dead-ended on the shore of the river, used only by fisherman when the stripers were running in early spring. It was desolate there now as the moon began to rise over the river in front of them, the top of the murky water glistening with a pretend freshness.

"I have to know what's going on," she said finally, blurting it out almost frantically, "he's nuts over the fact that I was with you, you're nuts over him. I could see you tighten up and go cold when he pulled up behind us. You do it every time his name comes up. And before, when he was yelling at me about you? There was real meanness on his face. His eyes were scary, like he was threatening me to stay away from you."

"Did he threaten you, or me?"

"No not you, me. Well yeah, sort of," she answered, in a way that seemed like she was trying to soften it. "He told

155

me that if I insisted on hanging around with you then he wouldn't let me come here anymore."

"What did you say?"

"I told him that if he was going to tell me who I could hang around with I wouldn't come here anyhow. Then he called me an 'ungrateful little bitch' and that I was always that way. Then he said I should leave."

"I'm so sorry I've brought this on you Sammy, it's my fault. You need to get away from me."

"You haven't brought this on me Wyatt; I want to be here. But I want to know, I *have* to know what's happening. I need to deal with him."

He considered telling her the whole thing, this minute, and felt pleasure inside as his loneliness vanished with the thought. He didn't know it, but any attempt at resistance short of simply getting out of the car and walking away, never to see her again, wasn't going to last. He'd let her in too far; there was no hiding it anymore; he would have to either walk away or take her with him.

"I don't want you to leave." He said finally, almost as a way of changing the subject.

"Wyatt, if you don't tell me everything right now, I'm going to drive you back to your house and drop you off. Then I'm going back to Brunk's house and get my dog and my things and I'm going home to Westchester. You'll never hear from me again. I can't be close to you if you're not going to be honest. There must be something really bad about you if you won't tell me now, especially after…"

"Sammy, I can't, it's so bad. It's not me, you don't

understand." He lowered his eyes and looked at her lap, sighing, shaking his head in resignation. Wyatt was at the crossroads, he had to choose; there would be no delaying it further.

She watched him intently; hopefully, giving him the opportunity to do what to her mind was surely the right thing. After a long silence she sneered softly, turned away from him and reached for the car ignition. "Christ, forget it," she said, shaking her head with a soft sad sigh. Then she started the car.

"No, wait." He reached up to the steering column to turn off the car and she pushed his hand away.

"You know," she said resentfully, with a touch of bitterness, "I was thinking that maybe you were too young for me, that maybe everything else was right but you were too young to be a man."

Wyatt puffed up. She'd struck a sour chord in the ear of his young pride. "It's not about that Sammy; I'm trying to protect you," the last three words were almost a yell.

"What? Protect me from what?"

That was it. The time had come. He was going to spill it all, he had to. Part of him wanted to. He looked at her directly; she saw his face, ashen colored, deeply upset.

"Brunk killed them Sammy, last night, I saw him do it."

She sat staring, completely dumbstruck. "He did what? He killed who? The two guys who are missing? You saw him kill them?" She was breathing hard, shaking, not knowing if this could be true.

He put his hands on hers and held them tightly. Then over the next half hour he told her the entire story, careful to be accurate about the details without being too gruesome about the scene of the men dying. He didn't go into his theory, yet, that perhaps Brunk had something to do with the death of her real father. She said little during his talk. There were a couple of points at which he was unsure if she was listening any more, staring as she was blankly over his shoulder while he talked. But he would pause and wait for her eyes to return to his face and then nod. She nodded back as if telling him to continue. Near the end of the story he began to inject his opinion about where it was all headed.

"I think he knows I was there, that I saw the whole thing. He put his hand on his gun while he stared at me this morning, at the ball field. Sort of like saying if I didn't keep quiet he was going to shoot me too."

"Shit Wyatt, am I the only one who knows this?"

"Yup, no one else is going to believe me."

"Ha," she said mockingly, "I'm not sure I believe you."

"How could I possibly lie to you about something like this? The other thing is, I think that detective Byrd, somehow he's figured out I was under the bleachers. He found the money I left for Alex, for the pot. And he saw the black mud."

"Black mud?"

"Yeah, under the bleachers it gets really muddy when it rains, and the dirt in there is black for some reason. It was all over my sneakers."

"I don't understand how you could live with this for the last day. How could you be so natural, well, except when Brunk was around?" She had a look of wonder on her face, shaking her head slowly as she spoke.

"I just try to forget about anything except what I'm doing at the time. O'Malley says that's what makes me a good ballplayer, the fact that I can do that. But anyway, it's been killing me really. I've been feeling like I want to puke all day. I made three errors at practice this morning and I never do that. I wanted to tell you, even before you knew something was up. I just didn't want to hurt you. When we were at the lake today and....when we did it, I forgot about everything except you."

"You have to just tell your father, then tell the cops," she said, not understanding the risk.

"Sammy, they haven't found the bodies. If I go to them with this story, they're not going to believe it, not about Brunk. They all think he's like a king of justice. Even if someone listens to me, it would take forever. There's no bodies, no *corpus delicti*. He'll get me before they get him."

"They'll figure it out eventually, there must be some evidence. They could force him to tell where the bodies are. You could ask for protection."

He shook his head. "It's my word against his. Hell, you even said you're not sure you believe me."

"It's just so incredible. I don't know... I don't understand," she said, sounding as if she was going to weep, finally.

"Well, I'll tell you this, in the time it takes for them to believe me and investigate, he'll kill me. I know it. He's got a gun. What do I have? I'm the only witness. If he gets rid of me, there's nothing left to threaten him. He may be thinking about getting rid of me right now, even before I tell anyone." She now understood the intense fear and unease that she had seen during the day; and began to feel the same way herself.

"Plus," he said, cautiously, ominously, "it could be this isn't the first time he's murdered somebody."

"What?"

"When you were talking about your real father today, how he got killed in a hunting accident only they never found the guy who shot him. And how he stole your mom from Brunk and then they had you. And, like, your dad and Brunk worked together and stuff, well...."

"Oh my God," she interrupted, "you think that maybe…"

"Well, I mean he's a friggin murderer," he interrupted before she actually said it, "you should have seen him when he shot those guys, he didn't even flinch. He just loaded the bodies into the car."

She began to shake. Her head was swirling from the final weight of what her life had been about. If what Wyatt said was true, her life was tied to a man who murders other humans, one of whom was her real father. There never has been and there would never be anything normal about her life. She was an oddball, different; her family history was tragic, insane and abnormal. Even if no one else ever knew about this, she knew, it was there now forever.

160

Somehow Wyatt sensed this. His short years didn't stop him from feeling empathy and imagining what it would be like to be her. It probably made it easier for him since his own family had failed. As she sat bent over in her seat, her hair fallen down shielding her face from his view, he lowered his head to hers.

"Listen, I'm here with you. We're in this together. I'll help you deal with it, you help me. It's pretty amazing really, how we just met and then this has gone on around us and we're together in it. If we stay strong and don't do anything stupid, it could turn out all right. Do you believe me?" he asked. She nodded her head and looked up at him.

"I'm sorry I said you aren't a man," she said, "you're more man than anyone I've ever known."

Somehow he managed a smile, "That's okay, it doesn't matter. What we have to say is that there's no proof he killed your dad also. I think it's what they call circumstantial. There's only proof that he killed Berelli and Stenman. I mean, I saw him, so there's proof for us."

She nodded again and looked at him with red eyes; her nose was running onto her top lip so he pulled the front of his t-shirt up and stretched it to her face to wipe her off. "You got my snot all over your shirt," she said, and managed a smile also.

"I don't care, your snot doesn't seem like snot to me." They paused and let their affection give them strength.

"So," he continued, "we have to figure out a way to get the cops on his trail without them knowing it was us that led them there, because if he figures it out, he'll try to kill us both."

"God, how are we going to do this?" she said, sounding hopeless.

"Do you think you could go back there? Go back and apologize to him, tell him you were wrong. Tell him you'll stop hanging around with me; that I'm not worth it or something. Could you do that? I mean could you handle being around him?"

"I don't know, I think so. Yeah, I can do it." he watched her recover; lift her head up in strength. He was marveled by the transformation she went through when confronted by a challenge. This was an amazing girl, he thought. She would surely be okay if they could just pull this off. "But then what am I going to do?" she asked, "I mean how are we going to make anyone see he's guilty?"

"I don't know, we'll figure something out. We need time. Maybe they'll find the bodies. Maybe there's something in his office or in the house that we can use. Keep your eye out for something, anything. But act normal, don't make him suspicious."

She laughed. "Act normal he says," she held her palms to the air, "sure, go back to the murderer's house, just pretend everything is A-O-K." She laughed again.

Wyatt didn't see the humor. "He can't know we're on to him. Think of it as survival, because it is."

"I know silly boy. I'm just trying to get you to lighten up. I'll handle that part. You figure out what we're going to do."

There was silence as she changed the mood, their faces

so close he could feel her breath on his eyelashes, smell her sweet warm scent as she let her air out on him. It was a scent that had now become familiar after the afternoon at the lake where she brought him to arousal and rewarded him with the delicious warmth of what was, he realized afterward, her never-ending desirability. He'd been inside her there, felt the contrast between the coolness of the fresh lake water and the warm surroundings of her insides. The memory returned to him as he again drank in the splendor of this young creature; how he floated her over to the rock and eased her up against it; how she welcomed him inside and with unspoken commands taught him to make her feel the same wonder he was feeling; how sensing her pleasure became his only real desire. It was something he'd never experienced before, because all his previous experience had been with girls, never a woman. The memory drove him crazy. He wanted to return there now. In the moonlight by the shore of the dirty Hudson River, she owned his heart.

Fifteen

Loretta Morton checked her interdepartmental mailbox on her way in the door on Monday morning, as she did every morning. She rarely finds anything there, since the majority of memos are now sent via email. But she checks the box everyday out of habit after so many years. She walked past the town clerk's office and made her way to her door, the office of the Tax Assessor for the Town of Nazareth.

It just so happens that the tax assessor is stationed directly next to the entrance to the police department. As the town grew over the years and office space came to be at a premium, the police continually take up more and more of it. Her department is viewed as the least needy one space wise, as the wizards in Town Hall figure number-crunchers can always be squeezed without any detriment. So the police and the clerk encroach further and further on her people every year. She doesn't care really; there's little glamour to this job. Visitors to her office are not there to sprawl out and the relatively austere conditions make for the impression that the money people in Nazareth are conscious about the use of tax payer dollars.

She took a job in this department in 1984 as Assistant Revenue Clerk when Tom, her husband, came to the school district as a guidance counselor. While he worked his way through the district and was eventually promoted to Assistant-Principal she served the assessor, an elected official, with loyalty and diligence. For forty years there had never been a challenge to the assessor in the bi-annual election. It's not a job sought by many. So when Porter Matthews retired finally in 2004, Loretta threw her hat in the ring and won the election. It was unanimous of course, with 1,471 votes cast, as there was no one else on the ballot for a voter to select. She had been running the department anyway for the previous ten years, so the promotion as it was, simply meant more responsibility and a little more money. It was attractive only because she'd be able to keep the job until she was ready to retire. When she did retire she'd have full benefits and a decent pension for the rest of her days. Not a bad gig for a working girl, if you can get it.

On her way in the door Detectives Byrd and Romundo were talking by the main entrance to the police department. They stopped abruptly and nodded politely at her, looking a little embarrassed.

"Good morning Loretta," Byrd finally offered.

"What the matter?" she asked, "you guys trying to keep the cafeteria breakfast menu a secret?" She smiled sarcastically, never one to let others get away with petty office intrigues. Byrd smiled and shook his head in admiration. The beauty of Loretta is that what you see is what you get. But he didn't answer, he couldn't think of anything smart at the moment and he certainly wasn't going to blurt out that their investigation had revealed her husband was having an affair.

She strolled in her office door appearing to not care

but silently wondering about what it was she interrupted. Those two rarely wasted time or energy spreading gossip. From the little she knew they seemed like pretty good cops. She walked into her tiny office and set her purse in its usual place. On the desk sat a five by seven glossy of her and Tom, pictured dancing at their twenty-fifth anniversary the previous year. They wore genuine smiles. Both appeared happy to be there; happy together. Over the course of the last few months though, she'd allowed desk papers to 'accidentally' obstruct the picture. Those who know her would think this strange, as fastidious as she is about her desk. But the portrait makes her feel guilty now, since she hadn't taken the time to have sex with her husband since, well, she couldn't remember when. He doesn't do it for her anymore. Sex with Tom is boring after all the years. He long ago stopped bothering to satisfy her; he simply did his business, rolled over and went to sleep. When it comes to the photo she's caught up in a no man's land of ambivalence: she can't bring herself to take it down, but she can't bear to look at it either.

If she knew about Tom's dalliance, things would be different. That's the kind of person she is, able to turn the page immediately when something makes her feel like she has been taken advantage of, and Tom wouldn't have cared, not really. But the question of his affair was moot. Her new indifference arrived from a different direction, the previous winter. On the first morning of work after New Year's she woke up, looked in the mirror and decided she wasn't at all pleased by what she saw. So she joined the local YMCA and began the grueling process of restoring tone to her fleshy body. She let her hair grow just to the shoulders, had it streaked to take away the gray and to restore the bouncy sandy blonde look that she carried in her twenties and thirties; the look that drew Tom's relentless interest all those years ago. After a few weeks of hard work she gained the ability to wear more contemporary and detailed clothing. She was back down to a size eight, no longer needed support hose and the styles available to her now complimented rather than covered up her sexuality. She looked years younger, a very attractive fifty-two going on forty-five. She became, at least to men of that age group, pretty hot. This was not lost on a certain single, quiet, and in a conservative way quite handsome veteran police officer. His name, she knew from the years of notoriety and years of watching him walk past her office door, was Victor Brunk.

"I figured somebody around here ought to pay some attention to the Tax Assessor," he said that morning, Valentine's Day, the fourteenth of February, as he stood at her office door with a red envelope, "so….well….I got you a Valentine." He followed up the pronouncement with a crusty smile; the closest Brunk could come to projecting a flirt.

"Well my goodness, thank you Brunk!" she said cheerily. It had been years since someone had thought to give her one of those. She was taken by complete surprise and deeply pleased.

"Yes, uhh… no need to get me one back, and, uh, you don't have to open it now, I just thought somebody oughta show some appreciation for you, uh, your good work." He awkwardly put it on her desk and shuffled back to the office door, "so, uh, anyway, happy Valentine's Day, Bye."

"Okay," she said, still surprised and nervous also, "you too." She giggled, "Bye yourself." She almost sang the words she was so uplifted.

Brunk was a frequent visitor to her office over the course of the next two weeks, as late winter turned to early spring. Sometimes he brought coffee to her; after he found out she liked mocha almond from Dunkin Donuts, with skim milk and one Splenda. This raised a few eyebrows in the office after the third time he did it, but most either didn't think much of it or figured Brunk, being such a scrooge, was probably just trying to work her for a lower assessment on his house. Loretta didn't care about his motives, but she was sure that it wasn't property tax related. She was just happy to have a man paying attention to her and, from where she sat, Brunk wasn't so bad. He was kind, thoughtful, friendly, trim and strong, good-looking, and for some reason he caused tingles in the base of her back like she used to get from Tom when she was younger.

Brunk would come in to her office now, with or without coffee, and sit in the wooden chair in front of her desk. They chatted about all kinds of things, the news, town politics, food, new movies that were out, the weather, anything. They developed an affinity and both looked forward to the next time he would walk in the door and park his big frame in front of her. Loretta had come to fantasize about him secretly, alone in her office or at night as she fell asleep. She never felt guilt about the fantasy, only that she hadn't come clean and told Tom she didn't want to be married to him anymore. For Brunk's part he had definite designs on a married woman; he was smitten by her beauty and the sound of her voice. He'd go with this as long and as far as she let him and hope that she felt desire for him also. They were a strange mix these two; her looking young for her age, him old for his.

One day in early April she was looking particularly good and they were having a particularly interesting talk in her office. The freshness in the air intoxicated him that morning, made him perhaps bolder than he otherwise might be. While she was explaining her idea that the school district should eliminate some of the "too too many" school buses it operated and require students who live within one mile of school to walk, just like she did when she was a young girl, Brunk threw out his idea.

"I think it would nice to have lunch outside the office for a change, what do you think?"

"Yes that would be nice," she said casually, as if it were a routine thing for her to have lunch with men from the police force, "shall we meet somewhere?"

He couldn't believe it was so easy; there wasn't even the slightest hesitation in her response. "I'm working the night shift tomorrow," he answered, "so I would be able to relax and not have to worry about the patrol car or anything."

"Good," she agreed with a confident smile, "I take as long as I like for lunch, where will we go?"

The details had never crossed his mind. He wasn't even planning to ask her today, it just came out. "Uh, let's go someplace in toward the city, someplace different than around Nazareth," he was stumbling through this, responding just as much as she gave him latitude to do so.

"You know, I don't really even care about eating lunch," she said, now with a wicked smile on her face, "I'd actually be happier to just go somewhere that we can be alone and relax."

"Same for me."

He took a room at a small hotel on a back avenue just outside the city. They met there at eleven the next morning and stayed well into the afternoon, much too late for her to return to the office. Brunk proved to be just what she was looking for, strong, patient, able to return to duty several times and give her all the pleasure she craved. Just as important she enjoyed his company. He paid attention when she talked, truly listening, not just shaking his head. He asked perfect questions about what she was saying, details, what she meant, encouraged her to tell him more about her life and desires. When she would pause and relax against his chest, content, he would bring her to arousal again and rise to the occasion for her. They carried on like that for hours. She didn't want to go home. While driving back to Nazareth she decided that people misjudge Victor Brunk. He's a kind and interesting man, unselfish and passionate. He's not the crazed vigilante they make him out to be. She felt this before they had sex, but being intimate with him made her understand more about what makes him tick.

During May, June, and now, July, they'd meet once or twice a week and spend the afternoon together naked in each other's arms. With no need for secrecy on his end, he'd often meet her on the weekend if she could get free and he wasn't on duty, keeping her time away from work to a minimum. He continued to arrive at her office for chats and bring coffee when he was able to. They grew quite close and the time spent together became important to them, though neither felt any great need to change their respective situations. The relationship worked the way it was, they were happier in life.

Today she was in another good mood; she was going to see her lover in the afternoon at their usual spot in the city. She spent the morning answering immediate issues, a few responses to requests for dispute of property value assessments and a short meeting with the Town Supervisor. By eleven-thirty the few important items on her desk had been cleared off and she was walking out the door. She made the fifteen minute drive to the hotel enjoying the summer air, hot as it was, knowing she'd soon be in a cool dark room underneath him, feeling him cover her up and enter her slowly, strong and hard but carefully allowing her to receive him comfortably. Sometimes it seemed like she could feel him between her ears, so deep was his penetration. She loved it. She'd orgasm almost immediately, which would invite him to do the same. It was always electric the first time, it felt so wonderful after anticipating it for days.

He wasn't there when she arrived, which was strange. He always made certain to be there early so she didn't feel awkward waiting for him in the parking lot. She didn't see his car, an aging Jeep Cherokee, anywhere so she pulled out of the lot and drove around the block to burn some time. When she passed by again he wasn't there still, so she again drove out and around the block. Two additional trips later there remained no sign of him so she pulled up to the curb away from the building far enough to not be noticed near the hotel but close enough to view it and watch for him. Nearly an hour passed and she began to worry. Not once had he been late or missed a date. She checked her cell phone several times to see if a call came in that she missed, but there was nothing there. She passed through moments of concern and worry to moments of anger and back to worry again. She kept coming back to the idea that he definitely would have called if he were able to. Something must be so terribly wrong that he's either unable to use his cell phone or get to a land line. He was not on duty that morning so he couldn't be in the middle of something police related. He might have been called in on an emergency but she was in the office all morning and he would have gotten word to her somehow. She decided that under the circumstances a drive by his house was warranted. If his car wasn't there, she would just go back to the office. Maybe, she hated to think it, but maybe he had just plain old stood her up. She didn't stop for a second to think that the disappearance of Berelli, who she had met several times over the years, and Stenman, the troublemaker, had the entire police force going flat out and in fact Brunk was called in that morning to make up the deficit.

She knew where his house was of course, but had never ventured over that way as she didn't want a chance sighting to give the impression she was looking for him. When she turned onto Clermont Street she prayed she wouldn't see his car there, unable to bear the thought that he might have simply stayed home and not bothered to meet her. The thought made her nauseous, but looking in the driveway she didn't see his car, only the blue BMW, which she correctly assumed belongs to Sammy.

Subconsciously she slowed in front of the house,

looking past the car to the garage door which was open. She saw Sammy standing in the opening, laying her eyes on her for the first time. Sammy turned out of the garage just as she drove by but didn't notice her. In her left hand Sammy carried a pair of men's boots.

The relief was only partial. She drove out of the neighborhood and made the short trip back to the office. It was still just twelve thirty in the afternoon and there were plenty of things to do. In addition she was so upset that going home and sitting alone or going shopping was out of the question. She also thought there was a chance he had left some kind of message for her on her desk, though that seemed unlikely since he would never leave a personal note lying around. The disappointment of it all began to bother her. She scolded herself briefly for becoming involved in this way. Here she was hurt like a school girl because her boyfriend didn't show up. She decided to straighten up and get over it; she was after all, the town Tax Assessor.

Sixteen

It was always this way he thought. Whenever they didn't understand, he couldn't go. The last time he was forced to venture outside the system and make sure a really bad guy paid the price, it was the worst, like now. That was a long time ago, but he remembered. Sometimes, in fact most of the time, he could force it out. But it was impossible now. So Brunk stopped grunting in futility at the urinal and put himself back in his pants, irritated, resentful, and spiteful of those who didn't understand him. The O'Malley kid was the problem. If not for him, there'd be no connection.

When they called early that morning to tell him the captain wanted everyone on duty today, he came in willingly as always, even though he had to play this cat and mouse game; even though if they knew the truth they'd put him away. The suits who oversee police work, the elected officials and the plain clothed town workers, none of them understand what a cop has to go through. None believe it takes a soldier to enforce the law and there are casualties in that war. Sometimes there's collateral damage. All of them, the politicians, the workers, the citizens, they all take safety for granted. They walk the sidewalks and drive the streets and let their kids ride their bikes to school and they expect everything to be okay. They forget it's him that does it. They'd forget about him even more if they knew about Berelli and Stenman. But then where would they be? They'd regret it someday but it'd be too late. He couldn't let them make that mistake.

He spent three hours in the briefing room this morning, giving that idiot Byrd and his flunky Romundo all his notes. The other guys gave them notes too. But Byrd didn't ask the other ones two and three times about what they did, making like he didn't get it or like he forgot some detail from before. He's slippery that one, trying to make a name for himself in this thing; trying to figure it out. And Loretta, poor sweet Loretta, she was another casualty of this war. She'd never understand either. When he left the briefing room to go to the bathroom earlier he saw her coming in, returning from the hotel. Her heels clicked sharply on the shiny tile as she walked the corridor, echoing off the painted walls. He could feel she was upset, sensed it. She pushed the door open to her office decisively after she saw him, making a statement. He chuckled at the memory. She has such a small mind, he decided. How could she possibly think he could DO IT today?

After seeing Brunk in the corridor, Loretta stepped to her office and sat at the desk. She began shuffling papers, pretending to herself that she had something to do there. Shortly thereafter Detective Byrd appeared at her door.

"Got a minute?" he asked.

"I suppose."

He sat down in the wooden chair facing her desk, Brunk's chair, perusing her official posture; wondering what she might look like when she relaxed; realizing he was about to throw a dagger at her and couldn't decide if he should feel bad about it or not.

"You've gotten to know Vic Brunk pretty well lately,"

he said, watching carefully for changes in her expression as he spoke.

"Is that a question?" There was just the slightest flinch in her head.

"Nope, I already know the answer. I'm just letting you know, I know."

"Okay, so now I know," she cocked her head to the side slightly and looked at him with narrowed eyes, "he visits me here in the office and we chat, he's a pretty interesting fellow and a good person to know; keeps me out of traffic court." She put up a coy smile. Byrd wasn't buying but nodded anyway.

"Does he visit with you anywhere else?"

"I beg your pardon?"

"You see the Supervisor has his Committee on Good Government, sort of our internal affairs division. Now I'm not on that Committee, but a couple of the other guys are."

"Is this some kind of official visit, Detective Byrd?"

"Nope, just the opposite."

"Oh? So you're asking me to talk to you off the record?"

"I think it's the best way."

"How so?"

Byrd leaned to the side in the chair and looked through the door, checking to be sure there was no one outside the office who would hear. "Well I'm what you might call privy to your friendship, so to speak, with Brunk. It would be best for all concerned at the moment, if my privies remain up here," he pointed to his head, "don't you think?" She maintained a stoic look on her face and didn't protest. Byrd knew he had her engaged. "So I've got this secret see, and you've got a secret too."

"I do?"

"Yes you do. I came in here to talk to you about Brunk, that's a secret," he looked side to side and turned his palms up and shrugged, "so far anyway." He paused a moment for effect then turned back to her. "Now as long as you keep our little chat a secret, then I'll keep your special friendship with Brunk a secret, and everybody will be happy."

She knew she had no choice, of course, and began to seethe again from allowing herself to become vulnerable in this way. "I'm listening," she said finally, and crossed her arms to pin down her hands and keep them from shaking.

"Were you with Brunk anytime on Saturday night from around six pm to eleven pm?"

"No, I assume he was working. He often works a double on Saturday, since no one else wants to work. We haven't talked since Friday."

Byrd said nothing but looked at her intensely, waiting for any sign to indicate she was lying. She'd feel pressure to say that she was with him, given what one would assume to be her natural desire to protect him, provided, that is, she thought there was a need to protect him. He saw nothing there.

"Are you investigating *him* for something?" she asked.

"I forgot to mention, you don't get to ask the questions."

"Indeed," she said sarcastically.

A part of Byrd wanted her to say she'd been with him. It would tie up another of those loose ends he dislikes. A part of him was more interested than before in the old cop's whereabouts.

"So you didn't talk to him at all over the weekend?"

"Nope."

"Did you notice him acting strangely today, like maybe things at work weren't going well? Anything like that?"

"I didn't talk to him today yet, we were...." she caught herself before her natural desire to spill it all took her too far.

"You were....what?"

"Shit," she cursed at herself and sighed before continuing, "We were supposed to be together this afternoon, but...."

"But he was called in to work? Right, sorry about that."

"I bet you are."

Byrd needed to ask her more about Saturday night. If she wasn't with him maybe she'd speculate on somewhere else he might have been. Two and a half hours with Brunk this morning gave Byrd no solid feel for where he was. His report was sketchy at best and there were no tickets issued, which was untypical for the guy. Saturday nights were always productive for him.

"Knowing him as well as you do, is there ever anyplace he goes while on duty?"

"I haven't any idea Detective. His step daughter is visiting him and his mother's in a nursing home over in Preston Hollow. I don't keep tabs on the man; I just have sex with him."

He nodded and slapped his hands on top of the two wooden arms of the chair, signaling he'd heard enough.

"So we'll keep this between us," he said as he stood up.

"You think you can contain yourself?"

He smiled at her testiness; sharp, he thought, even under the circumstances. "Have a good afternoon Loretta," he said and left.

She stared out her office window, overlooking the town hall parking lot; watched as Byrd walked out the back door, walked to his car, and opened the trunk. She picked up her desk phone and punched in the number for the Police dispatch desk.

"Hello Officer Barnes? This is Loretta Morton. Is Detective Byrd in this afternoon?... oh okay... well do you know what case is he working on at the moment? Oh yes, that's right, the missing persons, I should have figured that... no, I'll call him back later, thank you." The hot July sun had moved past midpoint in the sky and was streaming in her window, making the heat unbearable through the glass. She reached over to the blinds and turned them closed darkening the room and making it feel smaller, without the window to look through she felt closed in; agitated. She realized it wasn't wise to be there, she shouldn't have come back. Two property files sat to the right where she left them earlier, ready to be worked on when she returned the following morning. There was nothing there that she could concentrate on now. Fear of what Byrd was doing dominated her mind. Try as she may she couldn't dismiss it as 'not her problem'. The man she had been having sex with for three months was clearly involved in something, otherwise Byrd wouldn't have taken the risk. His little 'shared secrets' deal indicated something was simmering. Brunk appeared at the door suddenly and it startled her.

"Sorry about this morning," he said, "the whole place is running crazy with the Berelli-Stenman disappearance. The formal report was just posted this morning so the chief wants everyone in the mill. The press is going to be all over us within hours. I've been on duty since Sunday morning."

"You should have called, or gotten word to me somehow. I waited for you for an hour and a half. I was worried that something happened to you. Then I felt like a fool."

"I'm sorry. I was completely tied up in the briefing room, barely got free to take a leak." He smiled and sat in the chair. It could've been warm still, from Byrd. She felt better now, strangely, seeing him there in his usual spot. Although she was still angry and distracted by Byrd's questioning, she felt like she could breathe again.

"I'll make it up to you, I promise."

"I don't need that," she said curtly, "I just need basic consideration. I have an important job too."

"I know. I'm sorry Loretta, it's an unusual circumstance, The place is in upheaval."

She supposed she could understand that. But still, suddenly there was a look in his eyes she had not seen before, a pretense.

"You had a visitor?" He directed his glare at her.

She quaked. "Oh, you mean Byrd? He's a strange bird, no pun intended. He wanted to find out if I know anything about Mark Berelli or Stenman."

"Well do you?"

"Victor, what do you mean? If I did, Byrd wouldn't need to come see me." He didn't answer, just looked at the edge of her desk blankly. His eyes were dark circles, like he hadn't slept in days. She'd never seen him look this old, pale, abnormal. It alarmed her, he wasn't right.

"There are some bad people out there Loretta, bad people. It makes my job tough." He stood and moved to the door.

"What? I don't understand Victor. Have you been sleeping at all?"

"Well enough. I have to get back….just wanted to say, sorry."

"Alright, that's fine. But please, go home and get some sleep."

He said nothing further and left. When he returned to the briefing room the meeting had broken up. Byrd and

Romundo had departed and only a few of the patrol officers remained talking in a small group. A couple of them looked up as he stood in the doorway, thinking he was behaving strangely as well, but not particularly concerned since Brunk always behaves a little strangely. His moods range from boisterous braggart to introvert and there's no telling which you might get at any given moment. The standing joke is that he's Nazareth's version of the two faces of Eve. When they looked up again he was gone, out the back door and walking across the parking lot to his patrol car. Loretta had re-opened the blinds and watched him through the window as he walked, as she had watched him so many times before. This time Brunk appeared mechanical, with no spring in his step. She knew instinctively he was driven today by a personality she'd never seen before, an alien mover inside him firing his muscles and directing the way.

He got in the car and drove down Oakwood Ave. as he had hundreds of times, this time not looking left and right on patrol. This time his destinations were his only interest. The sign for the Animal Hospital came into view and he pulled into the parking lot, looking for the small green bicycle in the spot where Wyatt always parks it. There were several empty parking spots so he chose one and sat there visualizing his walk into the office and seeing the kid there sweeping or doing whatever that old coot veterinarian had him doing. He pictured the receptionist, what was her name? That's right Garret, Viola Garret, a strange bird too. She always greets him so friendly like, but he figures she's just trying to keep from getting a ticket. She never wears her seat belt. He knows it and she knows he knows it. She's just as bad that one, just like the old vet, giving Wyatt a job and protecting him from justice, prolonging what's going to become of him eventually regardless: locked in a jail cell somewhere. She'll have hers though. The kid has no sense of right and wrong. He imagined the look on his face if he should walk in the door to the hospital. He was closing in on him; the look on the kid's face would be entertaining.

But the bicycle wasn't there. He pulled out of the lot and drove to the ballpark, but found just a few kids playing on the fields in the heat of the July afternoon. He knew Wyatt would be showing up at the park today, sooner or later, for the team would surely be practicing before the beginning of the big tournament that night. He sat in the lot as he would any other day, in the cool of his air conditioned cruiser, looking out through the dark tinted glass. Only today he wasn't waiting for baseball moms to go speeding through the lot. He stared straight ahead through the windshield, out to the mostly empty field. Maybe the kid would show up before anyone else and he'd have him alone. That could be hours away though and there'd surely be other players around. He suddenly felt strange, as if someone was watching, the feeling you get when you're someplace you shouldn't be. What would they think if they saw him there, not doing anything just staring straight ahead at the emptiness? They'd think he was a kook.

He pulled out of the lot and drove over to Willow Street, where that other ne'er-do-well Scooter lives. Being in that part of town wasn't unusual for Brunk; he was always cruising through there, looking for 'Scooter' types. But the bike wasn't there either.

Seventeen

Wyatt went into work early that morning, early for him that is. He arrived through the back door of the Animal Hospital at 7:30, put his lab coat on and reviewed the list that the Doc had left for him. The main task this morning was to get the waiting room floor mopped before the first patient appointment at 9:15. The floor really did need cleaning so he didn't mind. He had come to take a measure of pride in his work at the vet's office, even though the old witch Garret would never believe that and treats him like a naughty dog no matter how hard he works. While he mopped he used a brush to scrub the corners where the floor and the walls meet. Then he rinsed the mop and went over the entire floor again, making sure all the cleanser was removed before the surface dried. At 9:05 he had picked up and put away his cleaning tools and returned the furniture to where it belongs. The waiting area looked and smelled clean, but Mrs. Garret had no comment when she came in and sat at the reception counter. He figured she was pissed because the smell of the soap was covering up the awful perfume cloud that followed her and which she probably figured smelled great. She offered only a curt, "Hello Wyatt," before she sat down.

Within a few minutes the first patient came in and Wyatt moved into the back area to continue with his list, a long one today, which meant he would be there well into the afternoon, which was fine because pre-game practice wasn't to start until five-thirty. Doc Sheehan was interested in the baseball tournament. A few days had passed and some patients had probably talked about it with him. Of course Wyatt's heroism at the plate had circulated around town and even got to the vet. Doc Sheehan had no use for the local rag, *The Searchlight*, on account of the fact that it was mostly an advertising circular, or so he said. Wyatt heard that the Doc was pissed because *The Searchlight* was running a half page advertisement paid for by the new Hi-Tec vet hospital, the one that offered 24 hour emergency treatment. Doc had provided 24 hour emergency treatment to the pets of Nazareth for 50 years, all you had to do was call him or stop by his farm. It didn't matter what of time day or night. And he remembered when *The Searchlight* building was farmland. Time was passing the old Doc by and he wasn't happy about it. Needless to say he didn't read *The Searchlight*, so it took a while for the details of the team's victory to reach him. Early in the afternoon Wyatt was helping to carry a big old German Shepherd to a recovery pen when the Doc brought up the subject of baseball.

"Big game tonight, eh Wyatt? I figure half of Nazareth will be up there watchin you fellas. Has O'Malley got you pitchin the first game does he?"

"Yes sir."

"How's your arm feel?"

"Feels pretty good Doc, I haven't pitched since last Tuesday, so I'm ready to go."

"It's gonna be hot out there, even though it'll be dark. Drink lots of electrolytes and eat a bunch of pasta today, spaghetti or something like that. Carbohydrates help fire the proteins, it'll give you more energy."

"Really?"

"Yup, and you may not realize it but energy is important when it's hot. Problem is a lot of athletes don't feel like eating this time of year, so they use supplements."

Wyatt believed anything the Doc told him; had never seen him be wrong about anything when it comes to living things; had seen dogs and cats come in here covered in blood and barely alive and walk out the door a week later like nothing had happened. "I'll do that Doc," he said finally, wondering if there was any macaroni or spaghetti at home. On account of baseball O'Malley didn't do a whole lot of cooking this time of year.

"After we get this patient settled in and the O.R. cleaned up you can knock off for the day. You probably have pre-game practice this afternoon, huh?"

"Yup, we do Doc, thanks."

"Tell your father I gave you the afternoon off. Use that time to relax and get your mind right for the game. Remember that if you have fun everything else will fall together. I'll see you up there if I can get out of here in time."

Wow, Wyatt thought, the Doc was coming to the game. That had to be a first. He couldn't remember seeing Doc Sheehan at a game, ever. Of course Doc didn't have a son, but had two daughters. Both were veterinarians.

He punched out at two-thirty and peddled his way home, not knowing that just after he left the hospital

Brunk pulled into the lot looking for his bike. When he arrived at the house he read the note that O'Malley had left for him on the counter but he missed that morning in his hurry to get out the door. It said to be at the field by five o'clock in full dress uniform. *The Searchlight* photographer was going to be there to take a team photo. Practice was going to be light, he was sure; maybe a little infield and some batting practice, but nothing heavy. Then they would load up in the cars and head north to the game. He grabbed two slices of bologna from the refrigerator, wrapped them in a slice of bread and went out the back door onto the screened-in porch. Some food and a little nap were needed before going to the field; he realized he wouldn't be able to eat pasta like the Doc had suggested. O'Malley must be leaving work early, he thought, then going right to the ball park. He always wondered how his father got so much time off from work this time of year. It was never an issue. And there were always tournaments they were going to, one of them this year just happened to be the World Series. *Just happened to be the World Series.* He thought about how funny that sounded, how he was taking it for granted.

Then the question of O'Malley's work returned; got him thinking of how little he actually knew about his father's job. O'Malley never talked about it, nor answered any questions about it in detail.

"I'm a computer analyst for the defense department," he answered last time Wyatt asked him.

"You mean you work for the government?"

"Yes."

"And you work with computers?"

"Yes."

"Well what's the name of your job, you know, guys ask me and I don't know what to tell them."

"I'm the Director of Technology and Information Development for the regional office here in the city, that's all," he answered casually, "just tell them that."

"So like when you go to Washington or Europe every so often, you're going there to like learn more stuff for your job?"

"Yep, I go there to learn more stuff."

"Well, like, do you have a boss?"

"Everybody has a boss Y-O."

"Who's yours?"

"My boss works in Washington; he has a big job with the government."

"What's his name?"

"Barack Obama."

Wyatt laughed, "Come on dad, he's everybody's boss,"

"Yup, anyone who works for the federal government."

"But don't you have another boss, somebody lower?"

"Why are you asking so many questions all of a sudden, you writing a book or something?" O'Malley tried to change the subject.

"I can't tell the guys you work for Barack Obama, they won't believe that."

"They won't recognize anyone else's name, well, maybe, Chuck Hagel."

"You work for him?"

"Yes"

"You ever get to talk to him?"

"Sure, when he needs something from me."

Wyatt inhaled the bologna sandwich and had nearly drifted off to sleep in the lounge chair when he heard a car pull up and the door slam around in front of the house. He got up and went part way around the stone walk that leads to the front, just far enough to see that the car in the driveway was a Nazareth police patrol car. He stopped in his tracks and walked back to the porch, into the house, and peered through a window from the dining room, the one they always do to check on who is in the driveway. He saw Brunk standing in the area where his bike was parked and looking toward the front door. "Fuuuuuuuck...." he said under his breath and moved quickly back to the porch and out the screen door again, this time accidentally letting it slam loudly as it closed, but not stopping to worry about the noise he was making. He ran to the fence separating their back yard from others, hopped over it, and ran toward the next street over. Hearing the door slam in back of the house Brunk ran around the side but was too late to see the kid jump the fence. He caught just a glimpse of Wyatt's back as he ran through the neighbor's yard and out onto Poplar Street in the distance.

By the time Brunk got into his car and drove around the block Wyatt had disappeared into the woods at the end of Poplar and was hiding along the bike path. It's the primary route that kids use to get between his neighborhood and Nazareth Plaza, a major strip mall. It's a network of paths actually, one of which follows the sewer line making its way down behind the plaza and ending at the sewage treatment plant sitting on the shore of the Motterskill creek. Wyatt dialed Sammy's cell phone.

"Where are you?" he said when she picked up.

"You're not going to believe what I found," she said on the other end.

"I don't have any time," he said, "Brunk's after me, I need you to come get me, he's gonna try to kill me, I know it."

"What?"

"Do you know how to get to the sewer plant down by the creek?"

"I think so."

"Drive by there in ten minutes. If I'm not there keep driving and then come back again. Don't stop until you see me."

"It'll take more than ten minutes for me to get there…."

"Just hurry up." He clicked off right as Brunk screeched to a halt by the beginning of path, grabbed the box cutter sitting on his seat and ran into the woods behind him. Wyatt jumped up and ran along the path that leads to the plaza. He heard the yell behind him, "Stop now O'Malley." He looked over his shoulder and saw Brunk standing in the distance with his hand on his gun, as if he were about to draw it. Wyatt decided instantly that there was no way he was going to stop, because Brunk was going to kill him regardless.

The path wasn't wide enough for a car. Since Brunk had seen Wyatt on the one that leads to the plaza, he ran back to his patrol car and zipped away, hoping to drive out and around the woods and into the front of the plaza quickly. Wyatt stopped briefly and looked back to see Brunk's car pull off with the tires squealing. It was just as he hoped. He back-tracked to get onto the other path and ran full speed to the treatment plant, about a half mile away. He sat in the bushes and waited for the sound of a car in the distance. Several minutes passed, it seemed like hours. Every second he remained there was one more second that Brunk had to figure out his destination was not the plaza, but the sewer plant instead. Finally he heard her coming, confirmed it was her by sticking his head out of the bushes, and then jumped out in front of her as she was nearly upon him. She screeched to a stop and he jumped in.

"Where do we go?" she yelled frantically.

"Just drive straight ahead, this road follows the creek and turns dirt and then comes out on Route 43 after a ways. We can't go back to Nazareth."

"Do you think anyone knows he was chasing you?"

"I didn't see anybody else."

"Where is your father?"

"He's at work. I'm supposed to be at pre-game at five. I think he's going there right from work. It's three forty-five now."

"Brunk won't bother you there, not with everyone around."

"I know, but I gotta get my stuff from the house, my uniform and glove and stuff."

"Listen," she said, "I have to tell you what I found."

"What?"

"Remember how you said to look around the house and see if there was anything?"

"Yeah,"

"I found his boots and I took them. They're in the trunk and they have black mud on them."

"Black mud?"

"Yes, didn't you say that Byrd saw the black mud on your sneakers that day? Well the same mud, I mean, I think it's the same, is on Brunk's boots. Wouldn't that tip off Byrd that he was there too?"

"If it's the same mud, but I wonder how Brunk got it there. He must have been under the bleachers. Christ, that's right! He must have checked under the bleachers after I left. Then why didn't he find the money for Alex?"

"It was dark, right? He didn't see it."

"Yup, could be."

"So all we have to do is get the boots to the detective. He doesn't need to know how they got there, just that they belong to Brunk."

Wyatt stared at her as she drove, realizing she had thought this out all the way. He realized also that Sammy is smart as hell.

"I don't know where I'd be if I hadn't met you," He said.

"Well you have Max to thank," she said and smiled, "he shit on the floor."

"He's gonna figure it out," Wyatt said after a moment, not seeing the humor in Max's accident under the circumstances.

"Who?"

"Byrd, he's gonna figure it out that I got the boots to him, that I must know what's going on. I'm the only one that knows about the black mud, me and O'Malley that is."

"It doesn't matter if he figures it out. He's not going to care where the tip came from, at least not right now. We'll worry about that later. We gotta get Byrd onto Brunk."

"Right, okay." He pulled out his cell phone and punched in 411 search. When the operator came on he said, "Nazareth New York, I need the number of a Byrd, that's B-Y-R-D, I don't know the first name." After a few seconds the operator came back with the number. "And do you have an address for that listing?" He waited while she searched. "Three twenty-two Homestead in Nazareth, thanks," he said. He didn't wait for the operator to connect, simply ended the call.

Eighteen

It was getting late and Rex would need to leave the office within the next hour. Monday afternoon traffic out of the city would be relatively light, but he still had a good forty minutes of driving from the parking garage to the ball field in Nazareth. This is one of the downsides of working in the city, but it was a relatively simple trade off since the Company has allowed him, as a veteran, to remain in New York even though much of his work requires constant communication with Langley. It would have been easier the last couple of years if he were still married, since he would have been able to count on Sheila to stay with Wyatt when mission analysis required his presence out of town. But he didn't blame her for leaving; the wife of an agent has little fun and his passion for baseball took up whatever free time he did find. Life without her required adjustments, but his sister welcomed the opportunity to stay over with Wyatt from time to time and Rex was fine without daily female companionship. Baseball was always his first love. In fact, while married to Sheila he'd forgotten their wedding anniversary several times but he'd never missed a playoff game on television unless a mission took him from it. This is a priority structure most women will not tolerate for an extended period.

Earlier in the day he sent out a query across the secure network. His Level 5 clearance afforded him access to nearly every federal, state, and local database without a sign-off - a countersignature - from a superior. The only higher clearance is Level 6, and only a dozen or so people in the country possess it. The information he was looking for would be as much available to a Level 5 query as it would Level 6. So he understood that whatever came back from the network would contain all of the 'official' information that can be found pertaining to this guy.

Rex is not unlike Detective Byrd, as it bothers him too when events appear or people do things 'untypical', which is why he has believed all along that Byrd is probably a good cop. It's why he understood when Byrd insisted that he figure out where Wyatt was on Saturday night. It's why he felt a strange connection with him when he said that his methods are different than Brunk's. It's why he believed his gut feeling that Wyatt's strange behavior of late had everything in the world to do with Brunk. And it's why, at this minute, Rex was waiting for a file to download onto his secure server that profiled the entire life of Patrolman Victor S. Brunk.

The history of the man, his place of birth, school, training, and family background were of little interest at the moment. On that regard, the life of Brunk didn't appear all that different from any other. In his service file there was an 'official' statement, some sixteen years ago, by Nazareth internal affairs regarding his divorce and the illegitimate child fathered by another officer on the force, a man who was subsequently found dead in a hunting accident. The child, he assumed, must be Samantha. A review of the file on the hunting accident revealed nothing but the coroner's report and the declaration by the district attorney that the case was unsolved two years later. There was no mention of any involvement on the part of Brunk.

He noted the complaint he had filed, two years ago, when Brunk had been giving Wyatt a rough time, and two others like it over the years filed by other Nazareth citizens complaining of Brunk's overzealous enforcement of the law.

The next file he requested was not regarding Brunk specifically. It was a file being sent over by the FBI as the result of a formal request to the Town of Nazareth Police Department for a copy of the GPS report showing all patrol cars during the period from midnight Friday night to midnight Saturday night. When combined with mapping software obtained under federal contract with Google Earth, O'Malley could produce a graphic display of the location of all Nazareth patrol cars during that period of time. He would then be able to sort through the GPS blips and eliminate all cars but the one driven by Brunk.

An alert on his screen went 'flag up' indicating the file had arrived. Working quickly O'Malley down-loaded it, sorted through to find Brunk's vehicle, integrated the Google software and converted the file to a time-lapsed graphic display. He studied the map of Nazareth to get his bearings and then used his curser to scroll through the day and into Saturday night. Between around five-thirty and about seven forty-five pm Brunk's car appeared all over town, making various short stops but not lingering anywhere for more than a minute or two. This seemed to indicate that he was not 'sitting' on traffic watch, but patrolling, as if looking for something. At seven fifty-nine pm his car arrived at the ball park. O'Malley could tell this very easily by the street names surrounding the location of the blips. Looking carefully, the mapping software even displayed the outline of the baseball fields and the location of the shed. The car remained parked by the shed for nearly two hours and forty-five minutes, until ten forty-one, when the blip began to move and O'Malley traced it back to the police station. Clearly that was the end of Brunk's shift for the evening.

He pulled up the duty reports filed for the night and sorted through to find Brunk's. The report stated that he was on moving patrol between five thirty-five when he finished his break for dinner and ten fifty-five pm when he returned to the station. It noted he issued several tickets during his day shift, two of them to Mark Berelli, but none were shown for his evening patrol. So besides Becca, he realized, Brunk was one of the last people to see Berelli before his disappearance. O'Malley stared at the screen and the blip showing Brunk's patrol car near the shed, stationary, as he scrolled through the hours after seven fifty-nine. Why would he be parked at the shed all that time? Cars weren't supposed to be in that area. Why would Brunk be there? It was dark by eight forty-five and it was pouring rain on and off throughout the period. Was Berelli's car parked there all that time? If so, Brunk surely saw it. O'Malley wondered if he included the sighting of Berelli's car in his reports to Byrd. Or if the car had been there and Brunk had seen it, he figured, it would have been a part of Brunk's general duty report for the night. There was no mention of him having been at the ball park at all. He wondered if Byrd had any idea that Brunk had basically misrepresented his location on his duty report.

At this point all of the peripheral circumstantial findings were combining to lead O'Malley to speculate that Brunk and Wyatt were together at the field at some time on Saturday night. There was the mud that Byrd had seen on Wyatt's shoes, purportedly from under the bleachers. There was the lack of accountability for Brunk in his report, but contradicted by the GPS tracking records. And most disturbing, there was the probability that Berelli was either there or had abandoned his car there and neither Wyatt nor Brunk had disclosed it. His mind went back to the discussion he had with Wyatt after he talked to the investigators at the ball park on Sunday morning. The kid seemed overly interested about what the investigators were doing with the cars.

O'Malley sat motionless staring at the screen, deciding his next step. He had to get out of the station and on the road so he wouldn't be late for pre-game practice. With all the tension about Wyatt and the disappearance, the trip to the World Series was missing excitement. He signed onto the website host domain that the Agency uses for non-traceable secure internet traffic and initiated an email. Then he pulled Byrd's business card from his pocket and typed in his email address. He bundled the GPS and mapping graphic into a .PDF file and selected it as an attachment to the mail. In the subject line of the mail he typed, 'Brunk location Saturday 2000 to 2230 hours,' and clicked send.

At the other end, Byrd sat at his desk shuffling through the reports he had collected during the day. He didn't see the flag go up as the info@peoplespower.org email arrived from O'Malley. Coincidentally, he had made a note to himself earlier in the day to check the GPS records for Brunk on Saturday night. He knew this would be difficult to do since the records are available only to officers who are part of internal affairs and he would not be able to requisition them without disclosing that his investigation might include a member of the force. Such an investigation cannot review employment or GPS records unless the union is notified prior and disclosed to the officer under investigation. The last thing he wanted to do at this stage was to alert the union or Brunk that he was a subject of any kind of investigation. So O'Malley's work had done Byrd a huge favor, all that was needed now was for him to read the email.

Instead, Byrd was distracted by a commotion out in the hallway leading from the reception area to the back offices where his desk sat. News of the missing persons had finally filtered to the media and a throng of reporters were gathered in the reception area and spilling out into the hall. Lights were on and cameras were rolling. Apparently the Chief of Police was preparing to make a statement. He couldn't imagine that anything the Chief could say at this point would have any basis in fact, because he was the only one who had any bit of evidence gathered and the Chief had yet not asked for a briefing. This was the Chief's job, where he earned his keep, making up bullshit for the media to digest and keeping them away from the guys who were really trying to do the crime solving, if in fact there was a crime here to be solved.

Knowing that he wanted nothing to do with the frenzy about to engulf the station, Byrd ignored the email, shut off his computer, packed up his notes into his briefcase and made his way to the back door. He was greeted there by another group of reporters, those who imagined that an officer or detective would be foolish enough to make a statement of some kind while going to his car. As he was confronted by a woman reporter yielding a microphone and being followed by a shoulder mounted camera he held up his hand, "The Chief is making a statement out front, that's all anyone is going to say." He moved quickly to his car and pulled out of the lot.

When he arrived at home, there was an object on the stoop next to his front door. His wife hadn't returned from work, so the black leather boots were still sitting there. He picked them up and looked at them, then noticed the dried black mud on the edges of the soles and in the cleats on the bottom. He simply stared for a moment, trying to understand what he was looking at and why. He did an about face immediately and returned to his car, opened the trunk, retrieved a large evidence bag, and carefully slid the boots inside. This was an interesting turn of events indeed. He sat on the stoop looking at the bag, trying to imagine who left them. It took mere seconds. There were only two other people, so far as he knew, to whom the black mud had any significance. He was willing to bet lunch that if he took these boots out to the ballpark and compared them to the footprints dried in the mud under the bleachers, they'd match.

Byrd is a man without deep experience in missing person investigations. There had been a few over the years, mostly teens or young adults, mostly runaways without malice. He investigated a child abduction which sadly, never produced results; the eight-year-old girl was never found. But he had never been part of an investigation which involved an adult that was reported missing and there wasn't a corpse found eventually. He figured one of two things was going to happen fairly soon. Either the two men would turn up alive with a plausible if ridiculous reason for their coincidental disappearance; or two bodies would be found and this would turn into a murder investigation. A murder that has been planned and executed is troublesome if the murderer took the time to dispose of the body carefully. Without a body, without the circumstances that surround the discovery of a body, an indication of murder weapon, time of death estimate, a location of the crime and any number of the tiniest clues the body could provide, it could be impossible to solve the crime. Even if an educated guess could be constructed about who did what, without a body there is no crime; *no corpus delicti.* This is painfully true, of course, unless there is a witness.

Detective Byrd made a career of investigating why people do things, which is why he had a low key job as a senior detective on a small police force in suburbia, even after a sterling record of solving crimes. District attorneys find it difficult to suffer through a Byrd investigation. They favor the tried and true investigative methods employed in inner cities: haul em in, read em their rights, make em crack and take a statement. It gives the powers that be the instant gratification they need in high crime locales. In little Nazareth, his nearly perfect record allowed the department to put up with his plodding ways. There is less urgency here, less tolerance for roughness, which afforded him the luxury now to sit on his stoop and think about the boots.

Why didn't they just tell him whose they are? He wondered what finger prints would be on them. That might lead somewhere, though surely neither Wyatt nor Rex had ever been printed. The owner's prints were probably on there; maybe he had a record of some kind. Maybe the guy had a blister and bled inside them or he left some sweat on the insoles. Maybe they could get a DNA sample.

If it was easy for Wyatt or O'Malley to talk about whose boots they were, they would have said, "these belong to so and so," but why the secrecy? It must be for fear of something. If O'Malley's prints appear on the boots, he could just ask him, force him to talk. Threaten that if he doesn't talk he'll arrest him for obstruction. But obstruction of what, trying to find out who owns a pair of boots? The possibilities presented too much for Byrd to delay his curiosity, his drive to know, until tomorrow. Not because he believed the boots themselves would bring about some clue that would help his current investigation, but because he couldn't stand not knowing why someone dropped them at his door. He picked up the evidence bag and walked to his car, put it in the trunk and went back to the house to write his wife a note. She was a great cop's wife, always understood about police work. There'd be good food waiting for him when he got home and if he was really late she'd help him wind down by asking him about the case. Even if she was asleep she'd wake up and talk, just to make sure he was okay. Sometimes she would ask simple questions about a case, so simple he'd have overlooked them if she hadn't asked; so simple yet so good. Maybe she'd come up with something special about this case. He might be unable to see the forest for all the trees.

Back at the station the first thing he did was to check the mud sample he'd taken from under the bleachers against the mud on the boots. It certainly looked the same. He took the sample and a chunk from the boots, put it in two separate small evidence bags and went down to the small lab in the basement. On the way back in to the station he'd called the part time lab technician who worked for the town, Mike Sarisi, and asked him to come in for a test. Mike was also the twelfth grade chemistry teacher at the high school and was working to complete his doctorate at City College. When that was done, Byrd figured, Mikey would take off to teach at a university somewhere and the department would be minus one great technician. Lack of equipment was the only thing keeping him from doing all the cool stuff, the really complex tests like DNA analysis, the way the big city police labs do. But Byrd felt confident that Mikey would be able to tell if two samples of mud came from the same location.

"There's no evidence tags on these," Mikey said as he opened one of the bags and stuck a sample probe into the clump of dried mud.

"They aren't evidence yet," Byrd replied stoically.

"So what do you want me to put on the report ticket?"

"You gotta have a report ticket?"

"If I want to get paid for my trouble tonight I do, can't just say I came in to test the Bunsen burners."

"Then just write 'two bags of dirt from detective Byrd.'"

"Where'd these samples come from Detective?"

Byrd paused to think about what he meant, but the answer was the same either way. "I'd better not say at the moment, since it isn't evidence and all."

"Well if I knew where it was collected from it would help me be sure it's the same or it's different."

"Can't you tell by tracing it?"

"Tracing what?"

"The compounds in there."

"The *compounds*, as you call them, are likely to be present in every sample of dirt in Orange County. We'll be looking for a common *non*-indigenous element, something extra which might allow one to say that the two samples came from the same place. For example, one would expect dirt from a vegetable garden to contain a high degree of nitrogen because of the constant fertilization, that sort of thing."

"Well both of them look the same and smell the same." Byrd thought this should be much easier than it sounded.

"I'll tell you what," Mikey said with a skeptical grin, "put Oprah Winfrey and Halle Berry behind a curtain naked with just their feet showing, paint their toenails the same color and have them both wear the same perfume. I'll tell you they're twins, and you'll believe me.... right up until they pull the curtain."

"I get it."

"Give me an hour or so and I should have something for you," Mikey said.

Byrd nodded and left the lab in the basement of Town Hall, then climbed the stairs to the first floor where his office is. The activity with people from the media an hour or so earlier had calmed down. He imagined he'd see the Chief's statement later on the eleven 'clock news. He sat at his desk and pulled the file for case interviews he kept locked in his bottom desk drawer. If he were only able to find out who Wyatt had left the money for, he'd have another avenue to get to a time line. He looked over the notes from the O'Malley interview again, the kid said so little there was nothing left to glean from it. He thought back about the expression on his face when he revealed the black mud on the sneakers. It wasn't a scared look, it was the look of someone who had practice at staying quiet before- probably a result of all the times Brunk tried to get him to talk. He'd seen the files, Wyatt O'Malley wasn't a bad kid, wasn't a trouble-maker. But at this stage, he wasn't afraid of cops either.

Byrd had taken the name and model number for the boots from under the tongue. They were Timberland model MP300. He turned on his computer with the intention of going to the Timberland website to find the model. When the computer screen came to life and his internet connection booted up, he saw the flag indicating mail. There's always mail. Much of it is strings of useless conversation from others in the office, so convinced of the importance of what they're talking about, they copy whoever they imagine would be remotely interested. Most of it he simply sends to his trash bin or reads after the string is over, not wasting his time until there is some hint the chatter has some importance. He scanned his inbox quickly and stopped at the one with Brunk's name in the subject line. The 'peoplepower' domain address had absolutely no meaning.

When he opened the mail and clicked on the attachment his security software kicked up a warning about the file. He nearly disposed of it unopened. But Brunk's name in the subject line was simply too tempting. He clicked on the 'ignore warning' icon and opened the file.

The .PDF file required a few seconds to load but finally filled his screen with an outline of the area near the ball park, the blips and lines were confusing. He simply stared at the screen in wonder, trying to decipher what it was telling him. Then he saw the blip for Brunk's car, parked near the shed for the more than two hours on Saturday night. He finally grasped the full meaning of the graphic and realized that someone else was shadowing this investigation; some person who must be deeply connected in order to get this information, and yet close enough to him to understand the significance. Again his mind raced to consider everyone he knew that was involved, trying to untangle who might possibly be aiding his research. Moreover, someone was out there telling him *what* to research.

A hazy movie was playing for him, a rerun of horizontal lines and obtuse sounds running through, with no continuity. All the circumstances put Wyatt and Brunk engaged in something. Their history, the mud, the graphic, all of it tied them to Saturday night. At least there was basis for that theory. There was no evidence for anything. Byrd was becoming convinced in his gut that there was a connection between all of this and the disappearance of Berelli and Stenman, but it was so murky it left him no place to nail something to the floor and take a good solid clear look.

His phone extension buzzed as he stared at the GPS graphic, just in time to punctuate his frustration at the garbled path he was on. "Byrd here," he answered after collecting himself.

"The only thing you got here," Mikey said, "is the fact

that this stuff is full of organic material, both samples"

"Organic material?"

"Yeah, you know, decaying plant life, nitrogen laden cellulose, skeletal cell walls floating in a soupy muddy admixture. Both admixtures are the same."

"So it's from the same place? I mean both samples?"

"Could be, the reason the stuff smells so bad is that the organic material is starting to work in the summer heat."

"Work?"

"Yeah, ferment."

"Oh."

"If you put this stuff in a bottle with water and capped it, in about a year you'd have some really rotten tasting alcohol. There's a lot of plant life in there."

"So they're from the same place, right?"

"Maybe, but if you're gonna try to use it for evidence you'll get your ass kicked."

"Why?"

"Because these two samples could be from the same place, probably are. It's probably someplace dark and wet with years of decomposed vegetation mixed in. And you could go back to that spot and get a third sample and you'd see the same stuff in it. But you could go to a million other places and find it also. So if you're planning to use the two samples to tie something together in an evidentiary context, you're screwed. My opinion is though; it's like ninety-nine percent the two came from the same hole."

"Thanks Mikey, that's all I need for now."

Byrd turned back to his computer and looked at the graphic one more time. He then did an internet search and pulled up the Timberland website. In the box for 'product search' he entered MP300 and after a blue line finished loading a picture of the boots came up. There they were; the same boots as those in his possession, right down to finished black nylon laces. Under product description it read 'The boot worn by Police and Military forces world-wide for over twenty years.' Byrd minimized the web page, put his password into the police department menu screen and found the section under department regulations that specified standard issue clothing for patrol officers. Under 'footwear' it listed three types of shoes; 'Dress,' General Service Duty,' and "Rough Service Duty.' In the box next to Rough Service Duty, it specified 'Timberland, Model MP300.'

Nineteen

Brunk circled the parking lot of the Nazareth Plaza several times without success. He wasn't surprised. When he watched the kid disappear down the path he held little hope of finding him on the other side. He parked his car behind the far section of the strip mall and walked the area covered by the overhang on foot. He passed by store fronts and looked in casually, pretending to be just the friendly town cop on the beat. After walking the entire length he returned to his car and sat with the engine running, knowing he would not get his hands on Wyatt this time, wondering if that might be best anyway. What would he have done with him? He couldn't slice his throat in public. He'd have to take him somewhere else. But that carried problems also; he couldn't depend upon being able to take the kid without being seen.

As the reality of what he was doing sunk in he felt tired, drained, wanting to sleep and get refreshed. He realized that Loretta was right; he hadn't slept more than an hour since Friday night. It occurred to him that perhaps his judgment had become clouded by the non-stop wear of his effort; that perhaps he was overly concerned about the kid and Byrd. He figured Wyatt was sufficiently scared at this point; that he would think twice about going public with what Brunk figured he'd seen. He needed to keep the pressure on him, but what would be the end game? If Wyatt remained alive, would there ever be a time when he wouldn't need to be concerned? Not likely, he thought.

But maybe he didn't need to be in such a hurry. There was no eminent confrontation brewing. If the kid decided to tell someone he'd have plenty of time to deal with him, as long as there were no bodies to back up his story. He decided he probably should worry more about the dead than about the living.

Being near the end of his shift, he drove by the doggie park on his way back to the station. He pulled into the ball park lot and took the left on the dirt road up to the maintenance building behind the doggie yard, then pulled up in front of the maintenance building and got out quickly, walking through the unlocked swing gate toward the area where he had buried the bodies. He noticed nothing out of place until he was nearly on top of the spot where he dug, then saw that dogs had been digging there, several holes were scraped out in the area a few inches deep but nothing had been exposed, yet. He didn't want to linger but kicked some of the dirt back into the holes with his foot none the less. It would do no good to fix it; they obviously smelled the bodies below and would only begin the process again. He was Amazed that an animal could sense that acutely. The scent would surely get more potent the deeper they dug, so something needed to be done. He walked back to his car thinking he would need to return later that night perhaps, uncover the bodies and move them somewhere else. He was so sure that the doggie park would be a good place. Few people walk there, animals do little more than run and piss and shit there. It seemed so perfect on that night.

Brunk was not a man prone to panic, but the pressure seemed to be coming from several directions. He started the engine and sat there thinking about it. He needed to calm down, to think it out logically and sort between threats that were real and those that were imagined. It was so hot that afternoon that the minor exertion of walking from the car to the doggie yard and back had put him into a full sweat. Or maybe it was the worry. Perspiration streamed down his forehead. His back was soaked against the seat and the air conditioner didn't do the job of cooling him off. Feeling as though he needed air he opened the car window, but more humidity just poured in. He closed the window again and abruptly put the car in reverse, aching to be moving, to get some breeze in the window. Without looking he cut the wheel to the right as he backed up and nearly ran directly into Byrd who was driving up on the left side of his car. He too was strangely drawn to the doggie park.

Byrd watched steadily as Brunk struggled to regain his composure after the near miss, and then pressed the window button for the passenger side so he could talk through it.

"What's going on Brunk?"

He didn't answer at first and couldn't prevent his dislike for the detective from putting a scowl on his face. "I don't report to you," he said after deciding to go on the offensive.

"You've been pretty stingy with answers lately officer, I'm beginning to wonder who's side you're on."

"I'm on the right side, been that way since before you were just a cadet. Did you ever do any patrol work Byrd, or did they just graduate you right into full-fledged gum shoe?"

"I did my time."

Brunk grunted. Bumping into Byrd made him forget all about his other anxiety. He turned his head away in pretense of having better things to think about. "I gotta go, my shift is over."

Byrd didn't take his eyes off him. "Yeah, you know I've been meaning to ask, you didn't run into the O'Malley kid on Saturday night did you? He won't talk about where he was. He told his father he was one place, then another, but it doesn't check out. Just a discrepancy, you know how that goes."

"He won't talk about where he was because he was probably doing something illegal, dealing drugs, or trying to get into some very young woman's pants."

"Right, he's bad, that one."

"Yup, he sure is."

"So with all the driving you did he was nowhere around huh? I imagine that if you were parked in one place all night you might've missed him, but since you were cruising all night you wouldn't have seen him if he was out, huh?"

"Is there a question in there somewhere?"

"Never mind, it's nothing. You know me, just trying to tie up loose ends. I'll get it figured out."

Brunk sneered at him and dropped the shifter into reverse again, this time looking behind as he pulled away from Byrd's car. As he drove out of the Maintenance building road the ball fields appeared in front of him. Players had begun to assemble on the field before the game, though neither Wyatt nor Rex had yet arrived. He hesitated before pulling out into the lot, thinking that he might hang around to see Wyatt's expression when he arrived. But with Byrd and Rex both likely to be in the vicinity, he drove on, knowing there would be plenty of time to intimidate the kid in the days to follow. And once he had relocated the bodies, there would be no evidence to be found and, therefore, nothing to fear whatsoever.

As he pulled out onto Home Run Road his cell phone rang.

"It's Brunk," he answered.

"Victor, it's Loretta."

"Hello," he answered formally, as if taking an official call, then pulled over on the side of the road to talk without driving.

"I'm sorry I was so upset with you this afternoon."

"Well you're entitled to your feelings, I should've called you but…"

"I know, you're right in the middle of the investigation, the whole department is, I understand. It wasn't like you, that's all."

"I'm tired Loretta, so tired."

"Can I see you? I miss our time together today."

"Tonight?" he sounded incredulous.

"Yes, right now. I have a few hours before I have to be home. Aren't you finished with your shift soon?"

"Well yes, but, uh… I wasn't planning… I was going

to do other things."

"Well then tomorrow night? Tom's going to watch the games all week and I'll have the nights free."

"Uh, well, I don't know, uh, maybe; if I don't have to work or something. There are a lot of important things going on Loretta."

"We have things going on too Victor, aren't we important? And there's something I need to talk to you about Byrd, he's…."

"What about Byrd?"

"You can't tell him. We need to talk about this in person, can't we meet?"

"What about Byrd, Loretta?" he barked into the phone.

"He can't know I told you this, he knows about us, he threatened to expose us."

"Christ, how the hell did he find out? Did you tell him?"

"No, he found out from one of the guys on the CFGG, I would never tell anyone about us. He knew before he came to see me."

"Why didn't you tell me about this when I was in your office?"

"I was nervous Victor, he had just left. I had time to think about it."

"Well what did he want?" Brunk was growling now, agitated and unable to maintain an even keel.

"He wanted to know if I had talked to you; if I knew where you were on Saturday night."

"And?"

"I told him you were working as far as I know, that's right isn't it?"

"Of course."

"Then why did he ask me? Isn't it in your report? Can't they tell where you were?"

"Yes it's in my report, they're just trying to discredit me Loretta, Byrd and his group have been doing that for years. They're jealous."

"Jealous? He's a detective, why would he be jealous?"

"The record, Loretta, they're jealous of my record."

She went silent over this concept, considering his arrogance, analyzing it for reasonableness. She didn't picture Byrd as the jealous, scheming type. Brunk interpreted her silence as skepticism.

"You know, many others have been climbing up my back, wanting to bring me down," he said.

"Well it doesn't make sense Victor….and you've been acting so strangely….why would he have to sneak around and interrogate me?"

"He's trying to gather up evidence to make me look unprofessional, and then he's going to unload it all by surprise. He doesn't want anyone in the department to find out what he's doing until his case is complete. There are so many things that go on that you don't know about, Loretta."

"It just seems so strange," she said, trying to believe him but not convinced. "If you were on duty, why wouldn't they know where you were? They have that new GPS tracking system and all."

This reminder came to him like a bucket of hot molten lead, burning through his face and causing his eyes to go to tunnel vision. The realization that an electronic record of Saturday night exists brought on instant panic. He forgot all about the damn GPS and wondered if they keep a recording of it and how far back it goes.

"Yeah, they could just check that couldn't they?" he said after a few seconds, managing to calm his breathing and regain his composure, sounding like that was a simple solution to the question, "then they'd see right where I was."

"But why does he want to know?"

"God dammit Loretta, how should I know? I'm not a goddam mind reader. Listen, I have to go, it's going to be busy the next few days and I don't know if I'll be able to talk to you. We should lay low anyway on account of Byrd. I'll contact you when I can…okay? …bye."

He didn't wait to hear her say goodbye in return but clicked the button on his phone abruptly without concern and let his mind go immediately to the issue of the GPS. He finished the drive back to the station and entered the back door as usual, knowing that Loretta could see him through her office window if she were still there. He didn't look up to check for her silhouette through the glass, but walked directly to the door with his eyes straight ahead, pretending he wasn't conscious of her, if she was there. He hoped to file his report for the day and slip back out the door before Byrd returned and without accidentally bumping into Loretta. As he stood at the duty counter and filled out his daily report the Captain walked by and stopped near him.

"You okay Victor?"

"Yes sir, fine, why?"

"You look tired and we haven't seen much in the way of traffic citations on your dailies, it's not like you."

"I've been working on the two missing persons, haven't had a lot of time to focus on traffic," he said this with a wry sort of grin on his face.

"I want you off the two MPs," the Captain said, "I have Byrd and his crew on that. I want you back on patrol."

"Well then tell Byrd to leave me be. I spent three hours with him this morning in the briefing room alone. He's got everybody giving him the same report two and three times."

"I'll talk to him."

"Yes sir, thank you. And uh….Captain, I was wondering, if I wanted to find out where a patrol car was a week or so ago, is there a record of it on the GPS tracking system?"

"Yeah, there's a record but you can't see it. You have to get approval from the Union. They don't want us going back and looking at that stuff unless there's a specific case requirement. Why?"

"It's nothing sir, sometimes I wonder where our guys are, it seems like I don't come across them as much as I should, you know, when I'm on patrol."

"Well, unlike you, most of them take a lunch and dinner break Victor," he chuckled and shook his head, then walked away.

This was good, Brunk figured. Byrd can't get access to the GPS record unless he's officially investigating and he wouldn't go official without something substantial to justify it. On balance, there was nothing right now and as long as he moved the bodies and got to the O'Malley kid before Byrd got to him, there'd be nothing later either.

Brunk finished his report and walked out the back door to his aging Jeep and drove out of the lot, heading home. He had plans for the night. He'd go get his things together and then go to the doggie park late that night and dig up the bodies when it was quiet and no-one was around. But before that he would take a ride up to the game that O'Malley's team was playing, just to make sure the kid knew he was there; that he would always be there. If he could keep him scared enough over the next few days, somewhere, sometime, he'd catch him alone. Then he'd deal with the issue permanently.

When he pulled into his driveway he parked next to Sammy's car and went into the house through the garage. He located the shovel and rake he would need for later and the roll of plastic he kept for when he did painting or other messy chores. His coveralls hung on the nail where he had left them early Sunday morning, still showing remnants of dirt from the doggie park that night; dried mud that had splattered onto the legs as he dug. Below the pant legs of the coveralls he saw the dried mud spot where his field boots sat before Sammy made off with them. It was more his notice that they weren't there, than remembering that he would need them. The space where the boots had sat was empty, an eerie absence to him, as if the emptiness above the dried mud puddle on the floor was talking to him. He looked all along the perimeter of the garage floor, against the wall, and then went out the back door to the breezeway, thinking he might have taken them off there after going through the garage. He found nothing of course and walked into the house confused and irritated. The misplaced boots were just one more frustrating inconvenience in a most inconvenient day. Sammy sat on the couch with her legs tucked up under her, reading a magazine. Brunk leaned casually against the jamb of the archway leading from the kitchen to the living room.

"Have you seen my boots?" he asked directly and without emotion.

"Your boots?" she asked in return, feeling her face flush, "which boots?"

"My field boots, they were in the garage, did you take them?"

"Pops, I don't know which boots you mean, but I wouldn't take them." She uncurled a leg, held out one of her small feet in front of the couch and smiled convincingly, "they surely wouldn't fit me. Did you look in the closet?"

He turned away slowly and walked to the hall closet, knowing all the while the boots would not be in there, but going through the motion while deciding whether to believe her or not.

"They wouldn't be in here unless you moved them. I took them off in the garage. They were covered in mud."

"Well I haven't seen them. Where did you get them muddy?

"Never mind, it doesn't matter"

He left through the kitchen grumbling and went back out into the garage, determined to find the boots, unable to believe he misplaced them after Saturday night. He knew they had sat in the spot below his coveralls for some time afterward. The black mud was there on the floor, left behind. The boots had to have been moved. He thought long and hard about whether he had touched them after Saturday night, just two days ago. He was exhausted. He could have taken them somewhere clean them and simply forgotten. It happens. But if he hadn't touched them there was only one other person it could be.

Sammy decided to get moving and escape the terror she felt from the conversation about the boots. She bolted out the front door and walked briskly toward her car. Brunk appeared at the garage door and gave her an inquisitive look.

"I'm going to the game tonight to see Patrick Burns play. I told him I'd see if you wanted to go also." She said as she opened the car door and unbuckled the locks on the convertible top.

"You mean the fat kid who lives in back?" He held his arm up and pointed behind with his thumb.

"That's mean Pops, he's losing weight. I think he

looks better than the last time I was here, and he's a really good guy. Do you want to go?" She knew he wouldn't.

"No, well I may drive up there later if I get a chance, but keep away from the O'Malley kid. Remember what we talked about. You promised."

"You're right, I promised. I'm going to the game and then I'll be right back," she said as she sat in the seat of the car and turned the ignition, "I won't be with any of the guys on the team, especially Wyatt." The BMW rumbled to life and she backed out of the driveway, waving to him as she began her forward motion. She yelled "ciao," and drove off.

Brunk went back into the house in a fury and made his way to the tall cabinet in the corner of the dining room. Fumbling with the key in the lock he finally opened the door and withdrew a bottle of whiskey and a short glass. He filled the glass halfway and raised it to his mouth, hand shaking. After draining the glass he stood there without moving, letting the elixir do its work. It had been a difficult day for the old cop; his secret was burning holes everywhere around him. He may need to resort to desperate measures. Events were out of control.

Twenty

The guys were in good spirits when they pulled into the parking lot of the baseball complex in Ridgewood Park. They'd played in some pretty big tournaments together over the years, so the edgy nervousness was familiar to them. But they'd never made it as far as a World Series. There were thirty-two teams here, from all across the United States, including Alaska and Hawaii.

Brackets and seeding were established by the tournament committee and it was pretty confusing for most of the players to understand how it worked until after a bunch of the teams were eliminated. The bottom line is each team would continue to play until it lost two games, until one team was left standing. So O'Malley told the guys not to worry about anything other than the team they were playing today.

They wouldn't have time for on field batting practice before the game so O'Malley sent the players to the batting cages adjacent to the field where coach Bastau would throw BP. O'Malley went to check in with the tournament committee and get apprised of any special tournament rules. When Wyatt walked up to the cages he hung his equipment bag on the fence and looked in it for his wooden practice bat, the one he used just before every game. When he found it wasn't there he remembered he lent it to Jed Rounder to use during BP back in Nazareth, during pre-game.

"Hey Round Dog," he yelled to the other end of the cage where Jed stood, "You got my bat?"

"I don't have your bat yo," Jed yelled back, "I put it by the fence where it was when you lent it to me."

"Wait," Wyatt asked sarcastically, "you telling me you left my bat at the park?"

"I didn't leave it there, you did."

"Numb nuts? You used it last!"

"I put it back."

"Oh man, Rounder, shit, I gotta have my bat."

"I'll call my mom; have her pick it up on the way here."

"I won't need it by the time she gets here."

"Sorry Y-O," Jed said, "my bad."

Wyatt didn't really need the bat, he could use his lightweight alloy game bat in the cages, but he never did that. Using his wood bat for BP was a pre-game requirement. It was a superstition, a good luck charm, it made him feel comfortable. When he swung it well in BP he always had a good game at the plate. He was out of sorts now.

"Damn," he said pulling his other bat out of his bag, "what a way to start."

He stepped into the cage and coach Bastau threw him fifteen perfect strikes right in the heart of the plate. Wyatt cracked each one of them hard and true, the loud ping of his alloy bat rang out with each swing. The other players waiting for their turn thought he hit the ball just fine, but Wyatt was pissed.

It was approaching seven-thirty in the evening and the stands were starting to fill up. Most of the spectators were parents and well-wishers for one of the teams but there were some college scouts there also, from a couple of large schools in the city and a couple of small schools on the outskirts. O'Malley knew who they were, but refrained from letting the players in on it, not wanting them nervous or thinking about anything but the game at hand. He wanted them to stay in the moment. Their opponents tonight were a strong team from the suburbs of Philadelphia, the West Chester Devils. O'Malley knew they'd have their hands full. The Devils always played deep into the mid-Atlantic regional and they made it to the World Series every few years. The coaches and the organization were used to this atmosphere. The players expected to be here. O'Malley knew the Hawks were going to have to jump on them early and hope that Wyatt had his best stuff on the mound, maybe hold the devils down for six innings, and then he'd bring in his closer, Matt 'Greasy' Barnum.

Greasy is a huge kid. When this was a team of twelve-year-olds in Little League and most of them were five feet tall, maybe five-two, greasy was five-ten. Now, at sixteen, Wyatt and big Patrick Burns are the tall ones at six-two, aside from Greasy that is, who stands six-six and weighs in at a tidy two hundred thirty pounds, all of it farmer boy muscle. With O'Malley's help, his father taught him how to play good old fashioned country hardball. He sometimes gets a few innings in right field where his glove will do the least damage and his arm makes up for most of his fielding gaffs, and Rex always wants his bat in the lineup because when he hits the ball it soars like it will never return to earth. But his real strength is his screaming fastball late in the game, after a craftier pitcher has gotten the other team used to looking for spin and trying to figure out what kind of junky curveball or change up is coming next. Greasy just comes in and fires pure heat. They had him at ninety miles per hour at one of the workout gyms in the city. He throws in on the hands, low and away, high and down the middle, and from time to time when he's feeling particularly nasty, he'll zing it right in on a batter's chin. If the bats weren't metal he'd saw them off. As it is, a miss-hit Greasy fastball will reverberate up batter's arms and rattle his teeth. Not too many sixteen-year-olds get comfortable in the batter's box when Greasy is serving late lunch.

If they were to win tonight, O'Malley knew but didn't let on; Wyatt would have to pitch the game of his life. They'd need him at his best for six innings. His Hawks could score runs. They were fast and dirty and they didn't mind getting drilled by a fastball if it meant taking one for the team and somehow getting to first base. They're good defensively and have strong arms in the outfield. When they get between the lines they focus on whatever it takes; the little things all the coaches talk about, that make a difference in the game. So the Devils would have their hands full also and O'Malley hoped that they were feeling just a little too cocky about themselves; making them too comfortable when the bell rings. If his guys could just get up a couple of runs early they'd have the edge they needed. But good pitching wins playoff games; no one knows this better than O'Malley. And good teams, really good teams, figure out a way to win even if they're behind. Wyatt had no idea how much his team was depending on the strength of his young arm tonight.

In the twenty minutes or so remaining before game time, Wyatt went to the bullpen on the third base side of the field with the team's number one catcher, Chucky 'Beans' Bennison, and did his pre-game pitching warm up. Beans is a stout kid, standing five feet eleven and muscular, owing to the fact he plays Varsity hockey every winter in school and carries that all the way through March every year with an AAU travel hockey team. He's a defenseman, tough, ornery and smart. The guys on the Hawks team alternate between loving and hating him, depending upon who his constantly running mouth is vituperating at the moment. But when he gets on the baseball field he calls a great game, doesn't let a wild pitch get through, throws a rope down to second base and being the wolverine that he is, nobody runs him over on a play at the plate.

When the plate umpire signaled five minutes to game time Wyatt and Beans made their way to the mound. O'Malley met them there for a short pep talk.

"You guys look good, how you feeling?" They both nodded a positive, but O'Malley could sense some tightness, nervousness, which is normal at the start of a game like this, healthy in fact.

"Good, now a couple of things to remember. Pitch to contact Wyatt, but keep the ball low in the strike zone Beans….right?" They both nodded, "You have a good defense out there and we want them fielding the ball off the grass and making solid plays. Don't try to strike out the entire line-up. Those guys are good so they'll be lookin to work you deep in the count. Throw first pitch strikes and get ahead in the count early so they expand the strike zone for you. Don't be afraid to intentionally walk the number five hitter if there are men on base. The scouting report says he hits it a mile and does it often. Remember too that as the sun sets and the lights come on the ball gets lost easy in the fading light, so keep them from hitting it in the air if you can. Okay?" They both nodded again. "Any questions?"

"What are we having for dinner afterward Skip?" Beans asked with a smile, "I'm gonna be hungry after chasin Y-O's shit in the dirt all night."

"Fuck you," Wyatt said with a nasty grin and they all chuckled.

"Go get em," O'Malley said and walked off the mound toward the dugout.

After Wyatt threw his regulation eight warm-up pitches the umpire called the first Devils batter to the plate and the kid stepped in. Once he dug his feet into the batter's box the umpire raised his right hand, pointed toward Wyatt and yelled, "PLAY." Wyatt hitched his left sleeve up with his right hand, stepped onto the rubber, went into his windup and threw a sizzling fast ball strike right where beans held his glove low and on the outside corner of the plate. The umpire yelled "HERRIIIIIIIKE," and the Hawks side of the field erupted in a loud applause from the stands. The 2013 appearance of the Nazareth Hawks in the Babe Ruth World Series had begun, and Wyatt started it with emphasis. The batter stepped out of the box to regroup as Wyatt received the ball back from Beans. O'Malley thought only that if Wyatt was going to get that low and away strike from this guy all night, it bodes well of his chance for success.

The kid went through the first three batters in the Devils line-up like a buzz saw, retiring one and three on four pitch strike-outs and getting the batter in between on a lazy fly ball to center that JR Shea fielded with ease. Three outs on eleven pitches and Wyatt bounded off the mound to the dugout feeling focused and energized. O'Malley worried only that he didn't relax thinking this was going to that easy all night long. He knew better.

In the bottom half of the first inning, the Hawks half, Jed Rounder led off and struck out. Next, JR Shea drew an eight pitch walk and then during Beans' at bat advanced to second on a pitch in the dirt that got by the catcher. They had a man in scoring position with one out. Beans then hit a long fly ball to right field which advanced JR from second to third. There were two out and big Patrick Burns strolled to the plate. Burnsy isn't exactly the best contact hitter in the world but he hits it hard and deep in the gaps when he does hit it and has enough power to send it over the fence, though for some reason rarely does. He's an imposing figure at the plate and really only fits well batting fourth, cleanup. Burnsy went up there swinging and a little too anxious, fouled the first two pitches - bad pitches - off, then settled down after O'Malley yelled at him and worked the next four pitches for a walk. It was now first and third with two outs and Wyatt, the number five batter, walked from the on deck circle to the plate. O'Malley stood in the coach's box by third base and wondered just how unsettled the Devils pitcher might be finding himself in this situation right off the bat. He really should be out of the inning since he had Burnsy with an 0-2 count and then lost him to a walk. The runner on third, JR, wouldn't be there except for the passed ball, and if the pitcher was thinking about all this stuff he might not be paying attention to all the possibilities in the present.

The rest of the infield seemed just a tad unsettled. The Devils were sleeping. The ideal play, the expected one, would be for Wyatt to look for an outside pitch and poke a line drive into right field, score JR, and get Burnsy to second. With two outs they weren't expecting a bunt and JR was occupying the third baseman's attention with a generous lead off the bag. The pitcher was going to try to throw a first pitch fastball for a strike given his control issues, so the element of surprise was perfect. It was early in the game and if Wyatt missed the bunt and JR was tagged out trying to steal home, the worst that would happen would be that Wyatt would lead off the next inning. When Both JR and Wyatt had their eyes on him he put on the sign down for the suicide squeeze bunt. If this was successful it would demoralize the other team and might lead to a big inning.

When they both realized what O'Malley was telling them to do, Wyatt and JR were shocked inside at such a ballsy move in this situation. They loved it. The instant the pitcher came out of the stretch and began his delivery to home plate, JR tore off toward home and Wyatt squared to bunt. The third baseman was caught looking and by the time he began to charge behind JR, Wyatt had laid down a perfect bunt into the no man's land on the grass down the third base line. By the time the pitcher got to the ball, JR had crossed the plate and Wyatt was almost at first base.

He didn't even bother to make the throw to first. The run scored, everyone was safe, and the Hawks side of the field erupted in cheers. On second base Burnsy was caught off guard too and didn't try to advance from second, which was just as well really, as being so slow he probably stood the best chance of being tagged out by a throw to third from the pitcher. But O'Malley, being the fundamentalist he is, implored Burnsy for not being alert and failing to move up. All was well though, as Johnny 'MoJo' Morelli stepped out of the on deck circle with a chance to give them a three run lead. The Devils were reeling at the moment while MoJo looked like he was going to a feast. The Hawks side of the field was in mayhem with cheers as he walked to the batter's box.

"This fuckin shit is mine man," he said, a little too loudly digging in, "this fuckin shit is MINE," this time louder and beating the plate with his bat for emphasis.

The umpire took exception and waved his hands in the air calling off further play, "MY TIME," he yelled and turned to MoJo.

With his finger pointing at him he said, "There won't be any talk like that here batter, this is your warning and you won't get a second one."

O'Malley was on the move as soon as the umpire called time and ran to the plate, not so much to take up MoJo's cause but to prevent him from saying anything vulgar to the umpire directly and getting thrown out of the game. He went to MoJo and pulled him away from the ump.

"He doesn't know he's saying it half the time, Sir, he

just gets excited and the stuff comes out," O'Malley pleaded, standing with his arm around the kid's shoulders.

"It took my Ritalin today Skip, I made sure of that, honest." MoJo said, finally realizing his mouth had caused the commotion and looking earnest.

The umpire didn't know what to do or believe. He'd heard, or been warned about MoJo, but had never been in this situation before and couldn't think of an applicable rule at the moment. "Well, you can't swear like that batter, not while I'm back here," he yelled finally, "if you can't control him coach, you're gonna have to pinch hit for him." He shook his head as umpires do whenever they're indicating they're not going to hear any more about it. The crowd on the Devils side was cheering loudly and calling for MoJo's ejection, while the crowd on the Hawk's side was yelling at the umpire telling him "leave the poor kid alone" and "quit picking on him and focus on the strike zone," and numerous other disparaging remarks.

Wyatt standing on first and Burnsy on second looked at each other and smiled. There was an over/under bet in the dugout earlier over the inning that MoJo's mouth would first get him in trouble. They both took the second inning and under. So they were sharing a moment of elation on that count, but also the fact that the general raucous he had caused would certainly upset the concentration of the Devils and be just *status quo* for the Hawks. Burnsy was actually nearing the point where he might start giggling. The Devils infielders were looking at the crowd, boggled. They'd never seen this kind of upheaval so early in a game before. The Devils manager came out of the dugout now as well, just to make sure his team's interests weren't somehow impacted in all the commotion. The umpire was standing near home plate with his arms up and hands facing each dugout, trying somehow to restore the game to order.

"All right, that's all. Managers get back to where you were." He pointed at both and then turned back to MoJo, "Batter….you step in the box and keep your mouth shut. If I hear any more out of you I'll, well, I won't like it and your team will pay the price and you don't want that!" MoJo looked at him like a deer in the headlights then nodded enthusiastically and dug his spikes into the clay. O'Malley and the other manager retreated and the umpire returned to behind the plate, waited for the catcher to get in position, pointed to the pitcher and yelled "PLAY." Wyatt and Burnsy wiped the smiles off their faces and got back into the game, taking leads from their respective bases. The crowd returned to cheering over the action. The Devils players probably should have pinched themselves, to make sure they hadn't been dreaming.

MoJo is not a very patient batter, but he has very good hand eye coordination so he has good at bats fouling off pitch after pitch. Although he rarely draws a walk he rarely strikes out either. A lot of the guys believe that he fouls off a pitch sometimes when he could have sent it into the field for a hit, just because he likes to drive the pitcher crazy; enjoys it, they say, even when he has two strikes on him. This at bat may have been one of those times because MoJo fouled off seven pitches in a row, smiling broadly after each and bringing cheers from the Hawks dugout. Wyatt and Burnsy were getting tired of it though, because each time he fouled one they would have to run half way or more to the next base.

Burnsy was huffing and puffing after the seventh, standing back on the bag at second and finally yelled in, "MoJo….hit the thing straight willya? You're killin us out here."

MoJo heard and gave him a blank stare, then realized what he was putting the two of them through and bore down. With an 0-2 count on the eighth pitch of the at bat MoJo swung hard and true at a high fastball on the outside part of the plate and hit the ball on a towering rope into the gap between center and right field. Burnsy was chugging down the third base line toward home by the time the center fielder picked up the ball at the base of the outfield fence and threw it in. Wyatt was hot on his heels, looking nearly like he'd pass Burnsy if he didn't slow down. Both of them crossed the plate safely. MoJo was cruising around second to the objection of O'Malley at the third base coach's box, putting both hands out toward him and yelling for him to stop at second. MoJo either didn't see him or ignored him completely and chugged full speed toward third base. The first baseman came off his bag and cut off the throw from the center fielder to home plate. He alertly threw a rope to third base just ahead of the sliding MoJo. In the dust and commotion the field umpire threw a pumping fist. The two runs had scored but MoJo was out on the throw to third. The inning was over though the Hawks led 3-0 on the strength of MoJo's almost triple to right. O'Malley helped him get to his feet after the play.

"MoJo, what the hell? I told you to stop!"

"I wanted to take out that third baseman Skip; he was laughing at me before."

O'Malley shook his head and managed to smile. The

Hawks crowd cheered for MoJo as he ran to the dugout to get his glove and get back to out right field for the next inning. Wyatt, on his way out to the mound, caught Sammy looking at him from the stands. He smiled at her discreetly before taking the throw from Beans to begin warming up.

Twenty-One

Wyatt began the third inning the way he left off the first. And with the confidence and security provided by a three run lead, he struck out the first batter on two screaming fastballs for strikes, a slider out of the strike zone that the batter didn't swing at, and a nasty change up that had the kid swinging fully well before the ball reached the plate. Four pitches, one out, and the Hawks crowd cheered again loudly. O'Malley was secretly concerned that this was going too well and there was still a lot of baseball to play. They had gotten four outs and there remained seventeen yet to go. When Beans threw to third to start the around the horn after the strike out, Wyatt looked over to the spot where the backstop fence meets the home team dugout. He felt a cold sensation from that direction, something drew his attention. What he saw took the air from his lungs. There stood Victor Brunk wearing blue jeans and an out of style brown golf shirt; pretending to the world that he was cheering for the boys from Nazareth, but truly there for one dark reason only; to scare the spirit out of Wyatt O'Malley.

Wyatt turned from him to the shortstop to receive the ball out of habit and nearly missed the throw to him as his vision lost the ability to perceive dimension in the world. He stared into the outfield in attempt to regain his reference, breathe a little and try somehow to face his task, pretending that Brunk was not there. He returned to the pitcher's rubber, placed his right foot on it and stared in to get the sign from Beans, who was fiddling with his mask while the next batter dug in. after a few seconds he got the sign for a slider, a slightly off speed fast ball with movement on it that makes it fall down and away from a right-handed hitter. It's a precision pitch that Wyatt would normally have no problem with while cruising through an outing such a today's, but with his knees suddenly shaking and with the dryness in his mouth, he shook the pitch off and waited for Burns to call for a straight fastball, usually the easiest pitch to throw for a strike. Wyatt hoped, at this point, to be successful in just getting his next offering somewhere near the strike zone. Beans cocked his head slightly at the shake off, asking why? Wyatt simply shook his head again and Beans realized he wanted to throw the fastball and complied with the appropriate sign.

Wyatt served up a juicy fastball right down main street, in the heart of the plate, lacking any movement whatsoever and without even the necessary speed that might get it by a decent hitter. The new batter thought he was in batting practice. He struck the ball right on the nose and drove it long and hard into the gap in left center field, then raced around the bases and pulled up at third base with a stand up triple. Wyatt kicked the ground hard while the kid ran the bases, then managed to remember his assignment and ran over to third to back up the throw from the outfield. O'Malley didn't say anything to Wyatt or anyone else, just watched as Wyatt returned to the mound and took the throw from the third baseman, Corey Gallup, who said, "It's no problem Y-O, lucky swing, let's get this next guy." O'Malley signaled the infield to play in on the edge of the grass in a prevent alignment, intending that a ground ball in the infield would be fielded quickly to hold the runner on third or throw him out at home. Corey, at third base, came in especially close in case there was a sign for the bunt.

Wyatt went into his windup again for the next batter, this time trying to throw a fastball on the outside corner of the strike zone. The ball went in the dirt and Beans successfully blocked it, keeping the runner on third from coming home on a wild pitch. The next three pitches were also called balls and the batter jogged down to first base with a one out walk. Wyatt was now actually in a better situation, in a way, since a ground ball would induce a force out at second and a throwback to first in time would mean a double play, getting Wyatt out of the inning. It was not to be though. Again Beans put the sign down, calling for the deuce, a curveball. Wyatt served up a hanging bender, leaving the ball out over the plate, which the batter drove to right field for a clean single. This scored one run and advanced the runner. It was now 3-1 with one out and men on first and second. O'Malley told Matt Morris, his number two pitcher and the planned starter for the next game to get warmed up. Then he jumped out of the dugout, signaled to the umpire for time out and walked to the mound slowly, using every second possible to delay; to allow Wyatt time to breathe and break the momentum that was building on the other side. Brunk stepped behind the dugout and walked toward the snack stand so that O'Malley wouldn't see him. But Sammy had observed his presence immediately and understood exactly what was going on with Wyatt.

"Getting exciting out here," O'Malley said when he arrived at the pitcher's mound. Wyatt exhaled loudly and looked away toward the right field line.

"Just give me a second, I'll be alright."

"It looks to me like your tempo has changed. Just go

back to basics. Slow down and relax. Reset yourself to where you were a few minutes ago. It's only one run, you don't have to be perfect." He looked at Beans who had joined them for the conference, "Alright, let's get a double play ground ball and get back to scoring runs ourselves, okay? Okay, go get em," he patted Wyatt on the butt and nodded to Beans.

Wyatt rubbed the ball with two bare hands and circled the mound while Beans returned to behind the plate and O'Malley stepped back down into the dugout. The umpire signaled "play" again and Wyatt toed the rubber. One brief glance back to the dugout confirmed Wyatt's intuition that Brunk had returned to his observation spot out of the sight of O'Malley. He had passed now, in just a few moments, from being completely upended by the killer's presence to burning anger at the situation, wanting to throw down his glove, walk over to the asshole and call him out right there. He knew that wouldn't do and again tried to hold this now different emotion inside and return to the task at hand. Anger, the new emotion however, is no more welcome in the mind of a pitcher than fear. His next offering, a fast ball that Beans reluctantly signaled for, stayed up in the zone and had so much zip on it that when the batter struck it on the nose, it sailed clear over JR's head in center field, over the fence and tumbled into the woods behind for a three run home run. It was now 4-3 and still only one out. Beans looked into the dugout at O'Malley, expecting to see him pop out again and pull Wyatt, in fact, hoping for it. The kid was done; Beans knew it, Wyatt himself knew it and O'Malley probably knew it too. But he didn't move just yet, waiting for Matt Morris to finish warming up. By this time Wyatt understood his only job was to prevent the next batter from reaching base; maybe keep him up there with a long at bat, allowing Morris just that much more time to get ready and then turn the ball over to him without any runners on base. He went to the back of the mound and bent down to tie his shoe. It didn't need tying but this alone gained Morris twenty precious seconds. When he stood up and went to the rubber he saw Brunk standing in his spot with an evil smile; so enamored with the terror he had brought he couldn't resist hanging around for just a few more minutes, hoping to bring more.

Wyatt battled through a six pitch contest with the next batter, but eventually lost him to a walk on a borderline pitch the ump could have called either way. O'Malley stepped out of the dugout again and signaled time. A second visit to the mound meant that Wyatt would have to be replaced in accordance with the rules. On his way out O'Malley stopped and turned 180 degrees to look and confirm once again that Morris was ready to come in. When he did, he saw Brunk slip away from behind the dugout, uncertain at first that it was him; incredulous that it was him. He went to the mound shaken now as well and immediately figured out what had transpired over the last few batters. He took the ball from Wyatt and put his hand on the side of his son's head and said, "Don't worry, we'll get em." The Hawks fans applauded warmly and sincerely as Wyatt walked to the dugout with his head down. Upon reaching the top stair he threw his glove violently against the back wall and sat down in the corner, alone and despondent. Greasy Burns, who was scheduled to be the closer today and wasn't playing in right field, came over and slapped Wyatt's knee.

"It's okay Y-O, you didn't have it today. Shit happens. We'll get it back," Greasy said with encouragement. Wyatt didn't say anything in return, only sat there churning inside but expressionless. He knew in fact he did have it today, but that son of a bitch took it from him. He wasn't going to let him take anything more.

When Matt Morris took Wyatt's place in the top of the second inning he dispatched the next two Devils hitters efficiently on seven pitches. The Devils pitcher settled down in the bottom of the second inning as well, in fact both of them put on a sterling pitching display for the next four innings. The Hawks were the home team and therefore enjoyed the last at bat of the game, so when they entered the bottom of the seventh inning they knew they had three outs to score a tying run or two runs for the walk off win. Morris had thrown only fifty-five pitches and would be able to return in the top of the eighth if they tied the game.

The Devils pitcher was at a higher pitch count, seventy-nine, but he had a chance for a complete game win and he still looked strong, so his manager let him return to close it out. There would be a very quick hook though, if he began to falter. The kid did a great job, striking out both Beans, batting seventh and Corey Gallup batting eighth. So there were two outs in the bottom of the seventh with no-one on base. The Devils were leading 4-3. Danny Bastau, the second baseman and the coach's son was batting ninth and although the kid didn't possess a lot of punch at the plate, he was a good contact hitter and was one of five Hawks players who had a hit in the game. O'Malley would often use him as a lead-off number-one hitter because he often finds a way to get on base; he's sneaky. So O'Malley figured they could be in a worse situation, batter-wise. The Devils pitcher figured he was facing the number nine batter and therefore the game was all but over. But after Danny battled courageously to work the count full on seven pitches, the pitcher finally began to tire and the pressure of the situation took its toll on him. Danny fouled off two more borderline strikes, then took the next pitch for a ten pitch walk. The tying run was on base now and the Hawks side began to come alive. The Devils manager popped out of the dugout and signaled to the bullpen for his closer, who was warmed up and ready to go.

Speedy Jed Rounder stood in the on-deck circle sizing up the new pitcher as he took his eight warm-up pitches. O'Malley often alternated him between batting lead-off like today, because of his speed, and batting third or fourth because of his power. He hadn't been on base yet in the game so the Devils had no real sample of his twin skills and assumed he was a typical lead-off hitter; a contact guy who could run. They had no idea how fast he could run. The situation was shaping up as best as O'Malley could hope under the circumstances, with Jed coming to the plate.

Rounder's approach to hitting could be confounding. Sometimes he would battle and battle and work his way on. Some days he'd be unconscious and have a four hit game. Some days, like today, he'd have three or four at bats and not even get a sniff. O'Malley was hoping that he'd battle here, answer the bell, and rise to the occasion. When Jed finally stepped in, he did so with one foot only at first, holding his hand back at the umpire, asking him to hold play until he was fully set. This is a good sign, thought O'Malley, because it meant that Jed was demanding time to get himself focused and it served to bring some impatience to the pitcher. In the Hawks dugout all of the players, even Wyatt, were standing up at the protective fence separating them from the field, yelling encouragement to Jed. The crowd on both sides was cheering loudly for very different results. Both the pitcher and Jed were on the spot. This would be a battle of power against power.

Jed was a smart enough to know that the pitcher, having been summoned at a moment like this would be a little, no, make that a lot nervous. A closer is generally not a crafty type. They learn how to throw heat, high hard ones, pitches that the batter cannot catch up with. He was sure this closer, all six-foot-five of him, would be no different. While the crowd yelled and O'Malley implored him from third base to "be patient" and "make it be your pitch," Jed had already made his mind up he was swinging at the first offering, which he was certain would be a screaming fastball right down Broadway. Jed wasn't feeling patient at the moment, he was feeling like he had it figured out. When the pitcher let go of the ball, it was just as he had suspected; a sizzler that bore down out of the huge kid's hand, targeted for the center of the plate. When Jed hit it, there was no feeling at all, just the sweet harmony of bat meeting ball in the exact perfect spot; as they say in golf, right on the screws. Jed had swung so early that he was way out in front of the pitch and he sent the ball out of the infield screaming on a rope down the left field line. Everyone in the park gasped as they tried to see if the ball would fly away foul. When it landed directly on the foul line, about twenty feet short of the outfield fence, it kicked up a spit of white chalk, removing any doubt that it was fair. By this time Danny Bastau had rounded second and his little legs had him steaming for third. O'Malley was giving him the windmill sign with his left arm, sending him home to tie the game. The Hawks dugout and crowd were on their feet and crazed with glee.

The left fielder, who had no idea of Jed's power, was playing him shallower than advisable and had to retreat full speed to deep left field to retrieve the ball. When it hit on the line, the spin sent it bounding into foul territory, into the corner of the fence between the left field line and the outfield. Running full speed toward the corner in pursuit, the fielder was right behind the ball when it struck the corner post of the fence and reflected violently back out into left field, in the direction from which he had come. This forced him to stop and turn around and pursue it again in nearly the opposite direction. The ball had rattled around out there, awkwardly away from the fielder. Jed, whose legs were but a blur as he ran, was halfway between second and third base before the left fielder finally got his hands on the elusive sphere. O'Malley didn't hesitate. He sent him home for the win. By the time the fielder planted himself and made a quality throw it was too late, Jed had crossed the plate, standing up, on an inside the park home run. The Hawks players swarmed him, even Wyatt, who somehow managed to recover from his episode with Brunk and feel part of the elation they all deserved. It had been and up and down day for him, but the end result turned poetic somehow; victory in the face of adversity, allowing him relief that somehow his 'problem' didn't bury the team along with him.

Twenty-Two

Brunk walked briskly out of the World Series venue after demonstrating his power to make Wyatt quake at will, feeling satisfaction at the impact on his young adversary. It reassured him that Wyatt would keep everything secret long enough for him to move the bodies then corner the rat alone and end his miserable life. He got into the Jeep and drove out the long entry road for the public sports complex; with several hours to burn before he could dig at the doggie park unobserved. Feeling relaxed and confident, he stopped at a favorite hamburger stand on his way back south toward Nazareth.

He sat at an outdoor table in the warm summer night and dined leisurely on a greasy cheeseburger, French fries and vanilla milk-shake, feeling the best he had in several days. Happy couples and families had Ice cream and hot dogs nearby as the sun waned in the west and the evening turned to nightfall. He credited their freedom to relax safely to men like himself - peacemakers - strong, brave men who sacrifice their private lives for the good of the community. His contentment kept him sitting at the picnic table biding his time, right up until closing at ten pm.

When it became evident the staff wanted to clean the tables and shut the place down for the night, he moved to his Jeep, got in and drove back to Nazareth. He went to his garage and put the shovel, rake, plastic and his gun in the Jeep, preparing to head over to the doggie park. It was still a little early being just ten forty-five. He didn't want to take any chance that someone might still be out at the park or walking their dog late on a Monday evening. But it was important for him to be out of the house before Sammy returned from the game, not wanting to raise any question in her mind about where he was heading. So he drove around town for a time, imagining he was on patrol, observing everything as he drove by. When he made his last loop around the by-pass and turned onto Oak Avenue toward the doggie park, he felt confident now that it was late enough to go about his work without being caught.

While Brunk was angling his way toward the graves, O'Malley had dropped Wyatt off at the house and left again to meet Becca for a late drink at Grif's. She called him on his cell phone while he and Wyatt drove back from Ridgewood Park. Although she was happy with the outcome of the game, the joy of it all actually depressed her once she was alone again and had time to think about how much Mark would have enjoyed being there and watching them do something special. No team from Nazareth had ever been to the World Series and it was a tragedy, she thought, that Mark didn't get the chance to see it. She was crying when she called so he found it impossible to say no, even as tired as he was. He told Wyatt to get a shower and go to sleep. Their next game wouldn't be until Wednesday but Wyatt had work at the Animal Hospital in the morning and they would have practice tomorrow night. He felt a little uneasy about leaving Wyatt alone, wanting some dialog with him about Brunk. The kid seemed unwilling to talk in the car on the way home but somehow he had to get him to open up. So Rex had his own issues that needed attention but Becca was insistent.

Wyatt alternated between fear and anger at what Brunk had done to him. He sat on the couch and watched Sports Center, staring at the screen without really paying attention. His insides ached and he felt trapped in the house, needing to move, to get out of there, and when he considered the possibility that Brunk may show up there since Rex's car wasn't in the driveway, he liked his chances out of doors - on the street - better than he liked them staying cooped up in the house.

Then he remembered his bat. Perfect. He pictured it sitting against the fence over at the park where Jed Rounder had left it and worried that someone might come across it there and he'd never see it again. He left a note for O'Malley on the counter, saying he was riding over to the park to get the bat and he'd be right back. As he rode out of the driveway he decided to take the most direct route to the park even though it would expose him to the highest possibility of being seen. The route was lit by street lighting except the last half mile or so which would take him over the short cut through the town park by the pool. As he cruised down Oakwood Avenue and through the stoplight at the intersection with Delatour, he passed in front of two cars waiting at the light. Detective Byrd was in one of the cars on his way home from his Monday bowling league. Wyatt didn't notice Byrd in the car in the darkness and Byrd wasn't really paying attention, but the green bicycle caught his eye at the last second and engaged him just in time to realize it was indeed Wyatt riding by. As the light turned green and Byrd pulled away, he wondered what Wyatt was doing out this late, especially since he had a curfew. He was riding in the opposite direction from the quiet street where he lives, but Byrd decided not to follow it up. He was tired and hungry and he knew his wife would have a plate of food covered and waiting for him on top of the stove. He hoped he wasn't making a mistake.

Rex had fashioned a tube made from PVC pipe on Wyatt's bike that allowed him to slip his bat in there and travel around with ease. When there was no bat in there and Wyatt got the bike up to a certain speed the tube would begin to whistle as the air passed over the opening. He learned to play a game with it as he rode, knowing the speed where the sound would begin and standing up and swinging the bike back and forth as he peddled causing the howl to oscillate. He had it going really well as he rode now and the sound made him feel like the world was normal again, though he knew in his heart it wasn't. Brunk would be looking for him for sure. But he had arrived at a new level of anxiety since the episode with his enemy earlier at the game. He decided that if he was cornered he would fight; he would avoid the man, run if he was pursued. But he was starting to feel deep anger about being in this place; he didn't deserve to be here and if he was caught, he was going to go down swinging, maybe even take a piece of Brunk with him.

The tube was howling especially well tonight in the perfectly still, perfectly quiet humid air. It was hot and sticky and he wondered if it was the atmospheric conditions which made the tube perform better or if it was the fact that the rest of the world was so quiet. As he rode through the deserted Town Park the noise he made began to concern him. He might be heard by the wrong person. When he saw the dark outline of the trees that enclosed the path to ball park he felt some relief. There was a sign at the front entrance which read, among other things, "Park closes at 8 pm." No such sign was posted at the ball park, so he knew that once he reached the other end of the path he'd no longer be doing anything wrong.

As he entered the well-traveled path there was little to see. A quarter moon on a humid July night doesn't produce much useful light and the streetlights in the distance, at the end of Home Run Drive, were diminished to almost nothing in the crowded forest. He traveled by memory, knowing where the big trees stand and where the thickest underbrush lies. He had ridden his bike over this route countless times both at day and at night. He knew exactly where to stay left on the path in order to avoid sliding sideways in gravel that had been put down to cover a muddy spot and where to duck his head down so that he didn't get whipped in the face by low hanging branches. He could hear the occasional car passing on the road and could see the mercury light on the side of the doggie park maintenance barn glimmer alternately through the trees in the distance. The tube continued to howl softly as he rode at a reduced speed.

When he broke through the trees at the end of the connecting pathway he could see the outline of the back stop fences and the shed. He could also see the lighted front of the Coke machine that sat there and into which he'd pumped countless quarters during games, retrieving a bottle of blue Gatorade. The figures grew larger as he gained on them and he began to think of his bat, praying it was still there, that no-one had found it. He knew if he'd found someone else's bat he'd never take it, never do that to them. He also knew there were a lot of kids who didn't have the same kind of respect for other guy's stuff. The question of whether or not the bat was there became almost an obsession. It was so important to his well-being; so much a part of his pre-game routine. He'd never, ever let someone use it again. If it wasn't there it would just figure, he thought. It'd be another sign of how bad things are right now.

He rode directly up to the gate in the fence on field five and walked through, and then over to the opposite side of the dugout where the bat had been leaning against the inside of the fence before Jed used it. It was so dark he couldn't tell if it was there with his eyes. He had to walk along and run his hand low on the fence. When he got to the exact spot his hand hit the bat and knocked it to the ground. "YES," he said out loud, not caring who heard him; feeling that now, for a minute, everything was all right. He picked it up and felt it just to make sure and although the wood was damp from the dew earlier it was surely his. He'd know the feel of the handle anywhere. He'd know it in his sleep. Elated, he walked out onto the dirt of the base paths and swung the bat fluidly in the dark, listening to it as it carved through the air, saying 'whoosh'. Maybe, Wyatt thought, if he hadn't left it behind his luck on the mound would've been better tonight. Maybe Brunk wouldn't have gotten to him so bad. He swung it several times; unable to see anything of what he was doing but in his mind's eye picturing his silhouette in the batter's box, the same way he does every time he takes a practice swing. Holding the bat out in front he looked for the label, but of course couldn't see it in the dark. Again he noticed the silence; he couldn't remember it being so quiet here before. There were always cars going by on the road, but not now, not this late.

Then he heard it, a low sound of metal, occasionally

clinking, punctuating gaps of silence. He looked up at the doggie park, from where the sound seemed to emanate and saw that there was much more light in that area than just what was produced by the security light on the maintenance building.

The sound he heard was being made by Brunk, who after returning home and getting his tools then driving to the doggie park, had begun what would surely be the gruesome task of removing and relocating the bodies. They had been buried in the soil now for nearly forty-eight hours; enough time for the process of decay to begin, and enough time for the bags of lime chalk he had poured on top of them to blend in with the fine gravel-sand mixture. This blend, combined with the moisture from the rain on Saturday when he did the digging and the subsequent drying over time had set up the ten or so inches directly above the bodies into nearly concrete. His shovel would barely dent it. He wondered how the dogs could smell the bodies through that admixture. And so he struggled with the digging, clanging the point of the shovel against it; frustrated that this chore was going to take him much longer and be much harder work than he anticipated. Finally exasperated with his progress he threw the shovel down, walked to the maintenance building, opened the overhead door and saw the John Deere model 2050 diesel backhoe sitting there, the answer to his problem. It would make much more noise than desirable, but one or two scoops with the machine and the work would be over. The urgency he felt - the need to exhume the bodies - pushed him to take a risk he might have avoided had he the clarity of mind to pause for a moment, stand back and assess what he was doing.

The machine was loud when he the engine fired up. It nearly woke him to his senses, but he pressed on, quickly driving it out to the grave site and aiming the work-lights mounted high on the rear of the machine on his task. He then planted the stabilizers into the earth and rotated his seat to operate the backhoe controls. It had been quite some time since he last worked a machine like this but he regained his familiarity fairly quickly and reached out with the mechanical arm toward the spot where he'd begun to dig by hand earlier. The teeth on the bucket dug into the soil easily, like a fork into pudding. On the second paw, the bucket accidentally exposed an arm, he had dug too deeply. Delicate is something a backhoe is not. Brunk swore loudly as he realized he was making a mess.

Down on the field Wyatt stood perfectly still for a few minutes, listening to the backhoe start up and begin digging. He hadn't experienced the varying tone of a large machine as the engine revved, increasing and decreasing slightly in RPM as load was added and then dropped and then added again, so he was confused as to exactly what he was listening to. After a spell he walked off the ball field, put his bat in the tube holder and rode over to the maintenance road leading to the doggie park. Once passing through the canopy of tree limbs at the beginning of the road, he dismounted and walked his bike the remaining distance up the gentle grade to the garage. As he drew closer to the top of the small hill he walked slowly, taking in the picture of the bright lights and the yellow tractor perched in the doggie yard with an outstretched claw resting on the ground. A few steps further, past the remaining tree blocking his view, he saw Brunk on his knees bending over and reaching into the hole. Being very still, now perhaps fifty feet away, he saw him pull out a swollen and blackened human arm. The grisly vision froze him. His stomach began to twist and salt welled up in his throat; a precursor of the vomit that threatened. Brunk himself coughed and gagged, momentarily overcome by the smell.

Twenty-Three

While Wyatt was stalking Brunk, Detective Byrd returned home and sat at his kitchen counter eating the plate of food his wife left for him. He was unsettled; not able to tolerate the unanswered question of where Wyatt was headed when he rode by at the stop light. It wouldn't be unusual for a kid to be on his way home at this hour of the night but Wyatt was riding in the wrong direction. Byrd got up without finishing the food, got into his car and drove back to the intersection and then took a left on Oakwood where Wyatt rode by earlier. Everything at the center of town had closed, except for Grif's of course. He'd already passed JR Shea's house and Wyatt's other best friend, Scooter, lived on the opposite side of the four corners. He wondered if the kid was heading out to the ball park to re-do the drug deal that went sour on Saturday. The prospect of learning the identity of other party to the deal interested Byrd. At the very least, it would be unusual for Wyatt to be at the Park the park this late, a reason for concern; although he could be meeting his girlfriend for a midnight rendezvous. He knew it was a popular place for kids to make out.

As he drove down Oakwood he felt an obligation to call O'Malley and report Wyatt being out after curfew, thinking he should extend the basic courtesy. If he subsequently discovered the kid was in the middle of something he shouldn't be, no one could say he had baited him or not tried to do something prophylactic. Byrd dialed

Rex on his cell phone and waited while it rang.

"Rex, this is Byrd," he said when O'Malley answered.

O'Malley was sitting at Grif's with Becca, nursing a beer at the bar and feeling good about the win but apprehensive over the episode with Brunk. He listened to her attentively while she used him as a sounding board over her grief about Mark Berelli. He was tired from the tension and excitement of the game but also interested in Becca and filling the part of good friend even though he had his own issues which needed attention.

"Geesh Byrd, don't you ever sleep?" Becca's head snapped to when she heard O'Malley say the name.

"Well I should be asleep Rex, but on my way home from bowling I saw your kid riding his bike down Oakwood in the direction of the ball field, so I changed my mind, decided that keeping an eye on him is much more fun."

"When?"

"About twenty minutes ago. You said he has an eleven o'clock curfew and it's about twelve fifteen. I figured I oughta give you a call."

"Thanks for being attentive detective. Since when did you become so community minded?"

"It's just a courtesy, that's all.

"Alright... okay," he looked at his watch and then at Becca, "Christ it is pretty late, what the hell would he be going to the park for? Oh yeah, you know what? He left his bat there before tonight's game, he probably went to pick it up before someone else does."

"Yeah, it's probably something perfectly explainable. Okay, just wanted to let you know Rex. If I see him I'll kick his ass home, seeya later."

"Wait… Byrd, Where are you now?"

"I'm almost at the park, maybe five minutes away."

"I'll call his cell phone, if he has it with him I'll clear this up."

"Whatever, I'm going to cruise out there anyway, if you talk to him call me." Byrd clicked off.

O'Malley called Wyatt's phone, the kid didn't answer when it vibrated in his pocket of course; he was too busy. Then he called the house and found no answer there either. He thought about Brunk then gathered up his cash from the bar.

"You have to go?" Becca asked.

"Yeah, something's going on with Wyatt. Byrd saw him riding his bike toward the park a little while ago."

"This late?"

"Yeah, I gotta go Bec, you okay to catch a ride with somebody?"

"It's no problem, I'll just walk. It's only a few blocks. Go… please, I hope everything's okay." O'Malley nodded and disappeared out the door.

In the noise and lights of the backhoe, neither Wyatt nor Brunk noticed when Byrd first drove into the parking lot down the hill and on the other side of the trees. But when he made a slow wide sweeping turn around the parking lot, letting his car lights wash across the fields while he looked for Wyatt's shiny green bike, the light eventually shone through the trees and up the maintenance road as he completed the sweep. This caught the peripheral vision of both Wyatt, in the shadow of the trees by the edge of the road and Brunk, in the grave retrieving body parts. Wyatt took notice of the car lights first and turned his head. When Brunk finally looked up, Wyatt was directly in his line of sight. The silhouette was eminently familiar, standing there holding his bike and turning toward the ball field. Brunk immediately leapt to his feet, both marveling at his good fortune and alarmed that the location of the burial had been discovered. There was no doubt in his mind about what he would do now. Wyatt stood just feet from his grasp.

When Byrd swung his car around he noticed the unusual lights up at the garage and stopped abruptly, listening to the idling backhoe and trying to imagine why a machine would be running at this hour. There was no public utility up there, no reason for a town work crew to be doing anything on an emergency basis. His lights illuminated the mouth of the maintenance road while he contemplated what could be going on and if Wyatt could possibly have anything to do with it. He turned the car off to listen more closely and extinguished his headlights in the hope of going un-noticed. After a few seconds he saw another set of headlights through the trees on top of the hill and heard the car engine and tires spinning in the dirt as it barreled down the road. In a flash, Wyatt's figure appeared under the tree canopy racing on his bike wildly, ahead of the car lights, bouncing out of control in the ruts of the road. When Wyatt turned to look back at his pursuer, the front wheel of the bike jammed into a particularly deep rut and flipped the bike over the shoulder, end over end into the deep drainage culvert that crossed under the beginning of the road. The bat was jolted out of the tube and flew through the air and landed in the road. Byrd opened the door and got out and watched as the chase car skidded to a halt across the entrance, shining its lights into the ditch to the left as dust swirled in the lights.

Brunk jumped out and ran through the hazy light in front of the car, then down into the ditch with his gun drawn. Brunk had not seen Byrd parked in the dark and neither of them was aware of yet another car pulling into the entrance road to the park. It was O'Malley, looking through his side window with interest at the activity around the car lights by the maintenance road. Byrd drew his own gun and ran to the ditch. Both Brunk and Wyatt were out of sight. He approached cautiously, gun first, peering over the edge. The first thing he saw at the bottom of the gully was Brunk's back, some ten feet below, bending over Wyatt lying face down in the muddy trickle of a stream. He held his gun pointed at Brunk and backed away so as not to be seen just yet. His intuition told him something was terribly wrong with the picture and quickly assessed that Brunk was not going to shoot Wyatt in the ditch.

Brunk grabbed Wyatt by the collar, rolled him over and pushed an eyelid up with his thumb. His breathing was irregular and the mouthful of muddy water he took in while lying on his belly fell to the back of his throat and made him cough and gag. Brunk slid his gun into his waist and grabbed Wyatt by the hair, slapping him with the other hand, trying to restore consciousness. The boy simply laid there and groaned. The knock on the head he'd taken from the fall into the culvert rendered him unable to open his eyes under his own power. Brunk grabbed him by the collar again and began to drag him up the bank. After a few feet he stopped to rest, nearly overcome by the exhaustion of dragging the big kid's body, gravity fighting him every inch of the way up the side of the ditch.

Byrd stayed well back from the edge and quietly moved to behind the front of Brunk's Jeep so that the bright glare of the headlights and the idling engine would shield him from being seen or heard as he peered over. He saw only the back of Brunk's head and shoulders as he struggled to pull Wyatt up the side of the bank. Then he noticed O'Malley's car arrive and park next to his own. He motioned for him to stop, putting a finger to his mouth to signal silence. Rex came to a halt in his tracks, shut his car off and said nothing. He got out of the car quietly and looked around, then stepped through the shadows in a wide semi-circle around the jeep, seeing Wyatt's bike in a heap on the side of the road and the bat lying in a rut. He looked intently at Byrd in the shadow behind the car lights, his gun drawn and pointing into the ditch. O'Malley bent down slowly and picked up the bat, then moved off again into the darkness.

Brunk was struggling mightily with the task of retrieving Wyatt, all one hundred seventy five pounds of him. As Byrd watched, he began to strategize about when to let his presence be known. He didn't want to make the old cop panic and shoot someone, but he also grew concerned about Wyatt's condition. O'Malley lurked in the shadows as well, having moved to a spot behind Brunk where he had a partial view of what was happening. Rex couldn't see Brunk's gun tucked into his waist as it was, but assumed from Byrd's posture that there was a weapon down there somewhere. He squatted in the dark, waiting for Brunk's head to appear over the edge of the ditch. Byrd stood completely still at the side of the jeep, his gun sighted with both hands on Brunk's head as he worked. Upon reaching the top Brunk sat on the edge and rested, holding Wyatt from falling back into the ditch. He could progress no further without the boy's help. So he drew his gun from his waist, pointed it to Wyatt's head and yelled,

"WAKE UP!" The boy didn't move so he shook him and yelled again, "WAKE UP!"

Still there was no response, although Wyatt's head seemed to move side to side under his own power and he groaned though no-one could hear it over the sound of the idling jeep.

"WAKE UP YOU LITTLE SHIT, SO I CAN LOOK INTO YOUR EYES WHEN I PULL THE TRIGGER!"

O'Malley was fit to be tied but his training kept him able to remain still, understanding that now was not the time to startle Brunk into a deadly response. He watched the gun held to Wyatt's head, reasoning that his son's life could end at any moment. He knew that Brunk would either shoot or use him as a hostage as soon as he caught sight of Byrd.

Byrd was banking on the hostage scenario. It was a standoff he felt he could win. He grew fearful that Brunk was in such a state that he might shoot him before getting him all the way out, so he moved out from behind the glare of the lights with his gun directed at the side of Brunk's head.

"Look at me Victor, and stay calm," he said evenly, "I have a nine-millimeter pointed right at your head. You make any other movement and it will be your last,"

Brunk brought his head up slowly and smiled at Byrd, staring him right in the eyes.

"Well Byrd, I wondered when it would come to this for you and me. I knew all along it would at some point, didn't you?"

O'Malley began to step in toward Brunk slowly, from behind, hoping the conversation would occupy him. Byrd didn't move his eyes from Brunk's face, but saw O'Malley faintly in his peripheral vision, pleading silently for him to stay put, afraid that any detection by Brunk would set off a chain reaction with Wyatt getting it first.

"This isn't going to come to anything Victor, you're going to put the gun down and we're going to save two lives, yours and his."

"My life can't be saved now anyway Byrd; it doesn't mean anything to me. So I'll just take the boy with me, how about that?" He stared Byrd in the eyes and smiled wickedly as he spoke; enjoying the dilemma he had posed.

Byrd smiled back, allowing himself to be a part of the discussion, hoping that keeping Brunk engrossed in the insane banter would buy time, a few more breaths for Wyatt, maybe enough time to talk him down from the ledge, so to speak; enough time for O'Malley to do something proactive. "Really Brunk? The boy isn't going to feel the bullet enter his skull; he's already out like a light. He'll just never wake up."

"Nice try Byrd, I've talked a few guys down too, in my time." Brunk laughed.

"But you'll feel the bullet enter your head," Byrd continued, "and it won't be pretty, the press photos I mean. I'm going to be alive to tell the world about how I ended your sad life. 'Yeah, he was a great cop once, he just went bad' is what I'll say. You won't be here to stick up for yourself."

This visual upset Brunk and his face turned angry. He focused only on Byrd, even allowing the nose of the gun to fall from the side of Wyatt's head.

"I DON'T HAVE TO STICK UP FOR ANYTHING," he yelled, "MY CAREER SPEAKS FOR ITSELF!" He waved the gun in Byrd's direction for emphasis, as if illustrating with a pointer.

When the gun came up Byrd flinched and nearly fired, but O'Malley had moved to within a few feet and Brunk was not pointing to shoot, only waving with it insanely. Byrd stopped himself from squeezing the trigger, hoping for one more moment that a relatively peaceful solution would arise.

Twenty-Four

Rex O'Malley was born with superb, more than superb, almost super-human hand-eye coordination. It was this talent which put him through Georgetown University with a baseball scholarship. And when he first became interested in the Central Intelligence Agency a few years after graduation, when he realized his minor league baseball career was at a dead end and a former college roommate encouraged him to seek out government service, his expertise served him well. He could shoot the cap off a plastic soda bottle from fifty yards. So along with his ability to smile and think clearly under pressure, his physical talents played well on his resume and he advanced through the ranks of the 'company' with great speed.

As he approached Brunk slowly from behind and prepared himself to swing Wyatt's practice bat into the would-be killer's back, perhaps knocking him unconscious, allowing time for him and Byrd to wrest Wyatt from his control, there was no doubt that he would hit the spot he aimed at. He'd strike him hard on the right side at the bottom of the rib cage, instantly sending the air out of his lungs and perhaps breaking a rib or two, but it would likely cause no permanent damage. When he reared back he wondered why he would spare this lunatic's life. He had tormented his son for years and was now willing to end his life; more than willing to end it, laughing about it. O'Malley couldn't see the sense of allowing Brunk to survive and continue to be Wyatt's reminder of terror anymore.

As he brought the bat around to strike, a moment of insanity took over in O'Malley. Instead of dealing Brunk a disabling but humane blow to the ribs, he altered the plane of his swing at the last instant and chose the back of the old cop's head as the target of his wheelhouse. When the barrel of the bat struck home, Brunk was finishing a sentence to Byrd, ending a rant about how his 'good work' had kept Nazareth a peaceful town for decades and if a few casualties had to be taken along the way, the end result was worth it. The point was well made and it was his last.

Byrd and O'Malley were both stunned by the sound as the bat hit Brunk's cranium; the sound a large rubber mallet will make when it strikes a brick wall, only louder. Pieces of scalp and bone sprayed into the air after impact and Brunk fell forward violently, unnaturally. Rex immediately grabbed for Wyatt, getting a hand under his armpit to prevent him from rolling back down the bank with Brunk. Byrd ran around from the roadside to help and after the two of them wrestled Wyatt back to safety he turned his attention to the Brunk, now slumped in a pile halfway down the bank. His pulse was weak and he wasn't breathing. His skull was caved in severely in the back and blood was oozing from it rapidly. Byrd now felt another, different urgency.

"We have to get an Ambulance here," he said

"He'll be all right, he's beginning to wake up I think," O'Malley said, referring to Wyatt, whose head was now resting on O'Malley's tee shirt.

"No, I mean for Brunk." Byrd was summoning a sense of decency that O'Malley didn't possess at the moment

O'Malley looked at Brunk lying on the side the slope, twitching. He sighed and turned back to Wyatt. "We're not going to call an Ambulance," he said with a solemn voice and then looked back at the man's crushed skull, "won't do any good anyway."

"We still have to call it in," Byrd said incredulously, wondering what O'Malley could be thinking.

"Nope, I'll have a cleanup crew here in an hour. By morning there won't be a trace."

"A CLEANUP CREW? WHAT THE HELL O'MALLEY?"

Rex said nothing further for a moment. He just sat next to Wyatt trying to figure it out. "So what happened here?" he asked finally.

Byrd went through the sequence of events for O'Malley, during which a light went on in his head. "So that's where the satellite and GPS imagery came from, it was you wasn't it?"

O'Malley nodded, then went to his car to retrieve a bottle of water and poured some onto Wyatt's lips. The boy began to stir and then fell off again.

Byrd stood and walked to the Jeep, turned it off and everything fell silent except for the backhoe idling up at the maintenance garage.

"What's that?" O'Malley asked.

"It sounds like a tractor. I'll go check it out. You better wait a minute before you call in your *crew*." O'Malley nodded again and Byrd walked up the road. When he arrived at the scene he saw the arm lying on the ground and walked over to the grave and peered in. The stench wafted up and repulsed him so he pulled out his shirt and put the tail over his mouth and nose. It didn't help much. He walked to the backhoe and shut it down. The fixture on the maintenance garage left enough light for him to assess what had transpired. Before he walked back down to where O'Malley and Wyatt waited, he took one last look at the grave site and shook his head in disbelief. He remembered standing in nearly that exact spot on Sunday afternoon without a clue of what lie below.

"You won't need your crew," he said when he returned to the culvert. O'Malley looked up blankly, "let's just get Wyatt into the back of your car and then help me get the body into the Jeep, you'll see what I mean."

After a few minutes of shaking him and yelling and pouring water on his face they managed to get Wyatt to his feet and over his objections told him to lie down in the back of O'Malley's SUV and told him not to leave the car until they returned. He was confused and disoriented but he resisted little and fell off to unconsciousness again almost immediately. Then Byrd handed O'Malley a set of latex gloves and they each put them on. They loaded Brunk into the back of his Jeep and drove up to the maintenance garage. O'Malley asked no questions along the way, but followed Byrd's lead, figuring he'd soon find out what was in store. He was amazed at the sight in the doggie park: the backhoe next to the grave, the smell of decay, a shredded arm and body below the spot where the claw of the machine had dug. O'Malley remembered standing very near the spot as well, just about thirty-six hours prior, talking with the other police, unaware that the men were buried there.

"He must have been trying to move them;" Byrd said finally, "maybe Wyatt rode up here and surprised him."

O'Malley nodded in agreement then asked, "What do you think the kid saw on Saturday night when he was under the bleachers?"

"I figure he saw act one. He must have been a captive audience. Then tonight he saw act two. Come and help me get the body," Byrd said and directed O'Malley to help him carry Brunk behind the backhoe, being careful not to make any drag marks on the dirt. Then he parked Brunk's car over by the garage and went through it thoroughly to be certain there were no obvious traces of them having been in there. O'Malley watched with interest as he went about the activity methodically, without discussion. Byrd then returned to the backhoe, started it and set the brake. He got down off the machine and looked at the rear wheel. The tire was nearly five feet tall with deep cleats protruding from it. Then he turned to O'Malley.

"All right, you take his feet."

"Where are we going with it?"

"Just get the feet over there, to your right." Byrd lined up Brunk's head directly behind the left rear tire, then set him down. He opened the tool box at the rear of the machine and looked inside. After rumbling around inside he withdrew a heavy metal tow chain. He hooked one end of it around the axle of the machine, scattered the length around the area, and then placed the other end on top of Brunk, on his chest, as if he'd been working with it. He looked at the way Brunk was lying on the ground and adjusted him slightly to make his posture look more natural. Then he got back up onto the back hoe, released the brake, shifted the machine into reverse and backed the left wheel onto Brunk's head, crushing it in the process and allowing the machine to jam against the body, using it as a wheel chock. He slipped the machine out of gear and into neutral and left it there, held from further movement by the jammed body, the engine idling away. The gruesome crushed skull repulsed even the normally stoic O'Malley, but the sense of what Byrd had done was undeniable under the circumstances.

"The Coroner won't have a whole lot to investigate there," Byrd said finally, "my sister's got a farm out in the western part of the state, this kind of thing happens occasionally."

O'Malley grunted in agreement and realized that, though it was atrocious and shocking, what Byrd did was exponentially more civic-minded than anything his cleanup crew would have done. Justice had been served, in a twisted way. At least the families would know the truth about the disappearances. His only real worry was for Wyatt, how the whole affair would impact him and for how long; though someone else did come to mind as O'Malley looked around at the carnage one more time.

"I sure feel bad for the poor bastard who drives up here and finds this first thing in the morning," O'Malley said, "he's gonna have a lousy day."

"Come on," Byrd said, "we better get moving."

Twenty-Five

Early the next morning Byrd got the call he was expecting. The dispatcher on the duty desk received a call from a delirious maintenance worker describing what he discovered at the doggie park. Byrd told him to send two patrol cars and tell them he would meet them there immediately. When he arrived at the scene he began his investigation into what had occurred as if he'd never seen the place, allowing the uniformed officers to describe the various items they found and where, listening to their various theories and assumptions of what had transpired. Two assistants from the County Coroner's office arrived an hour later, sealed off the grave site and started to further exhume the bodies. Byrd spent the entire morning taking pictures and gathering evidence samples.

By noon everyone pretty much agreed about what happened. Brunk had killed the two in the grave at an earlier date and buried them there, returned the night before to remove the bodies, and for an unknown reason was under the backhoe trying to connect a chain when the wheel rolled over his head. It didn't seem as though there was going to be much call for a detailed criminal investigation, although the coroner's office would perform a forensic evaluation as a matter of procedure. As the bodies were being pulled from the hole, Byrd smeared some Vicks Vaporub under his nose to mask the smell and went over to have a look at the faces. The distortion caused by rigor mortis and decay made it difficult for him to affirm that either one looked like Berelli or Stenman, but the circumstantial evidence was overwhelming. The assistant Coroner noted what appeared to be bullet wounds on the corpses as they laid the two side by side in the dirt. Byrd asked for a phone call as soon as the dental records confirmed who they are and if there was a traceable bullet lodged in either one of them.

By three o'clock the town was ablaze with the news. All the local television and radio stations had crews set up at the ball park lot and at Town Hall. The streets were crawling with reporters of all kinds. The news about the Hawks' success the night before was pushed way back onto the back burner. Out of respect for the families O'Malley reluctantly cancelled the practice scheduled for that night, which gave Wyatt time to recover both mentally and physically from the night prior. O'Malley himself called in to the office first thing, taking the day off. His cell phone rang incessantly all morning though, between calls from Washington by those who have no respect for a senior agent taking a day off and other baseball people in the community wanting to talk about the atrocity. At eleven-thirty a.m. Wyatt was still asleep in bed when Rex's cell phone rang once again, this time it was Becca.

"My God Rex, did you hear?" she squealed when he answered.

"Yes, I'm so sorry Becca, is there anything I can do for you?"

"No, not really, I'd pretty much made up my mind he was gone. Now it's just the visual of him lying there in a hole. It's so dreadful, so sad."

"Well, if it makes you feel any better," O'Malley said in his best therapist's voice, "the last day he spent on earth he spent happy with you."

"Yeah, I know," she paused, "umm... Rex?"

"Yeah?"

"The truth is, it wasn't all that happy. I mean we had sex and all, and our sex was always good. But..."

"But?"

"I told him on Saturday that I couldn't do it anymore. I was tired of being the other woman. I knew he'd never make me anything *more* than the other woman, so I was sure that would be the end. But the truth is...."

"The truth is?"

"The truth is I couldn't stand him anyway. He wasn't a friend, he always talked about himself and if it wasn't about him, he didn't have any interest in it. He never cared about anything that I think or feel."

"Becca, you never told me this, how long has it been, I mean, how long have you *not liked* him?"

"I think that, well, and don't take this the wrong way, but I think that when I became friends with you I realized I would never be friends with him."

"Oh."

Becca went on talking about how she was feeling, how much she felt free from Mark, in a way, and how this meant a fresh start for her. The town had grown so small with him in it. She couldn't be with him openly, yet she couldn't be with anyone else. That was over and she felt liberated. O'Malley listened to her intently, interested, as any true friend would.

In his bedroom, Wyatt's phone was ringing too. It was Sammy.

"Hello" he said. He was groggy.

"Hi, it's me."

"Oh, hi… what time is it?"

"God, were you still asleep? It's almost noon; didn't you have work this morning?"

Wyatt tried to get a handle on where he was, what day it was. His head throbbed. He looked at his left arm, which was bandaged at the elbow and stinging with pain. The last thing he remembered was Brunk chasing him and flying through the air into the culvert. He gathered himself, trying to think.

"Yeah… uh, well, I think I fell off my bike last night, I must have hit my head pretty good and banged up my arm. Shit, I gotta get up, I gotta find out what's…"

"Wyatt, did you hear what happened?"

"No"

"They found them, the two guys." Her voice began to crack but Wyatt didn't notice.

"Who did?"

"A maintenance worker went up to that place by the ball park, where people walk their dogs. They were buried in a hole and…"

"I think I saw it last night, I don't know, maybe I was

271

dreaming."

"And?"

"I think I was dreaming. Brunk was chasing me down the road," he looked at his elbow and remembered the feel of the impact in the ditch, "it couldn't be a dream."

"WYATT!" she yelled into the phone.

"Huh?"

"Listen to me," she lowered her voice after getting his attention, but then it quaked when she said, "Brunk is dead."

There was silence while this sunk in. He wondered if he was still dreaming, then he felt the pain is his head.

"Dead? How?"

"I'm not sure, the Police have been here all morning. They said a tractor ran over him, up by the place where they found the two guys. They had a warrant Wyatt; I had to let them in the house to search everything. They just left, said they'd be back later."

"Christ, HE"S DEAD? Jesus Christ." He couldn't help feeling a sense of relief flow over him, liberating him, like diving into a lake on a brutally hot summer day and feeling the cool water peel off the sweat and grime. Then he remembered her, "Shit, are you okay?"

"Yeah, I think so. I mean, he was a murderer, Wyatt. He scared me so much. But I never imagined he'd just suddenly be dead. I don't know, it's strange right now, I don't know how I feel." Her voice cracked again; this time he heard it.

"Sammy, I still feel like I'm in a dream. We need to be together. Can I come over?"

"I'll come get you," she said, "I don't want to stay here right now."

"All right. Well, I gotta take a shower. Just come on in when you get here."

"Okay, it'll be there in a few minutes."

"Sammy?"

"Yeah?"

"It's gonna be okay, I swear it."

"Okay," she said in a cracked voice and she hung up.

Wyatt closed his cell phone and laid there looking up at the ceiling. On the one hand his body was dancing inside, like he dreamed he hit a home run to win the World Series, not the one he was playing in now but THE World Series. On the other hand he ached for Sammy. He'd been so busy running for his life since Saturday he never took the time to imagine how this would turn out; how it would impact her if her, well, whatever he was to her – Brunk, turned out to be dead at the end.

He got up slowly. Everything ached. But he made his way out to the kitchen where his father sat at the counter talking on the phone with Becca. He wondered if O'Malley knew Brunk had chased him the night before.

"I gotta go," O'Malley said, "Wyatt just got up and he looks like the walking dead." Oops, he thought to himself; poor choice of words under the circumstances. They said goodbye and hung up.

"How come you're not working?" Wyatt asked.

"Don't you remember what happened? I stayed home to take care of you."

Wyatt put his hand on the lump on his forehead. "I remember falling off my bike into the ditch and my head hit something really hard."

"Yeah, you fell about ten feet into the culvert."

"Then everything went black. And I remember I was laying down in the backseat of a car and you were talking to me." He went silent for a moment and thought about it. "That's all I remember, I don't remember what you said."

O'Malley was encouraged. "It's a good thing I came looking for you, good thing you left me the note. It got late and I got worried. See? Communication is always good."

"I know Dad."

"They found Berelli and Stenman."

"Yeah, Sammy told me. She told me about Brunk too. She's pretty upset. She's gonna stop over okay?"

"Yeah, sure," O'Malley said softly, "I feel bad for her." He didn't care what happened now, Wyatt was safe and he remembered nothing.

"Do you know how he was killed?" Wyatt asked.

"Which?"

"Brunk, I mean, the other guys too, yeah, but I was wondering about Brunk mostly."

"I guess it was some kind of accident with a backhoe,

it ran over him. They're pretty sure he was the one that killed Berelli and Stenman; he was digging up their bodies when it ran over him. That's what I'm hearing anyway."

"Who told you about it?"

"Well, Joe Morelli told me first. He has the cleaning contract at the town hall and hears all the stuff. Then Becca called a little while ago, she heard the same thing."

Wyatt expected to get some questions from O'Malley, like, why were you riding your bike over by the culvert? And, did you see Brunk while you were at the park? But nothing seemed forthcoming, so he decided to test the waters.

"It seems funny that we didn't run into him. You didn't see him did you?"

O'Malley shook his head with a 'beats me' frown. "Nope."

"He must have been there after us I guess."

"Must've been."

The pregnant pause made Wyatt want to say something. O'Malley's skill at this kind of cat and mouse dialog let the silence bear fruit; though he was really just as happy to leave certain things unsaid.

"Listen, dad, I, uh... nah, never mind. I gotta get in the shower, Sammy will be here soon."

"Try not to get that bandage wet. We have to get you healed up before the game tomorrow night."

"Aren't we having practice tonight?"

"No, I cancelled it. The town is in shock and the families, well; it wouldn't be very respectful would it?"

"No, I guess not." Wyatt turned to leave for the bathroom.

"Did you want to tell me something else?" O'Malley asked casually.

"Nah, I'm just glad Brunk isn't around anymore, it's pretty shitty to say that I know, but I'm glad."

"Me too," O'Malley said warmly. "Now get in the shower. Don't leave me out here to entertain her while you're powdering your nose, I'm no good at that stuff."

"Yeah you are. Becca thinks you are," he taunted, "she's been calling a lot lately O'Malley, what's up with that?"

"Git outa here," O'Malley made a move to chase him and Wyatt jumped into the bathroom and closed the door. Things were better already, he thought, way better.

Wyatt never did go to the doctor that day, at least not his regular one. O'Malley told him that a specialist in head injury, a doctor buddy from the city, was going to be at the house at five pm to give him a checkup so he needed to be home by then. And he wasn't to be doing any driving; Sammy would have to do the honor today. After she picked him up they drove out to Parker Lake. Although Wyatt didn't feel much like swimming they floated out to the rock, the 'Sur le Pointe' rock, and warmed themselves in the afternoon sun. Sammy was remarkably comfortable in spite of the tragedy. She didn't even bring it up again until they sat on the boulder and day-dreamed while gazing across the lake, side by side.

"He was chasing you?" she asked.

Wyatt nodded, "Yes, he was going to kill me."

"Why didn't he catch you? I mean, you fell of your bike, was he right behind you?"

"He was so close. I was peddling like hell. If I'd gone down in the road he'd have run right over me and never thought twice about it."

"Then why didn't he kill you after you went down, he was right there?"

Wyatt shrugged. "The next thing I knew I was in my bed and you were calling. Well, I think I remember a little something in between….my head was pounding and my ears were ringing, but I think I remember O'Malley over me, telling me not to get out of the car. I think Byrd was there too."

"Oh my God, Byrd?"

"Yeah, I think so. It could have been a dream. I don't know for sure."

"If they both were there, and they rescued you, then maybe they chased Brunk away from you or…."

"I… I don't know Sammy, but it doesn't matter because it's over and, well, I don't really even care. I mean, do you?"

She shook her head.

"It's just over and he's not going to hurt us and we don't have to be afraid, and think about it, we can walk down the street or go anywhere we want and I won't have to be looking over my shoulder for him."

She managed to smile, but struggled with a feeling of loss that her thoughts told her she shouldn't feel. "I can't help remembering so many things about him. Some of them are good things."

Wyatt finally realized that it was going to take a long time for her to move past Brunk's death. No matter how bad he was, they had a long history. He stared at her hand as she fingered the wet tail of her tee shirt, unaware she was doing it; churning inside. Ignoring the sting in his elbow he put his left arm around her and pulled her into him. Then he put his lips against the side of her head and spoke in a low soft voice, "No matter how long it takes Sammy, I'll help you forget." She felt the vibration of his warmth as much as she heard it.

"Just hold me," she said, "make it go away."

Twenty-Six

All day on Tuesday and into Wednesday the people of Nazareth endured revelation after revelation as the police department investigated the carnage at the doggie park and the findings circulated. In a small town, people in the know get information about things that never become part of an 'official' release. Macabre jokes were invented and circulated on emails. One displayed the Official Town seal of Nazareth with a heading that read, "Welcome to Nazareth New York, the only place in the world where your dog can dig up the dirt on your neighbor." Another was a mock proposal from a concerned citizen suggesting the town help relieve its budget crisis by auctioning the backhoe on eBay. The media pushed the Chief of Police for a press conference which he promised as soon as all the facts were gathered. The atmosphere at Town Hall had reached a circus like crescendo that no small government could possibly cope with. Business as usual had come to an abrupt halt.

Detective Byrd remained as far from the rumor mill as possible, for multiple reasons, offering no opinion aside from the written report he was preparing to file on Wednesday afternoon. He listened carefully to what everyone else opined though, and was mildly entertained by one of the theories that evolved. A fellow detective postulated that Brunk was a member of a conspiracy, that there was no way he was working alone, that the backhoe couldn't have rolled over him but was driven over him mistakenly by a partner in the crime, who may be a town maintenance worker. The conspirator then fled the scene from fear, supposedly, when Brunk was accidentally crushed. After this idea made its way over to the town highway department, workers began to look at fellow workers askance.

On Wednesday afternoon, two days after Brunk was killed, Byrd sat at his desk reviewing, for the third time, a group of reports from the ballistics lab and the Coroner's office. The report he was in turn crafting would be first reviewed by the Chief of Police and then forwarded, if acceptable, to the District Attorney's office and the Coroner's office with a recommendation for action or no action, depending upon the evidence. At the end of a long dry description of evidentiary procedures used in the investigation and his subsequent findings, he wrote the following:

> In summary, the report from ballistics confirms that the projectile extracted from the spinal column of the corpse of subject 'A' (deceased Stenman) originated from the weapon issued to Patrolman Brunk. Also confirmed are traces of expired gunpowder discovered on the sleeve of a uniform shirt found in the home of Patrolman Brunk. It is the contention of this investigation that Patrolman Brunk fired the shot which killed subject 'A' sometime in the days preceding the discovery of the bodies at 0825 hours on the morning of Tuesday, 16 July 2013. The Coroner's office has placed the time of death at approximately 2100 hours on the night of Saturday, 13 July 2013.
>
> Referencing subject 'B' (Berelli), there is no conclusive evidence the death occurred by a shot from

Brunk's weapon, as no projectile has been recovered. However, the Coroner's report contends that the wounds inflicted upon both subjects were made by projectiles of the same caliber and that the time of death for both subjects is substantially identical. It is therefore the contention of this investigation that Patrolman Brunk fired the shot which killed subject 'B' also, in spite of the fact that the evidence is merely strongly circumstantial.

Referencing subject 'C' (Brunk) the Coroner's office cites evidence at the scene of death which supports a contention that the subject was killed accidentally. The backhoe which crushed the skull of subject 'C' inadvertently or for unknown reasons rolled onto the subject while he was beneath it working.

In conclusion and as to a positive course of action, this investigative unit sees no virtue in a criminal investigation into the cause of death for any of the subjects, but will defer to the District Attorney and the Coroner if opinion exists otherwise.

Submitted 17 July, 2013,
Harold C. Byrd,
Chief Investigator
Nazareth Special Investigations Unit

Satisfied with his creation, Byrd looked up the email address that O'Malley had given him for use on any official communication, cut and pasted the report and sent it to him. He then deleted the sent mail and any remnant of the address from his contact list.

When O'Malley received the email he was getting ready to leave the office and drive to the ball park for pre-game practice. He read the email quickly and saved it for later when he would have more time. But the gist of it was that Byrd had done a thorough job in reviewing the evidence, found nothing to implicate either of them in the result, and swept the whole thing under the rug; just as he had hoped. He knew they had broken several important laws and if they were found out the consequences would be dire, but he also racked his brain about what could go wrong in their cover-up and could come up with nothing.

That night, the Nazareth Hawks played a courageous game, holding a 2-2 tie with a team from Hawaii, the Honolulu Sharks, all the way until the seventh inning. The Sharks were just too big, too good, too deep, and when Greasy fired a ninety mile per hour fastball across the plate after he got one out in the top of the seventh, the big third basement teed off on it and sent it over the center field fence for a home run and a one run lead, making the score 3-2. In the bottom of the seventh the Sharks closer came in and threw B-B's, getting three outs in succession to preserve the win. The Hawks were devastated and although O'Malley really wanted that game, in fact came to believe, after thinking initially the Sharks were going to shellac them, they could win once they tied it up 2-2, he was in the end enormously proud of his guys. They were playing quality baseball against national programs and that was something that no group from Nazareth had ever done. Regardless, it was a double elimination tournament and they had lost only once, so they were down but not out. They would play again on Thursday against another team that had lost once also. Win that one and they'd be right back in it, loser goes home. He was sure Wyatt would be up to the task once again, he hadn't pitched since

Monday and hadn't thrown many pitches at that. Just as important, there was no Brunk around to make him crazy.

On Thursday night they returned to the World Series to play a team from San Diego, the California Suns. Wyatt was indeed ready to go and pitched superbly, taking a one hitter through the sixth inning in a 0-0 scoreless tie. The Suns pitcher was dealing aces also. The Hawks had loaded the bases on him in the second and fifth innings, but couldn't succeed in pushing a run across the plate; the kid was too good. And so it was really a matter, it seemed, of which pitcher would tire first and force the manager to go to his bullpen. In the top of the seventh the pitcher for the Suns walked both JR Shea and Burnsy to start the inning, but then struck out Greasy, Wyatt and Mojo Morelli to get out of trouble. O'Malley figured if they could get through the bottom of the inning without losing the game, it would probably the last they would see of the other pitcher; that he was now surely out of gas and there would be a pitching change.

He reluctantly sent Wyatt out to the mound again knowing that one little slip from a tired pitcher and the game would be over. The 2013 Hawks trip to the World Series would be over as well. As it was his own son he worried a little more than usual about the prospect of Wyatt giving up the game winning run, but the kid would not take no for an answer and O'Malley looked around his bench and decided that a tired Wyatt was probably better than any other pitcher he was able to put out there in relief under the circumstances. None of them had pitched relief in this situation before.

Wyatt retired the first batter on a seven pitch strikeout,

not exactly what O'Malley was hoping for, as his pitch count was now around 120 pitches and he still had at least two batters to face. The next batter worked a six pitch walk. Balls three and four were borderline pitches that could have been called strikes and O'Malley argued fervently after both pitches, something he was not known to do. But the umpire was not going to relent and in fact issued a warning to him when the batter trotted to first base and O'Malley was still yelling unpleasant things with regard to the calls. When he stopped ranting he told Danny Bastau to get warmed up again. Danny had been warmed up three times in the last two innings, but he figured this time it would be the real deal. Wyatt walked the next batter on five pitches to put two men on with only one out. O'Malley, frustrated and still upset at the umpire, called time and went to the mound. Wyatt was gassed. He had nothing left in the tank. When Rex got out there he stuck his hand out and Wyatt put the ball in it with emphasis, pissed that he was being pulled, pissed that he had run out of steam.

"You pitched a hell of a game Y-O, we just didn't score any runs for you."

"That fuckin fat lazy prick is tryin to end this game," Wyatt said between his teeth, referring to the umpire, "he doesn't want to go extra innings."

"Chill out buddy," he patted Wyatt on the butt as he walked by, "go have a seat and let us fill in for you."

Wyatt said nothing further and left the mound to sincere applause for the job he had done that night. When he got to the opening to the dugout he threw his glove against the back wall in frustration and said nothing to any of the guys, One by one they walked by over the next few minutes while Danny warmed up and patted his leg or gave a hand slap in appreciation for his work. He had pitched a one-hitter and he felt like he failed. Baseball is a strange game sometimes.

Danny Bastau is a crafty pitcher. He's a little smaller than most guys his age so he doesn't over-power a hitter. In fact his fastball is no more than a little below average. But he throws a curve, slider, sinking change and straight change all for strikes, and he nibbles at the corners of the plate. He induces a lot of ground balls and strikes guys out with the change, which also makes his fastball look like a hundred miles per hour in comparison. In short, he drives the batter nuts. When Danny was warming up, he didn't throw anything but fastballs, not wanting to show the batter what anything looked like. And true to form, they were licking their chops on his below average heater. After his seventh warm-up pitch the Umpire declared "one more" in anticipation of resuming the game. Beans, the catcher, walked the ball out to Danny instead of throwing it back, knowing full well this would sacrifice Danny's allowed eighth warm-up pitch, but the kid didn't need any more and Beans knew it. He'd already warmed up in the bullpen three times. Beans wanted to talk about the pitch selection instead of putting the sign down, knowing the runner on second might see the sign and in turn signal to the batter what was coming.

"Put the sign down for a fastball," Danny said as soon as Beans arrived," but I'm throwing the change-up first pitch." This was a ballsy move, but Danny knew they wouldn't be looking for the off speed. Of course, they didn't know Danny Bastau, he'd throw any of his pitches at any time, and he could throw them all for a strike.

"If he bites on that, we'll throw it again, they'd never expect that. If he doesn't bite on it, you call the next one," he said to Beans, "just keep me out of the middle of the plate."

Beans nodded and went back, squatted behind home plate and the Ump pointed to Danny and yelled "play." The secret to a change-up is that the arm speed the pitcher shows is the same as that for a fastball, he only changes his grip on the ball so that his hand slips off of it instead throwing it full speed. So the batter sees fastball tempo but the pitch is at least ten miles per hour slower. It can make the batter look silly when he swings off balance and way ahead of the ball.

With men on first and second and one out, Danny was pitching from the stretch. He has a very good pick-off move so he waited and waited for the runner on first to relax with a big lead. When the runner took another small step toward second Danny spun and fired to first, nearly picking him off. Now that he'd shown his move, the opposing manager wasn't going to let the runners take that big of a lead anymore at this stage in the game. When Danny got the ball back he went through the routine again, but this time threw his pitch to the plate. It was a sweet change-up as planned and the batter swung way ahead of it hitting an awkward dribbling ground ball down the third base line. This pulled the third baseman off the bag to field the ball and he had no other play but to first base for the sure out. The runners on first and second advanced, and there were now two outs.

With men on second and third, two out, first base

vacant, and the number eight batter coming to the plate, O'Malley sent in the sign for an intentional walk. This would load the bases and set up a force play for the third out at all bases. Beans stood up, made the mandatory indication for an intentional walk, and the batter trotted to first after Danny intentionally threw four pitches way out side for balls. It was now show time.

The runner on third was being a distraction. He was advancing well down the third base line as Danny went into his stretch. Corey Gallup, the third baseman, knew that the runner had no idea of the quality of Danny's move to third base, and was risking pick off by being so bold. Corey stood a couple of feet from the bag, ready for a predetermined play to move quickly to the bag should Danny signal that he was going to throw over. In his set position Danny stared at the runner, delaying, trying to catch him off balance. The signal to Corey was that he wouldn't take his eyes of the runner, and if he smiled, making certain the runner saw the smile, letting it take his mind off the situation, he was going to throw over. When Corey saw the smile he counted to three and moved quickly to the bag, Danny pulled his left leg up, appearing to throw the pitch home, then in a move that barely stayed within the balk rules, shifted his weight toward third and threw the ball to Corey instead. This indeed caught the runner off guard and the ball arrived in plenty of time to pick him off. But instead of waiting until the ball was firmly implanted in his glove, Corey moved his hand to apply the tag just a fraction of a second too soon. The throw deflected off the webbing of his glove and skittered away behind him. The runner got up off his belly and tore for home, reaching the plate just prior to Corey's recovery throw, and the Suns had won on an error. The famous season for the Hawks was over. They would go home tonight thinking about what might have been.

It could have turned out so differently. If Danny had thrown home, the batter might have hit a harmless fly ball, or grounded out anywhere to end the inning. If Corey had waited one micro-second longer, caught the ball and made the tag, he and Danny would have been heroes. They'd still be playing. If Danny had thrown the ball just a little lower, it may not have deflected off the webbing of Corey's glove. But as it was, the tiniest error, the smallest movement in Corey's glove, ended a season. One of the most difficult things about baseball is that there is a very fine line between being a hero and being a goat.

The boys were deflated, feeling robbed, frustrated and angry that they had been beaten in such a small way. There wasn't a sound to be heard in the dugout or in the Hawks section of the stands. Everyone listened but turned away as the Suns ran onto the field and celebrated. The Hawks players made their way off the field slowly with their heads hung low, not wanting to watch as the Suns hopped and hollered and jumped on each other at home plate. Before they lined up to shake hands with their victorious opponents, a gesture that would be difficult and that no-one wanted to do, Wyatt pushed aside his disappointment and his own feelings of self-indulgence and went over to Corey Gallup, who was walking off the field as white as a sheet. This was a tough one for Corey and Wyatt knew it. He walked up to him, threw his arms around him, hugged him and said, "It's my bad dude, if I hadn't walked him he couldn't have scored." Wyatt hoped this would help, and the bottom line is, it was true.

O'Malley gathered all the players in the outfield and told them to take a knee. No-one wanted to hear what was coming, although they knew that O'Malley would be sincere. Maybe he would say something that would take the pain away.

"First," he began, "the runner who scored shouldn't have been there. The umpire made a bad call on the fourth ball to him and he walked. So don't get down on yourselves but chalk it up to the nature of the game. Everybody gets bad calls; sometimes they mean more than others. We've won our share over the years that way…. right?"

They all nodded as the weight began to come off. Each of them had been thinking of the point in the game where they might have done something differently to change the outcome. Deflecting the blame to something out of their control was the best thing that Rex could do for them at the moment.

"Take the positives from this. Who's got a positive?" he looked at Mojo Morelli, deep in thought as he listened. "Mojo, you got a positive?"

Mojo tried to keep from smiling and squirmed before he spoke. "Yeah, I got a positive Skip, I got a big positive. The babe who's working the snack stand is comin to pick me up tonight in her old man's car, a friggin Mercedes, and duuude….she is friggin hot!" They all laughed, some shook their heads marveling at how quickly Mojo could change gears and go right back to the throb he constantly felt between his legs. "BUT…" he said loudly, holding his hands up to get everybody to be quiet, "about the team, I mean, about us. Well, I know we wouldn't be here without everybody doing good stuff at one time or another, so that's pretty friggin cool too." Greasy yelled, "YEAH!" and started to clap. Everyone else joined in, even Corey Gallup, who was now smiling.

"Okay," O'Malley said after they settled down, "on Saturday afternoon the town Supervisor wants to honor the team at a ceremony at the ball park. They're gonna give speeches and have food, and afterward we'll have a parent-son game, okay?" Everybody groaned about the game.

"Damn, Skipper, you mean we gotta play you old farts again?" Beans said, "the stuff gets boring you know…."

"Yeah, I know Beans, but this year, cut us some slack willya?" O'Malley asked with a mischievous grin on his face, "we barely beat you little shits last year, what was it, like fifteen to two?"

"You did not." Beans argued and again a rousing chatter developed between them all.

After a couple minutes of reverie and cross challenges O'Malley decided it was a perfect time to cut it off, parents were waiting. "Okay, one more thing," he said loudly, and then he got quiet as they settled down. "I've been around the block a few times in this game and I want you all to know, this is one of the best teams I've ever been a part of." They remained silent, thinking, knowing that indeed O'Malley had played on some really good teams in his time. They also knew he must truly feel that way, because they felt no need for him to say it.

Twenty-Seven

On Saturday afternoon second term Nazareth Town Supervisor, Jim Callahan, used the opportunity to do what politicians do: smile for the cameras and try his best to deliver a rousing speech. He spoke of the importance of being involved in the community and praised the organizers of Nazareth Babe Ruth Baseball for their good work, "producing fruit which," he said, "has grown from a vine extending all the way from this ball park in wonderful Nazareth to the site of the Sixteen-year-old World Series." 'Such eloquence,' O'Malley thought, 'for a guy who won't give the league five thousand lousy dollars to put new dirt on the infield, but will spend twenty thousand to fence in four acres next door so that six dogs can run around inside it and take a dump.'

Callahan requested a moment of silence for the "the tragic loss of two good friends to baseball and to the community," meaning of course, Berelli and Stenman. "Model citizens," he called them, "who gave their time selflessly, without reward other than the satisfaction of helping our youth to excel in sports and become better humans." At least half of the three hundred or so people winced in silence; realizing once and for all that Callahan has no idea of what he is talking about. O'Malley wondered if Mark Berelli - the self-absorbed serial cheater, or Peter Stenman - the drunken wife beater, had risen from the grave to become Callahan's speech writer. There was no mention of the 'tragic loss of Victor Brunk'; probably a tragedy the town leadership would like everyone to forget.

The team stood side by side in a line across the infield grass in front of the pitcher's mound, slightly at attention as Callahan droned on at a podium and microphone in front of them. Wyatt was at the far end of the line, standing next to Mojo Morelli, who made fart noises with his mouth during the occasional applause. This caused Wyatt, Beans, Burnsy and others to be unable to keep from laughing, especially since they knew whenever a break was coming for applause, so was a group of farts. It was vintage Mojo and Wyatt was deeply happy to be able to appreciate it after the hell he survived the weekend prior. He felt settled as he looked around slowly at the surroundings and the crowd while Callahan talked. He saw Becca in the crowd, actually caught her staring at O'Malley, and wondered what might become of that. He saw Sammy sitting there, amazingly unfazed during the talk of the tragedy, or at least hiding her emotions well. She smiled at him when he caught her eye and he thought that meeting her made the whole ordeal worth it. All the guys were once again amazed at his prowess, being able to attract the hottest babe around; this one in fact, *older* than him and driving a BMW. They attributed it partly, to him being a pitcher, a big stud, on the hill.

He looked over to the bleachers, the ones he hid underneath that fateful night. For a moment the vision of Brunk pulling the trigger, coldly eliminating human life, came back to mind. Then his eyes moved to the right, to the spot where Mark Berelli and then Stenman stood slinging the shovel wildly; then further right to where Brunk stood and pulled the trigger. You'd never know that anything had happened there, that just a few inches below the surface likely lie traces of their blood. The place looked so civilized now, full of people sitting attentively as a big shot from the town spoke to them. If only they knew.

O'Malley, at the other end of the line, noticed him looking over at the bleachers, staring at the spot with a solemn expression. He wondered what the boy might be seeing. He figured all along the bleachers had something terrible to do with the Berelli-Stenman murders, but he didn't want to know the details. He didn't want to put Wyatt through what it would take to learn the details. When Wyatt felt him looking at him they caught each other's look for a long second, then both smiled, knowing, but then again not knowing.

After the ceremony O'Malley announced the forthcoming parent-son game, that it would last a maximum of five innings, and invited all interested parents to come onto the field and 'suit up.' Detective Byrd hung around to watch, and when it turned out there were only eight parents willing to risk heat stroke to play, because Ricky Burns insisted on being the umpire, Byrd went to his car and got his sneakers and took a place in the outfield. He even got a couple of chances at fly balls and fielded them cleanly, then made weak but accurate throws back in to the cutoff man. Fun was had by all and the Hawks players, try as they may, couldn't tee off on the junk that pitchers Rex O'Malley and then Art Bastau threw to them during their at bats. Since there were no adults capable of squatting long enough to be catcher, the Hawks catchers, Beans and his backup, Danny Oster, were required to take turns catching for the them. After four innings, the score stood at 3-2 in favor of the Hawks. It was the top of the fifth and the parents were at bat with their last chance to tie or win the game. Wyatt had come on in the fourth inning to pitch and was doing a good job of being fair, knowing that few of the adults except for Rex or coach Bastau would be able to hit anything he threw other than simple little three-quarter fastballs in the middle of the plate. He knew that if and when he faced Rex, however, he'd have to pitch to him, because Rex would yell at him if he threw anything that looked like a sympathy pitch, or if he did throw such a pitch, Rex would simply tattoo it out of the yard. He thought he remembered that Rex was batting fourth in this inning and he didn't want to face him exactly, because he didn't want to give up a home run to his old man. That would be funny, he thought, but then again not so funny.

Art Shea led off the inning and popped out to the infield. Then Jed Rounder's dad, Marquis, got up and hit a weak ground ball to third which Corey fielded casually and threw to first way ahead of the sweating and grunting Mr. Rounder. O'Malley and Byrd stood on the side lines watching and smiling in spite of knowing they were down to the last out and with Wyatt on the hill this game was very close to being over. Joe Morelli, rotund and fiery Italian that he is, stepped into the box. O'Malley was officially on deck, but he didn't move out there, allowing Joe the full stage. Joe turned to Ricky Burns, umpiring behind home plate, and said as he stepped in,

"If there's a play at first you better run your fairy ass down there to get a good look and make sure you get it right."

"If there's a play at first," Ricky retorted, not smiling behind the mask, "I'll run down there backwards and beat your fat ass."

O'Malley and Byrd saw the two of them jawing at the plate, their body language hinting that they weren't exactly exchanging playful barbs. Beans, the catcher, looked over at O'Malley and shook his head, feeling the misfortune of having to be between the two of them. Wyatt saw the exchange as well and looked in to O'Malley smiling, knowing the opportunity existed to make this interlude interesting by throwing the right pitch. O'Malley gave him a playfully stern look and shook his head, knowing what the kid had up his sleeve. Wyatt turned away still smiling then looked in to Beans and nodded, before a signal even went down. After Joe had dug in Wyatt went into a mock windup and threw a sweet, smooth, meaty batting practice fastball right in the heart of the plate; the kind of fastball that a twelve year old hits a mile. Joe took a mighty swing and hit the ball right on the sweet spot, sending a line drive into left field that any player on the Hawks team would be proud to have hit.

Joe geared up and steamed toward first base, all five foot nine and 240 pounds of him, chugging and grunting as if running for his life. JR Shea, playing left field instead of his normal short-stop, causally fielded the ball, not imagining that 'Mr. Morelli' would challenge his arm and try to stretch the hit into a double. It was a clean base hit, he figured, we'll give him that. But when Joe rounded first base wildly, flailing his arms and trying to get his body turned in the direction of second, JR watched with amazement and then threw a bullet toward Danny Bastau who was playing short-stop and covering the bag. Every one of the parents were standing shell shocked at the sight of Joe Morelli in such a state, knowing once JR released the ball, the old fat guy didn't have a chance. But the play was closer than it might have been, because Danny Bastau knew what was barreling down on him from first and there was no way he was going to be out in front of that runaway train. He was afraid if Joe didn't slide and then ran into him while he tried to apply the tag, well, that would be ugly for sure and it would hurt, a lot. So Danny stepped off the bag to make room for Godzilla, and when JR's throw bounced low in the dirt in front of him, he bobbled the ball at first but then recovered quickly enough to apply the tag, standing off to the side, as the meaty, big and bouncy Joe Morelli did in fact slide by in a cloud of dust.

Ricky Burns, umpiring behind the plate, couldn't believe his eyes when Joe turned toward second trying to stretch a single, figuring at first it was a clean base hit, that Joe would stop at first and there would be no need to leave his spot behind the plate. But when he saw the flailing arms, Ricky knew there would be a play at second and ran as fast as he could toward the base in order to not miss the call. At about mid infield he watched the rotund Joe Morelli put down a pretty good slide, but in the end, he didn't touch the bag with his foot before Danny's tag. Ricky took one more leap toward second and in mid-air threw an animated wheelhouse fist in the direction of the bag and yelled "YOU'RRRRE OUT!"

Everyone was laughing, it was the most fun they'd had all game. Danny Bastau made a mock wipe of his forehead before he bent down to see if Joe was all right still lying in the dirt. The entire forty or so people who were watching burst into laughter and applause as well, everyone was having a ball, except for Joe Morelli, that is. He rolled over onto his belly so that he could get up on his knees before standing and yelled at Ricky, "You got to be friggin kidding me!!! You blew the call, I knew that was gonna happen, goddammit." Then he stood up.

"I didn't blow the call porky; you were out by a mile. Now pull up your pants and get out of here." Ricky moved away toward the dugout, the game was over.

"You calling me porky you little maggot filled piece of shit? I been real peaceful with you so far this season, but I've had enough of your crap…."

Everyone was dumb-founded. O'Malley knew it had been too good to be true. There was no way these two guys could go through an entire season without at least one threat of a fist fight. Big Patrick Burns watched his father turn toward Joe, his face twisted in anger. It wasn't the term 'maggot filled piece of shit' that bothered him, but he couldn't stand being called 'little'. Patrick ran over from first base and got in front, trying to pull him away. MoJo Morelli ran in from right field at full speed. O'Malley worried because he didn't know if MoJo would try to stop the fight or jump right in. Wyatt came over from the pitcher's mound with the intention get between the two of them but decided he didn't want to bear the brunt of a wayward fist.

O'Malley and Byrd were standing together by the dugout. "Somebody oughta write a book about this place Rex," Byrd said shaking his head, "you couldn't make this stuff up."

"Yeah," O'Malley said, nodding, "somebody oughta."

* * *

ABOUT THE AUTHOR

Dwight Mathieu is an exciting new author arriving at the forefront of contemporary American fiction. Having honed his thought at Boston University under the tutelage of renowned philosopher Alasdair MacIntyre, he now turns his attention to intricate and transporting suspense novels. His first, *The Big Hit*, will be followed by *No Men of God* (spring 2014) and *Bella* (summer 2014). Mathieu is a longtime baseball coach, avid golfer, airplane pilot, business owner, and musician. He lives in Albany, New York.

www.ingramcontent.com/pod-product-compliance
Lightning Source LLC
Chambersburg PA
CBHW021319250626
47155CB00002B/544